CW00507981

SONG OF THE FAE

BOOK ONE IN THE WILDSONG SERIES

TRICIA O'MALLEY

LOVEWRITE PUBLISHING

SONG OF THE FAE
THE WILDSONG SERIES
BOOK ONE

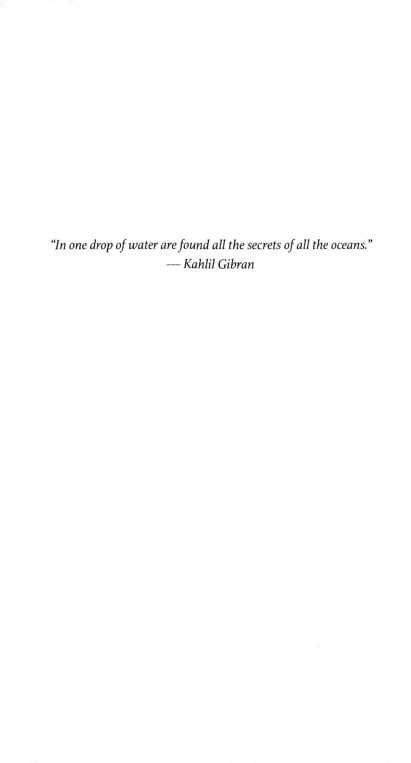

"In one drop of water are found all the secrets of all the oceans."
— *Kahlil Gibran*

The Fae Realm

Danula

The Light Fae ruled by the Goddess Danu

The Elemental Fae

The Royal Fae Court of the Danula oversee
the Elemental Fae

Water Fae

Earth Fae   Fire Fae

Air Fae

Domnua

The Dark Fae ruled by Goddess Domnu

PROLOGUE

For each Elemental,
A child shall fight;
Born of human and Fae,
Darkness and light;
The Elementals will fall,
Stolen powers in the night;
If the child lives on,
The dark loses their right.

"Sister."

The words were a hiss on the wind, their coldness wrapping sinuously around Danu's body, threatening her next breath. Goddess Danu sighed, flicking her sister's magick away with the tip of her crystalline nail, turning from where she studied the prophecy inscribed on the wall of the portal cave. As always, seeing the madness swirling in her twin sister's eyes twisted Danu's heart. Domnu was coldly and terrifyingly beautiful, with obsidian eyes and wildly curling hair that ended in fangs. Dark to Danu's light, Domnu's quest for power of all factions of the world – both human and Fae – would destroy her if it didn't first ruin them all.

"You know better than to use your magicks on me." Danu stepped away from the prophecy, keeping her back to the wall. "It didn't end well for you the last time, did it now?"

"The Four Treasures should be mine." Domnu shrieked, her hair screaming along with her words. "It was but a slight miscalculation on my part, is all."

"Was that all it was?" Danu tapped her finger against her lips, trying to judge how far the madness had consumed her sister. Both Goddesses, they'd separated when they'd come to the land of Inisfáil, known today as Ireland, and her sister had realized the Four Treasures – gifts of impossible power that would guarantee the owner world domination – would give her the power she so desperately sought. It had only been by the fierce determination and sheer courage of a plucky band of humans and Fae – the Seekers and the Protectors – that had saved Ireland, and the world, from certain destruction. At the time, Domnu had been banished to her dark realm to oversee her cruel faction of Dark Fae, and Danu had delivered the treasures safely back to the Goddesses, forever ensuring that they wouldn't slip into the wrong hands. Now, two decades later, it seemed that the next prophecy was being realized.

"Of course." Domnu sniffed. "I was distracted and perhaps I underestimated those human Seekers of yours. Humans seem so weak to me."

"They weren't completely human, were they? They each had their own powers. As do these children of the Elementals." Danu gestured to the inscription on the wall that glowed lightly of its own accord, as though molten gold had been poured into the deep etching. "What are you planning, sister?"

"Me?" Domnu twirled a lock of hair around her finger, laughing when it bit her. Danu wasn't surprised when Domnu sucked the blood that had blossomed on her pale skin. "My Domnua children are restless. It seems that the Elemental Fae might be interested in coming to our side, dear sister. They used to distrust the Domnua, my sweet children, can you believe that? But now the Elementals are learning that the Danula Fae aren't as great as they claim. Perhaps it is time for a new Royal Court, dear sister." Domnu checked her finger, smiling at the skin that now showed no wound.

"My Danula rule the Elementals with pride," Danu said, keeping her tone even, refusing to let her sister provoke her. "We've long worked with them in a solid partnership, and the world has benefited for it."

"Perhaps," Domnu said, and shrugged one shoulder. "And perhaps not. Maybe you shouldn't be so confident in your people's reign anymore."

The centuries-old frustration dragged at Danu, and she pinched her nose, before meeting her sister's eyes.

"It didn't...and it *doesn't*...have to be this way, sister," Danu said. Why did she still try? Her sister had descended into darkness, and madness had claimed her ages ago.

Yet still, a part of her hoped to reach something good, *anything*, that might still be buried inside of Domnu. She sighed. "You will bring war to our world once more?"

"I won't rest until Inisfáil is mine."

"And to what purpose? You'll destroy...everything."

"Maybe that's for the better. Then my people will rise, and we will populate the world with our magicks." A flicker of gold rippled through the darkness of Domnu's eyes.

"You'll fail," Danu said, her tone harsh. "The Danula Prince is already in Ireland. As are some of his greatest warriors. We've defeated you once before, and we'll do it again."

"Will you?" Domnu twirled around the cave, her dark skirt flaring out behind her, her voice in a sing-song lilt. "Your prince is vulnerable now, don't you see?"

"What have you done?" Danu asked, fear gripping her.

"Prince Callum is in love. And, as we both know, love is nothing but a weakness, darling sister. Even now, we take his fated mate, for a prince without his heart is nothing."

"Domnu!" she yelled, but her sister disappeared in a flash of light and laughter. Rage and sadness raced through Danu. She'd hoped it could be another way, that the prophecy would prove to be untrue. Tracing her fingers over the molten gold words, she hung her head. "I'm sorry, my children. I'm so very sorry."

1

THE MAN BECKONED to her from beneath the silky surface of the sea. The familiar unease unfurled in Imogen's core, and instead of turning away as she usually did, Imogen met his gaze and tried to study him objectively.

The man's grin widened. He was really more of a creature, she supposed. His skin was so white that the pearlescent sheen of it gleamed in the soft light from the moon, reminding Imogen of the underbelly of a salmon. Eyes of milky opalescence blinked at her, flashes of pinks and greens shimmering in their depths. Both beautiful and terrifying, Imogen swallowed against her suddenly dry throat as the man raised a hand and beckoned to her once more. The most surprising thing? A part of her wanted to follow him. To dive into the wintry cold sea, sinking into the inky depths, and deliver her mind over to the delusions that had danced on the edge of her consciousness for years now. When that urge became dangerously close to engulfing her, Imogen turned from the bow of the boat and shuddered, gulping in a few deep breaths and forcing herself to break the pull she felt from the creature in the water.

That she'd seen most of her life, that is. In her dreams as well.

It was always the same man who followed her – slipping silently just below the ocean's surface – during stormy nights or calm blue-sky days. A part of her hated this creature, for his appearance threw her own sanity into question, and yet another part of her yearned to go to him. It was as though he was a missing link in her life, but Imogen didn't have the time or inclination to dissect just what he symbolized for her. Maybe, someday, when her boat was paid off and she could take a moment to breathe, Imogen would plop herself down on a therapist's couch and pour out all of her fears. But that day had not yet come, and Imogen doubted it ever would. The luxury of analysis and self-improvement was not afforded to a person like her, who spent every waking moment trying to build her business and keep her deck crew employed.

Annoyed with herself, and the direction of her thoughts, Imogen strode across the deck of the *Mystic Pirate*, her very own charter boat, and locked the wheelhouse. They'd arrived in Grace's Cove that morning, the harbor hugged by rolling green hills with colorful houses dotting the winding streets. It was a charming village, and Imogen had been scouting for longer charter trips for the American tourists that visited each summer. She wanted to meet with a few B&B owners to see about offering a land and sea package holiday. Imogen's instincts told her that a package that mixed the best of what Ireland had to offer would be well-received, particularly by tourists who had limited vacation days.

Imogen leapt onto the dock, pausing to slip on her shoes, and then walked toward the village, still feeling the familiar rocking of the boat beneath her. It was always that way when she stepped onto land, Imogen thought with a bemused smile on her face. At sea, she was most stable, while on land she felt off-kilter and out of sorts. With no family to speak of, and very few friends, the gentle rocking motion that plagued most sailors when they went to land was a comfortable reminder to Imogen of where she really belonged.

A captain of her own ship, controlling her own destiny on the water that she loved. *Her home.*

She'd never fit in the regular world anyway, for she had no frame of reference for how the usual things were done. She'd never had birthday parties or played sports and had just enough schooling to get by. No, Imogen wasn't going to bake a pie with a baby perched on her hip. The very thought made her laugh, as the vision of that life seemed more delusional to her than the creature that followed her at the ocean's edge.

A recent rain had left puddles in the streets of Grace's Cove, and they reflected the lights of the shops and restaurants that clustered together, winding up the street toward the top of the hill. Imogen strolled along, her hands in the pockets of her fleece jacket, and hummed a song that had been niggling at her brain for a while. It was one of those things where she just couldn't place the tune, and it had been driving her wild for months. She heard the song in her dreams, and she caught herself singing it during the day while she helped to clean the boat or tallied their provisions. It was a melancholy tune, almost heartbreaking in its need, and Imogen still hadn't been able to discover where she'd learned of it.

Opal eyes blinked at her from a puddle on the street and Imogen skidded to a stop, her stomach twisting, as the creature from the ocean smiled up at her. *This was...this was new.*

Sweat broke out across her brow. Fear gripped her and she turned to run, only to slam directly into a wall.

Well, at least what felt like a wall. Hands gripped her arms, steadying her, and Imogen's breath caught as her gaze rose from the buttons of a flannel shirt and up, up, up to the face of a glowering man. Stormy gray eyes, a rough beard, and a chiseled jawline would be enough to make any woman swoon.

For Imogen, it was like a plug finding a socket, and strange energy coursed through her, making her feel both alive and inconceivably resilient.

I want to kiss him.

The thought shocked her enough to step back, cutting their physical contact, and the hum of energy lessened...but it did not entirely abate. Imogen was not a lusty person, oh no, if anything she found sex to be tedious or boring most times. Which is why it had been ages since she'd let a man touch her. And yet now, it was like all her senses woke up and she wanted, well, things she shouldn't want from a stranger who was glaring at her on the street.

"What was that song you were singing?" The man's voice, like honey spilled on gravel, caused her insides to go liquid so she just stared at him in confusion for a moment until his words registered. *What an odd thing to ask.* Heat crept up her cheeks when she realized she was just standing there with her mouth hanging open like a fish out of water.

"Um, sure and it's just a made-up tune, really. A bit of nonsense at that." Imogen cleared her throat and took another step back. *This man was so intense.*

"Is it?" The man's brow furrowed, and he seemed to be considering his next words carefully. Imogen wondered if she should take this opportunity to flee, but the confusing mix of feelings that toiled inside her kept her rooted to the spot. A door from the restaurant behind her swung open, and a patron stepped onto the street. Laughter, music, the clinking of silverware, along with the delicious scent of garlic danced in the air, and Imogen was grateful that she wasn't alone on the street with this stranger. A man easily double her size, built of muscle, with a storm cloud of emotions on his handsome face.

"I believe it to be, yes." Imogen spoke her words carefully, taking another step away, though her body urged her to step forward and back into his arms. It had felt safe there, though why Imogen needed to feel safe, she couldn't be certain. Her mind flashed back to the creature in the puddle. Okay, sure, maybe a big strapping man by her side wasn't a bad thing. Maybe just not *this* man...

"What are you?" His tone was clipped, and Imogen's eyes widened when he clenched his fists at his sides.

"Surely, you've seen a female before, haven't you then?" Imogen arched a brow at the man. She rocked lightly back on her heels, her hand going to her waistband where her favorite knife was tucked. Imogen had learned a lot working the docks, and protecting herself had been at the top of the list.

"You heard my question." The man glanced to the sky, his worry flashing across his face as lightning exploded in the velvety darkness.

There were no storm clouds.

Imogen swallowed, worry filling her, as the man's eyes sought hers once more.

"And I answered it." Imogen lifted her chin.

"Something's wrong." The man moved to brush past her, but stopped just at her side, and looked down at her. "Be careful with your songs, little one. You don't know what you're doing."

"Excuse me?" Imogen whirled as the man raced up the street, preternaturally quiet. Unease slipped through her at the faint purple tinge glowing in a soft silhouette around the man. It wasn't the first time she'd seen such a thing, but it was something she decidedly tried to ignore. Much like the faces in the water, Imogen wasn't interested in trying to explain why she could see people's auras. At least that's what her research had led her to believe. One big problem? From what she'd learned, auras came in all colors.

Imogen could only see *two* aura colors. Silver and purple. Neither of which helped convince herself that she was, indeed, normal.

While a pint and a bit of home-cooked food had initially been what had drawn Imogen from the *Mystic Pirate* and into the village, now she turned abruptly and made her way back to her boat, hurrying as another bolt of lightning lanced across the night sky.

Whatever problems plagued Grace's Cove were not her own, Imogen decided, breathing out a sigh of relief when she stepped back onto her ship. Unlocking the door to her wheelhouse, she slipped inside and locked the door behind her, and then clambered down a short flight of stairs that led to the galley and lounge area. She crossed the gleaming wood floor and opened a cabinet to pull out a bottle of Green Spot which was usually reserved for the guests and poured herself a healthy glass. Leaning against the counter, Imogen took a sip, and the familiar heat of whiskey soothed her throat.

What are you?

The man's words drifted back to her.

"I wish I knew," Imogen said out loud, before lifting her glass in a silent toast to the strangely glowing man she'd met on the street. "Trust me, sir, I wish I knew."

2

NOLAN LEFT THE WOMAN, the enchantress that she was, and rushed to Gallagher's Pub where he knew he'd find his people. It bothered him deeply just how much he didn't want to leave the red-headed woman whose voice had caused him to turn mid-stride and stalk the village until he found her. The song had been a punch to his gut, and it infuriated him that he'd felt almost no control over his need to find the source. He didn't like things he didn't under-stand, and this witchy-eyed woman with the intoxicating voice didn't fit neatly into his world.

Well, technically he wasn't in his world, was he? Nolan reminded himself of that fact as another bolt of lightning shattered the sky, and his shoulders tensed. He could read the signature of magick that hovered in the air in the wake of the lightning.

The Prince of Fae was angry.

Which meant Nolan had a job to do. As a Royal Court advisor to the Fae, and Prince Callum's best friend, Nolan could count on one hand the number of times that the prince had summoned a storm like this one. But now, as clouds raced across the sky and unleashed a torrent of rain on the streets of Grace's Cove, Nolan ducked into Gallagher's Pub, his eyes seeking one of his own.

He found them, tucked in the corner of the busy pub, one human with added powers and one Fae, diving into a plate of chips. Ignoring the curious looks of the locals, Nolan strode across the packed pub and dropped into a seat across from Bianca and Seamus, his gaze meeting Seamus's worried eyes.

"Has something happened?" Seamus asked, and Bianca, a woman with blonde hair and dancing blue eyes, glanced at her husband in question.

"What's going on?" Bianca looked between the two Fae, worry marring her pretty features.

The door to Gallagher's Pub slammed open with such force, that the windows rattled. The Prince of Fae had arrived.

Judging from the furious wave of energy that crackled around him, as though he controlled the storm itself, Prince Callum was ready for battle.

"Oh shite," Bianca breathed. In seconds, Seamus muttered a complicated spell and threw a magickal bubble across the room, concealing Callum from the view of the crowd. For a moment, everyone looked around in confusion, and then a woman jumped up and ran to close the door. From outside the spell, it would look as though the group at the table continued to enjoy an easygoing conversation.

"Just the storm blowing the door open." Cait, the owner of Gallagher's Pub, shot Callum a look from where she manned the bar.

Thunder roared overhead, shaking the windows of the pub, and Cait ducked under the passthrough and went head-to-head with the Prince. Though she wasn't Fae, Cait had a magickal bloodline that fueled her confidence.

"That's enough of that now. You'll be replacing any windows you break." Cait's voice was low. Callum brushed her aside like she was a gnat, and Bianca's swift hiss of breath was understandable. Very few people were ballsy enough to treat Cait that way. Not to mention the fact that it was rare for Callum to be outright rude.

Which meant something was very, very wrong.

In all the years he had stood by his side, both in battle and in overseeing the Royal Court of the Fae, Prince Callum led with a cool head. But right then, the hair on the back of Nolan's neck lifted, as though darkness slithered over him, and his eyes held Callum's as the prince skidded to a stop at their table.

"Prince." Seamus bowed his head.

"Lily's missing." Callum's words fell like an icicle shattering to the ground. *Callum's fated mate and one true love.* No...

Nolan was the first to speak.

"What happened? I can leave immediately. What should we do?"

Cait surprised Nolan by appearing at Callum's side once more, and she did something that no Fae would ever dare to do – she tugged Callum's hand until he was sitting on a chair in front of the table and handed him a whiskey.

"Tell us," Cait insisted.

Bianca's eyes darted to Nolan's, the pretty blonde having picked up on the break in Royal protocol, and he made a mental note that she might be useful for whatever lay before them. Because if something bad *had* happened – here in Grace's Cove and not in the Fae realm – well, they would need help navigating this world. Both Bianca and her husband, Seamus, had successfully supported the Seekers on their quest to save the Four Treasures from the Domnua, the evil Fae, over two decades ago. If the Domnua *were* involved, these two would be invaluable resources.

Pulling his eyes back to the prince, Nolan waited until Callum had swallowed the whiskey and then schooled his breathing. Outside their magickal bubble, the band played on and a few people had pushed chairs aside to throw themselves into a measure of complicated dance steps. Any other night, and Nolan would have joined them. When he was on duty, Nolan allowed nothing to distract him from the job. But, like all Fae, Nolan loved celebrations and where there was music, there'd often be Fae dancing just outside the awareness of humans.

"It's the Water Fae." Once more Callum leveled a fierce look at Nolan, and his insides twisted. The Water Fae were the faction of Elemental Fae that Nolan himself commanded. It was his duty to oversee and manage their concerns and needs – which meant something, likely the Domnua, had forced the Water Fae to act out.

"You're certain?" Nolan asked, his words sharp.

"Aye, sure and I'm certain."

"Sir, I met with the leader just this week," Nolan said.

"And what was the resolution of this meeting?"

"I met with the Water Fae on their turf – in their protected cave deep in the sea. I was quite confident that we'd left the meeting with a mutual respect and understanding. They'd brought up some concerns for me to address, and I've already made good on one of them."

"Which one?" Callum asked, his fingers clenched tightly on the whiskey glass. The rest of the table remained silent, their eyes bouncing between Callum and Nolan like they were watching a tennis match.

"They desired that the path of the humans' cargo ships be amended slightly as it crossed too closely to their nurseries in the kelp. I adjusted the currents of the ocean to force the boats to give a wider berth to that particular area." Nolan had been proud of this particular feat, as it had taken careful management of many natural elements, not to mention adjusting human behavior without them being aware of it. He'd also been pleased to be able to help the Water Fae quickly, so they would understand that he was working on behalf of them as a representative in the higher realms of Fae Court.

"And that's all? Nothing else...untoward happened in this meeting?"

"No, sir. It was one of our better meetings. Frankly, I'm surprised by this. I was quite pleased with the results of our negotiations, and it had sounded like the elders were as well. Can you tell me what happened?" Nolan took a careful sip of his whiskey, the liquid burning a hot trail to his stomach.

"I only left Lily for a moment." Callum's voice was ragged, his eyes haunted. "I'd promised her I was going to light a fire as humans do." Callum waved his hand in the air. "You know, with the wood, and the flame, and the tinder...all that nonsense. She wanted to see if I would have the patience to try it without my magick, you see. It was a game, really. We were having fun...laughing. I went outside into the storm to get the firewood from the shed. She'd...she'd been standing in the doorway, just a touch in the rain, laughing out at me because she wanted to watch me do manual labor."

Bianca looked as though she wanted to make a comment most likely about how building a fire was not really manual labor, but shut her mouth when Seamus touched her arm briefly.

"When I came back...wood in my arms...she was gone." Callum slammed his fist down on the table and a flash of lightning lit the sky outside the pub. In seconds, thunder followed, shaking the room with its wrath. "The door was wide open. And...just this."

Callum pulled out a piece of parchment paper and put it on the table. Nolan leaned over, not touching it for Fae magick was tricky on an easy day – and read the words.

We trade a love for a love. You've stolen our power. Now we steal your heart.

Below the words was a sketch of a talisman etched with an intricate Celtic knot. It was a drawing of the Water Fae's amulet, which was unimaginably powerful in the wrong hands, and only worn by the leader of the Water Fae. Each faction of the Elemental Fae had a ruling talisman such as the amulet, and the leader always had it on hand lest it be stolen and used for wrongdoing. Panic slipped through Nolan as he met Callum's eyes.

"The amulet. It's missing."

"Aye, and they think *we* stole it."

3

Love is an ocean both powerful and healing.

The song drifted across the water to her, and annoyance laced with a healthy dose of fear flashed through Imogen. It was the same song she'd been singing unintentionally as she'd wandered the streets of the village. Now, as the storm unleashed its fury over the harbor, a thread of fear wound itself through Imogen at the song. Maybe she shouldn't have come here.

Imogen crossed to the window on her boat and looked out to where lightning lit the glowering gray clouds that spat out heavy streams of rain. The ocean roiled, the waves slapping against the hull, and Imogen closed her eyes against the shape she saw moving in the water.

She still remembered, clear as day, the first time her mother, Shauna, had taken her to the ocean. Imogen had been hardly tall enough to see over the stubby rock wall that had lined the small village harbor, but she'd instantly felt like the water was welcoming her home. It had taken her mother's promise of sweets to pull Imogen away from the water. But not before she'd seen a face grinning at her from the waves that lapped gently over the algae-covered rocks.

"Mam, why is the water smiling at me?"

"Hush, now Imogen. You're simply imagining things." Her mother's grip had grown steel-like, and she'd hauled Imogen away from the wall with single-minded determination.

"But...I saw..." Imogen protested, her lip pushing out as she had tried to dig in her heels. For the first time ever, Shauna turned and raised a hand to her. Imogen had ducked in shock, but the blow had never landed. Her mother had caught herself and then dropped to her knees in front of Imogen and fiercely gripped her daughter's arms.

"Listen to me, Imogen. If you never remember another thing that I tell you, remember this." She'd given her daughter a little shake to emphasize her words. "Do not speak of what you see in the water. Ever."

"But..." Imogen's lower lip trembled, and her stomach twisted at the scary look in her mother's eyes. "There's a man..."

"Stop. Immediately. Don't speak of it. Don't talk to anyone about it. Do you hear me?" Another shake at this. "Do you? You will ruin your life if you do."

Tears had filled Imogen's eyes. She couldn't understand why she was getting in trouble.

With that, her mother had hauled her up the street, refusing to wipe Imogen's tears or acknowledge any more questions. She'd given Imogen the silent treatment the rest of the day – a first for young Imogen – and that moment had crystalized in Imogen's memories.

It hadn't been the last time she'd seen those faces in the water, oh no, not to mention numerous other unexplainable things. During her teen years, when rebellion had set in,

Imogen had broached the subject once more with her mother. That night Shauna had followed through on what she hadn't when Imogen was younger, and Imogen had greeted the morning with a bruised face and an empty home. Her mother didn't return for weeks, and Imogen had been left to see herself to school and cook her own meals. When Shauna had finally returned, without an ounce of apology, she had resolved to never speak of what Shauna referred to as Imogen's delusions.

Because, really, that was the only explanation for the beings she saw that slipped easily through the water. Or the colors that danced around people when she first met them. Or that she often was able to command the natural world – seemingly with nothing but a thought. Nope, she *definitely* wasn't going to think too long about that last little bit. Imogen had dealt with the pain of rejection from her unstable mother for years now, and one of her greatest fears was that she would slowly follow Shauna into madness.

Another low roll of thunder sent shivers down her back, and Imogen turned from the window and twisted her braid around her finger. She'd taken to tugging on her braids as a young girl whenever she felt unease or was forcing herself to remain quiet. Imogen paced the ship's galley – four steps forward and four steps back – unable to settle. Tension raked through her body and her skin felt electric, like the lightning that lanced the dark clouds hanging over the small village of Grace's Cove.

She had the boat to herself tonight, as her crew would likely seek companionship in town, something Imogen herself rarely did. Instead, she had planned to go over her marketing proposals for her charters. She needed this season to go well because hopefully within a year or two, her boat would finally be her own and not partially owned by the bank. Her stomach still twisted at the thought of how much money she'd had to borrow to buy her own boat – a gently-used Aqualine Houseboat – but with enough hard work and essentially ignoring any semblance of a social life, Imogen was finally nearing the day where she could come up for air. If all went to plan, in five years, she'd be able to have a healthy savings account set up for herself and perhaps actually be able to take some time off.

An image of sunny skies and tropical waters floated through Imogen's mind, and she smiled to herself at the thought of the dream vacation she had promised herself once she had finally paid off her loan. She was going to strap on the tiniest bikini she could find, order the biggest and most ridiculous frothy cocktail – perhaps one of those served in a coconut with a little umbrella – and relax in the sun on a tropical beach somewhere. Well, not *too* long in the sun as her fair Irish skin would burn in seconds. Imogen mentally added a wide straw hat to her vision.

The *Mystic Pirate* was her baby and all she knew of the world. Hard work and long days were the norm for her, and Imogen briefly wondered if she even knew *how* to relax. More than likely, she'd sit still for ten minutes on that tropical beach and then pop up to race into the water or to do... something. Anything. Idleness wasn't a gift that someone like her could accept easily.

Imogen glanced once more to the window before deciding to return to her Captain's Quarters. It sounded more luxurious than it was, because the space was hardly bigger than the galley she'd just left. But it was hers and she didn't have to share it with anyone, which on a boat was truly a blessing. Even though Imogen had saved and scrimped all her tips and charter profits to pour back into the boat, she'd still managed to create a homey environment for herself in her bunk. A soft woven wool blanket in shades of a stormy sea at dawn covered her neatly made bed. The blanket had been an absolute steal at a thrift market years ago, and it still made Imogen happy to this day. With a nod to the fanciful, Imogen had also strung up some copper wire twinkle lights around her ceiling, and they glowed softly like stars splashed in the sky. A few moody seascape paintings, bought from a street artist, were tacked up on her walls.

Imogen changed into a simple sleep tank and pants, before pulling the wool blanket over her and propping herself up on her pillows. Immediately soothed, she automatically reached for the gold ring tucked in the drawer of her nightstand before opening her laptop. The ring, a worn and weathered gold, was set with a faceted aquamarine stone which matched the color of her eyes almost exactly and was the one piece of jewelry that Imogen owned. In a weird way, it had become a good luck charm – reminding her always that she oversaw her own destiny. She never wore it, for jewelry could catch and cause her harm while running the ship, but every night before bed Imogen would take it out and twist it around her finger in a mindless habit while she worked on the administration side of running her business.

It was never-ending, really. If she wasn't answering guest emails, she was responding to crew issues, ordering parts for the boat, or updating her supplier lists. The *Mystic Pirate* might be her beloved baby, but it was a demanding one.

"Well, now, that's a nice thing to see, isn't it?" Imogen murmured to herself as she read a recent review posted from a guest who had been on a charter a while back. The *Mystic Pirate* operated both daily charters as well as three-day charters for those who wanted to experience Ireland from the water. While it wasn't as glamourous as some of the larger luxurious yachts where guests could take a week to tour the Irish coast in the lap of luxury, Imogen prided herself in making up for it by providing excellent customer experience.

For daytrips to the Cliffs of Moher, Imogen could take up to fifteen passengers on the boat and provide them with a made-with-love Irish meal, an epic storytelling of various myths and legends that surrounded the famous cliffs, and even a proper whiskey-tasting for those who were in the mood. For her longer charters, Imogen had four well-appointed cabins that allowed for an intimate experience for a group of friends or a family who wanted to enjoy the breathtaking views of Ireland from the water. No, her ship wasn't mighty – but it was hers – and Imogen was proud of what she'd created.

Checking her booking schedule, Imogen was more than pleased to see that in a month or so they would start their high season and the calendar was solidly booked for months after that. For the next few weeks, the crew would see to any upgrades or fixes the ship needed, and generally shine the *Mystic Pirate* up until she all but glowed.

A crackle of heat raced down her palm and Imogen glanced at her ring and caught a momentary flash of light emanating from the aquamarine stone. She stilled, schooling her breathing, as her heart began to race. This had happened only a few times over the years, and Imogen had been unable to summon any reasonable explanation for why the ring seemed to glow. Per usual, she'd chalked it up to her imagination or exhaustion, and had tried to put the unusual experience from her mind.

But now, since she had arrived in Grace's Cove? The ring had warmed to her touch each night. Pushing her laptop aside, Imogen held the ring up in front of her face. Her stomach twisted as unease danced through her once again. There was something in the air here, Imogen decided, as the energy had just felt off since she'd arrived. Imogen trusted her instincts, honed from years on the water, and made a mental note to call her crew in the morning and move on from Grace's Cove. Between the strange encounter with the man on the street and the storm that raged outside the boat, Imogen was deeply unsettled.

"It was left for you."

The words came to her, along with her mother's haggard face, as they always did when she studied her ring. Her mother had given it to her as a sixteenth birthday present, when Imogen had been packing her bags after Shauna had opened the door and invited her to make her own way in the world. Imogen supposed that had been Shauna's birthday gift to her – freedom – but at the time, being kicked out had been terrifying. Just before she'd reached the door, Shauna had handed her the ring. For a moment, Imogen's heart had warmed, and she'd thought her mother was giving her something meaningful.

Instead, Shauna's words dripped with bitterness and very little explanation before the door to Imogen's home had been shut neatly in her face. At the time, Imogen had blinked back tears and shoved the ring in her pocket, reluctant to look like a fool standing on the doorstep of her own home with her bags at her feet.

So, she did what she'd learned to do in times of distress – Imogen had gone to the water. There she'd proven herself as an adept and able dockworker, and soon Imogen had been given a chance to get out on the ocean as a crew member.

She hadn't left the water since.

4

ICY RAIN BATTERED Nolan's face as he followed their small group across the rain-slicked street to a flat Cait had offered for their use. Nolan welcomed the pain, as the sharp bite of the storm heightened his senses and caused the magick in his blood to warm. Ready for battle, Nolan drew a sharp intake of breath as a man – Dark Fae, of course – appeared silhouetted in a shimmery silver light at the top of the street. The wide smile on the Fae's face confirmed Nolan's suspicions. Raising his hand, Nolan drew energy from the storm and directed a searing bolt of lightning at the Domnua, but he was already gone, only the silvery threads of his manic laughter lingering in the cold night air.

"What was that?" Callum addressed Nolan immediately from where he paced the small living room of the apartment. Naturally, the prince would have felt the ripple of Fae magick in the air.

"Domnua." Nolan spit the words, as though he'd taken a bite of rotten food, and leaned his back against the door. Bianca and Seamus both drew in sharp breaths, the two knowing full well the danger that the Domnua could bring.

"I'll kill every last one of the spineless bastards," Prince Callum vowed, his hand already reaching for the dagger tucked into his waistband. While the dagger looked unassuming to the casual observer, it held mercurial and violent magick.

The Domnua, otherwise known as the Dark Fae or the bad Fae, had spent centuries trying to wrest power from Nolan's people, the Danula. Over two decades ago, they'd nearly succeeded in their quest to reclaim the legendary Four Treasures – which would have given them free rein of modern-day Ireland – but luckily the good Fae had managed to find the treasures and run the Domnua back to their dark realm.

Until now, it seemed.

"I thought the Domnua were no longer a threat? After we'd beaten the curse and claimed the magickal treasures? Wasn't that kind of the point of the quest?" Bianca asked, her voice tentative. While Bianca was technically human, she'd been such an asset in the great Fae battle that the good Fae had bestowed upon her some extra magick.

The Royal Court of Danula Fae were the strongest in all the Fae realms. It was a point of pride for Nolan that he'd been able to gain such a top role within the Royal Court. He'd done so through dedication, unwavering loyalty, and a willingness to call the prince on his nonsense when Callum was being difficult. It was a fine line to walk, but he'd navigated it masterfully, and now his mind was torn between rage at the Domnua and worry for the prince's love.

"Would you like me to call a meeting with the other Royal Court advisors?" Nolan asked. Callum didn't stop his pacing as he considered Nolan's questions.

"How many advisors are there?" Bianca, ever curious, piped up.

"We have many advisors," Nolan said, his eyes never leaving the prince. "However, the highest standing are ones like myself – who oversee the lesser divisions of the Elementals. Through us, we're able to maintain a natural order to the world and humans are none the wiser for it."

Bianca's eyes widened and she pressed her lips together, clearly holding back more questions as she considered his words.

"I don't know much about the Elementals," Bianca finally said. "I really only know about the Fae through the quest for the Four Treasures. I'm not going to lie, though – the Domnua make me feel stabby."

"And rightly so, my darling love." Seamus ran a hand down Bianca's arm. He, too, stood at attention next to where Bianca sat on the sofa. "They did try to kill you on more than one occasion."

"They underestimated me," Bianca said, a savage smile widening on her cheerfully pretty face. Nolan revised his opinion of her and upgraded her from potentially helpful to an asset. She was coming with them wherever they needed to go.

"How can we sit here and just..." Callum raised the hand with the dagger and gestured to the room, anger roiling across his face.

"Because they *want* you to race blindly into the night searching for her. It's a trap, and a smart one at that. They're not after Lily, Callum. They're after you." Nolan's words stopped Callum in his tracks, and the man took several deep breaths, his gaze on Nolan. Unease prickled over Nolan's skin as he waited for Callum's response.

"Why now?" Seamus stepped forward. "It hasn't been all that long, at least in Fae time, since we banished them. How are they able to make this move?"

"Well..." Bianca said and all the men swung on her. Her eyebrows shot up and she blinked at the angry prince. "Um..."

"Speak," Callum spit out.

"I'm just trying to think like the stupid Fae that they are, you know? And, well, the whole curse of the Four Treasures? That curse lasted centuries, right? The Dark Fae have been clinging to this hope for hundreds of years that one day they would come to power. And, sure and that has to sting a wee bit when they lose, right? So, now, they're likely not thinking straight. Have you ever been so mad that you just wanted revenge? You didn't stop to talk it out or think up a better plan? Sure, and I think that's what's happening now, right? If I were them..." Bianca trailed off and tucked a strand of blonde hair behind her ear, blinking up at the men who all stared at her.

"Go on," Callum ordered. He was listening, at least, Nolan noted.

"I guess if I couldn't immediately be striking back at the Royal Court...you understand? Since we kicked their slimy arses so badly and all, I'd probably start stirring the pot in other ways until I saw my chance again. Looking for a chink in the armor, right?"

"What do you mean stir the pot?" Callum had stopped directly in front of Bianca, hands on hips, and stared down at her. Nolan saw her swallow at the intensity of the prince's stare but gave her credit for continuing to speak.

"So, like, I suppose it would really be something like... well, the Elemental Fae are lesser, as you said, right?"

"They are still vitally important to our kingdom," Callum said automatically.

"Right, sure. I didn't mean to say..." Bianca glanced quickly at Seamus, who gave her an encouraging nod.

"What I meant was lesser in power. It sounds to me like your Royal Court oversees the Elementals, but also takes care of them, right?"

"Correct. We attend to their needs and provide them with assistance depending on what their issues are. We also provide protection and nurturing," Callum said.

"But...technically, you're still the more powerful Fae. You could stop them from doing something they wanted to do. Or put rules on them. Restrictions, right? They don't get free reign?" Bianca pressed on.

"That is correct. While we do value a certain level of autonomy and free thought between all factions of the Fae world, there are some rules that the Elementals must abide by. If only so as not to upset the natural order of things."

"Right, so, say I want to upset that balance? I'd probably..." Bianca tapped a pretty pink nail against her mouth. "Well, I'd likely start pitting the Elementals against each other, but also maybe against the Royal Court. I'd probably try to turn the factions on each other. You know...like saying the Fire Fae.... Are there Fire Fae?" Bianca turned in question to Seamus who nodded down to her.

"Aye, love, there are."

"Well, then, maybe I'd make up lies and say the Fire Fae were getting better treatment. Or rules. Or gifts. Or whatever it is you do." Bianca waved a hand in the air. "Then once I'd created a level of dissatisfaction between all the groups, I'd start directing their angst at you, the Royal Court, that is," Bianca swallowed again. "Classic move, you know? If the Dark Fae are starting an uprising, that is. It's easier to create a division, topple the kingdom, and then when the dust settles, they'll bring the Elementals together to unite against a supposed common evil – you."

"Shite," Callum swore and turned, resuming his pacing.

"Unless, of course, they can get to you first. If that's their goal. If so, they will hit you where you are vulnerable. Which, would be...Lily," Bianca said, her tone gentle.

This was why it was important to never fall in love, Nolan thought to himself. Love clouded a person's thoughts. Nolan couldn't afford to be distracted, which was why he'd never taken more than a few nights with a lover before. He'd seen more than one Fae lose his edge once he found his fated mate. Maybe that was fine for some, but he needed to keep a clear head if he was going to protect the prince.

"What do you think of this?" Callum swung and crossed to Nolan. "You've been mighty quiet."

"I'm just as surprised as you are, Callum. I'm listening and taking it all in. Because, despite the seriousness of the situation – we can't be rash. I have to assume that the Domnua are behind this – as I just saw one of the Dark Fae outside. Which means, they are causing trouble and you know when they do things like this, your family are the targets. Which means, we have to be smart about our actions. When we move, we do so in a protected manner. Racing into the storm with no direction to go on is foolish."

"I can't just sit here," Callum spit out.

"You're of no use to Lily if you're dead," Nolan said, his tone even, as he waited to see how the prince would handle his response. Lightning shattered the night sky and thunder followed closely behind, shaking the windows of the building.

"Cait's gonna be fiercely mad..." Bianca whispered to Seamus, who squeezed her arm with a smile.

"Wait!" Callum's head shot up and he held his hands to the ceiling. Instantly, the storm quieted, and the prince strode to the window, staring out into the darkness.

"What..." Nolan bit his words off when the prince shot a heated glare over his shoulder.

"She's calling to me. I can hear her in my mind. She sings our song..." Callum closed his eyes, and for the first time Nolan saw the fear etched across his face. The prince's hand tightened around the dagger.

"Are you able to track her? If she continues to sing?" Nolan asked, his voice soft. His mind danced to the witchy-eyed woman and her song earlier. Was she a trap set by the Domnua to distract him? He'd all but run through the village looking for her.

"Aye, I think I can track Lily. We'll need a ship." Callum turned and looked between Seamus and Bianca. "She's here. In this world. They haven't yet taken her to their realm."

"A ship? But why? Isn't it dangerous to go out on the ocean if the Water Fae are the ones..." Bianca gulped when Callum turned on her and Seamus jumped in front of his love. Though he was built like a lanky string bean, he had a quiet confidence that resonated with Nolan.

"They wouldn't expect us to go by water for exactly that reason," Callum supplied and looked up at a soft knock at the door.

"Food and drinks." Cait's voice came through the door and Nolan moved. He allowed the door to open just a crack and scanned the hallway before ushering her inside with her tray. "Sure, and I'm appreciating you stopping the storm, Callum."

"Cait, we'll need supplies. And a boat," Nolan said, having grown to like the diminutive bartender over the last few weeks. She was a woman of action, quick thinking, with a strong backbone.

"Of course. The boat may be a touch tricky, but I'll start calling around now. In the meantime, I'll have packs organized for you and ready to go within the hour. Will that suit?"

"We can't wait days for a boat," Callum said. "But we'll take the packs."

"What are you thinking then?" Nolan asked.

"Leave the boat to me." Callum's smile was dangerous in the soft light of the living room. For a fleeting moment, Nolan wondered what it would be like to love someone with that level of intensity. Brushing the thought aside, he turned to Cait and took the tray from her.

"We'll accept the packs. The sooner the better, as I don't think we'll be able to keep Callum here much longer."

"I don't blame him. Lily's special. You'll bring her home." Cait's words were for Nolan and he smiled briefly at her.

"Aye, we'll bring her home."

5

IMOGEN SAT up in her bunk, blinking the sleep from her eyes, as her brain scrambled to separate itself from the silky threads of her dream. Her heart hammered in her chest and sweat dampened her brow. It was the same dream she'd had for years now, and it always, *always*, left her deeply unsettled and questioning reality.

It was the man from the water. Every time. Both terrifying and enchanting, he visited her in her dreams, and while every time the dream was different – the message was always the same.

Come to me.

The man would beckon to her, just as he always did when Imogen would see him flitting beneath the surface of the ocean. But in her dreams, the pull to join him was so much more powerful. It was as though he held the answers to her life's greatest questions. And all she had to do was dive below the surface of the water and join him. Scary, really, when she thought too long about it, because even Imogen knew that throwing herself into the icy cold ocean on a blustery winter's night was a recipe for certain death.

But this time? The dream had been different.

He hadn't just asked her to join him this time, oh no. This time? He'd cut his finger and held it up for her to see. A trickle of radiant bluish red blood had trailed down his pearlescent finger as the man's grin widened in his face.

My blood. You belong with me.

It was that moment which had shattered Imogen, and she'd shot upright in her bed, her chest heaving as she gasped for breath, thinking this man could be her father. And what a silly thought, really. But Imogen supposed that if a person had never had a father figure, maybe anything could appear as one in her dreams. Daddy issues, much? Imogen laughed to herself and tried to shake off the unsettled feeling that the dream had left her with.

Something...she wasn't sure what...caused her chin to come up and she cocked her head. Taking a second, she remained motionless as she schooled her breathing. A soft glow emanated from the crack in her bedside drawer and Imogen eyed the light with confusion. No sounds or anything untoward greeted her, and yet, the light still pulsed gently from her drawer.

Well, this was new, Imogen thought, as she slid the drawer carefully open and looked down at the aquamarine ring. Sure enough, it glowed softly – like a nightlight in a toddler's bedroom – but significantly less soothing. The light felt like a warning, and fear slid through her to create a knot of tension at the base of Imogen's neck. The boat rocked quietly on its mooring, the storm having subsided, and nothing unusual seemed afoot.

And yet...

Imogen stood and, leaving the ring where it was, she reached for the knife next to it. It was one of her favorite blades, fitting neatly in the palm of her hand, and she was rarely without it. While the knife came in generally useful around the boat for all things maintenance, Imogen had honed her skills with throwing it over the years. There had been many a bored night where she and her crew had created their own amusements while docked. Though Imogen hadn't allowed knives to be thrown on board, because, well, she knew the price of teak wood. Between that and several self-defense courses, something Imogen had found useful more than once through the years, she felt confident in her ability to defend herself. It was why it never bothered her to sleep on her boat alone.

She still remembered the wife of the very first warehouse manager who'd given her a job helping to offload cargo ships. The woman had turned a blind eye to her doctored documents, proclaiming her older than she was and instead had taken her under her wing. The first order of business? Self-defense classes. While the other employees had eventually become a loose, albeit crude, family, Imogen had come to learn that not everyone abided by the same moral code. She'd surprised more than one man who had limped away after testing her boundaries.

Perhaps she'd been lucky so far, Imogen thought, as she eased the door to her cabin open silently. Padding quietly through the wheelhouse lit only by the soft glow from the instruments at the dash, Imogen paused at a door with a small window and peered out into the darkness. Again, nothing was amiss that she could see, just the faintly twinkling lights of a village that seemed to be sleeping. Deciding she would feel better if she did a perimeter check anyway, Imogen eased the door open and stepped onto the deck.

The cold wind slapped her skin and Imogen immediately regretted not grabbing a jumper to pull over her sleep tank. Made of thin cotton, the tank molded to her body in the wind, and her nipples perked at the rush of cold. Ignoring the weather, Imogen crept barefoot down the dock, her eyes scanning quickly for anything out of place.

"You should drop the knife."

The words, heavy with warning, caused her to whirl. The knife was out of her hand and flying in the direction of the voice before Imogen could blink.

"I'm not in the mood for this." The man, visible in the faint glow from the dock light, snagged the knife out of the air and pocketed it neatly in the leather coat he wore. Imogen froze.

No normal man could move that fast.

It was him. The man from the street earlier that evening.

Her pulse raced. The man – or whatever he was – instantly brought two opposing reactions in her body. The first? Well, it was the same damn one as before. Imogen wanted to cross the boat and pull this man into a heated kiss, wrapping herself around him, and letting him feast upon the gift of her body. *Yes*, her heart seemed to whisper. *Go to him.* It was the most powerful reaction she'd ever had to someone before, and Imogen gasped against the confusing emotions that rocketed through her, her body responding to the heat in his gaze.

The second emotion was, of course, fear. Not just because this man was clearly lethal, but also for the faint color she could see emanating softly around him. Imogen swallowed against her dry throat, offering nothing to the man, and lifted her chin.

"You don't need to make this more difficult." The man, or God, or whatever he was, sighed and ran a hand through dark hair that almost reached his shoulders. He was built like a tree, or a mountain, Imogen decided, carefully trying to rate her odds against his strength. Though she remembered what it had felt like to run into him before. He was all muscle. Thick legs were defined in fitted leather pants, and broad shoulders and arms filled out the jacket he wore. Working man's boots, a chiseled jaw, and a *screw-you* glint in his eyes completed the package of deadly confidence.

The punch of power she felt from this man terrified Imogen, and yet...

And yet.

Something in her rose, seeking to challenge him, seeking to know him, seeking to...well, best to push that thought aside. No, this man was a threat, plain and simple, and needed to be dealt with. Fast.

"Sure, and it's not me making things difficult now, is it? 'Tis my ship, and you've clearly lost your way." Imogen said, taking a step back and to the side. He mirrored her movement.

"I'm exactly where I'm meant to be. Though I'll admit, I wasn't expecting you again..." His raspy voice sent a shiver across her skin. She could imagine his mouth at her throat, that delicious voice whispering decadent words against her skin, and lust pooled low in her body. What was wrong with her? Imogen widened her eyes, furious with herself and with this man for creating such thoughts in her mind.

"Well, that makes two of us," Imogen said, sliding further from the man. He echoed her movements, prowling forward, forcing Imogen backwards. The stern of the boat was behind her and if she could just take a few more steps, she could disappear quickly over the side and into the door to the engine room. Imogen knew all the passages on the boat, and he was certainly at a disadvantage. She just had to...

"We don't have time for this, Nolan."

Imogen whirled at the fury-laden voice that came from

behind her. Instantly realizing her mistake, she kicked back as the first man's arm circled her waist and slammed her firmly back against his chest. It was like hitting a stone wall, and Imogen gasped out a short breath before reeling forward and slamming her head backward, trying to catch his nose with the back of her head.

"Stop." The man cursed low and long, dodging her attempts to head butt him, and kept her neatly locked against his body no matter how she tried to twist and turn. Angling her foot, she kicked it back, trying to catch him between the legs, and gasped when his thighs closed around her leg, capturing her. "I said...stop. You'll only hurt yourself."

"I wouldn't be so sure about that," Imogen bit out, turning to glare at him over her shoulder.

Gray. A stormy moody impossibly gray color were his eyes. Imogen paused, caught in his look, and he seemed equally stunned. The moment hung suspended, before Imogen wrenched an arm away and shot her elbow harshly into his ribs. A soft gasp escaped the man's lips, but his hold didn't weaken.

"We're commandeering your boat." The second man, his gaze fierce and his tone commanding, stared at her. "But you'll be driving it."

"Like hell I will," Imogen said, blinking at the sight of the same purple color dancing faintly around the second man. Was this it then? The final slippery slide into delusion? Glowing purple men and faces in the water...rings that lit from within? Maybe she'd finally stepped neatly into her own fantasies and the real world would no longer matter.

The second man walked forward and grabbed her chin with his hand, holding her face steady as he bit out his words. Imogen paused. His eyes...well, they were enchanting in the most terrifying of ways. Fear, fury, and sadness danced in them, and an ancient power – one which Imogen would have no chance against – caused her to wilt against the man who held her.

"You have no choice in the matter."

"I understand." Imogen hated the words, but her survival instincts had kicked in. She knew as much as she knew the sun rose in the east that the man in front of her would kill her if he didn't get his way. Imogen was a fighter, but she also wasn't stupid.

"You'll do my bidding?" the man holding her chin asked.

"For now," Imogen bit out.

"Nolan. You'll watch her every minute. I don't trust her not to cause problems."

"And rightly so!" This time, a woman's voice. The tone of it immediately soothed Imogen, and she looked past the furious man in front of her to see a pretty blonde woman boarding her ship.

"What in the world are you doing?" the woman demanded, seemingly unbothered by the fierceness of the two men who currently caged Imogen in. "Sure, and there's a better way to be asking to borrow a boat, isn't there? Look at the poor thing...she's half-dressed and likely terrified. Did you pull her from her bed? I'm sorry..." This, the woman addressed to her, and pushed past the angry man in front of Imogen. Concerned blue eyes met hers. "I'm Bianca and these gentlemen...well, I'll explain later. Did they tell you what is going on?"

"It appears they are commandeering my ship, and I'm meant to be their captain," Imogen bit out, squirming against the rock-solid grip across her stomach. She was likely to have bruises in the morning.

"Erm, well, yes, that's technically true. But it's a rescue

mission, you see? This one..." Bianca pointed to the second man. "His name is Callum. His fiancée has been kidnapped. We need to go after her."

Imogen's eyes widened. Surely the woman was being sincere, but...

"Why wouldn't you just call the Gardai? This seems a bit odd, no?"

"Um, yes, well, that's the part that might be needing a touch more explanation," Bianca admitted. "But...unfortunately, we really do need your help. The missing woman is... she's a friend of mine."

A ragged look of sorrow crossed Callum's face at Bianca's words, and it was then Imogen made her decision.

"Aye, I'll help. But only because you've asked, Bianca. I need an explanation. And I'll need to be letting my crew know where I am. They're family, you see. They'll be heading back to the boat..." Imogen cut off when Callum lifted his arm.

"Nobody else shall board!"

"Right. Well..." Imogen looked at Bianca.

"Can you drive this thing without the crew?" Bianca asked.

"This thing is called the *Mystic Pirate*, and she is a majestic and infuriating boat. Of course, I can captain her alone. But it won't be easy. It's really best to have some crew..."

"Nobody else." Callum swore and a lightning bolt flashed across the sky.

"I'll just need to contact my crew." Imogen held up a hand to stop Callum's words. "I can't leave them here with no explanation. They'll send the Gardai to look for me as well. It wouldn't make sense to them."

"She's not wrong. Let her contact them. If you're worried

she's going to send someone after us, we can read the messages." Bianca looked between the two hulking men.

A drop of sweat slithered down the back of Imogen's neck, the parts of her body pressed into Nolan's alive with heat. She wondered if he could feel her reaction to him. Imogen hoped not. Because as much as she hated being caged in his arms – well, her libido certainly didn't seem to mind. His strength both overwhelmed and intoxicated her, and Imogen suddenly had a new appreciation for those captive romance novels a co-worker of hers used to read.

"How soon can we leave?" Callum directed the question at her, and Imogen had to pull her mind away from thoughts of Nolan.

"Within the hour. I'll need to get the engines going, chart our course, check the weather..." Imogen looked up at Callum. "You do know our course, don't you?"

"We'll figure it out."

"Grand, just grand." Imogen let out a breath and stepped quickly away from Nolan when he finally released her. Refusing to turn and meet his eyes, afraid of what he might see in her, she looked at Bianca. "I don't trust these two. But I trust you. Promise me you'll cause me no harm."

"I can promise you that none of *us* will harm you," Bianca said.

"How many is us?" Imogen demanded.

"Just one more!" A cheerful face popped into view. A lanky man with a shock of red hair and a bright smile on his face came into view.

"That one's mine. Hands off," Bianca said, shooting the new arrival a saucy wink.

"No bother about that," Imogen said. "I've sworn off men for the foreseeable future."

"More's the pity to you then." Bianca grabbed her arm

and pulled her past Callum. "Let's get those messages sent to your crew and the boat on the way before Callum explodes."

"I don't like them." Imogen glanced over her shoulder and glared at Nolan. His eyes caught hers and held, a ripple of awareness moving between them, before Imogen turned away.

"Well, sure and there's extenuating circumstances at the moment. Perhaps in time you'll see they're not so bad," Bianca said.

"I doubt it."

6

"Why don't you get some clothes on? It's a bit cold out," Bianca said.

"Aye, I'll do that." Imogen's mind whirled as she crossed to the door that led into the wheelhouse and through that to her cabin. Bianca followed, glancing around the small room when Imogen flipped the lights on.

"Well, this is nice, isn't it? Cozier than I expected."

"It suits me." Imogen grabbed the wool sweater hanging on a hook by her door and tugged it over her head, not bothering to put a bra on. Though she was well-endowed in that department, Imogen just wasn't comfortable with changing in front of a stranger even though Bianca was doing her best to be kind...at least that was how it seemed. Imogen paused and looked over at the woman. Perhaps this was all a ruse – like the good cop/bad cop routine on television shows. The men were the bad cops and when that approach didn't work, they sent Bianca in to smooth the way. She narrowed her eyes.

"What?" Bianca asked, tilting her head at Imogen in question. Imogen looked the woman up and down. In any other light, she was an attractive mid-fifties woman wearing a bright blue sweater, fitted denim pants, and sturdy hiking boots. She could've been Imogen's mother if Shauna had eaten well and stayed away from her demons.

"I'm just trying to decide if you're running a scam on me," Imogen admitted, straightening and pulling her braid out of the collar of her sweater.

"Sure, and I'd be thinking the same, wouldn't I?" Bianca nodded approvingly at Imogen. "May I?" Bianca gestured to the bed and Imogen shrugged her acquiescence.

"I have questions."

"I would hope so," Bianca said, settling onto the bed and turning to look at the paintings tacked to Imogen's wall. "These are nice."

The move relaxed the tension at Imogen's shoulders. If the woman considered her a threat, Bianca never would have taken her eyes off Imogen.

"Thanks. A street artist I came upon during a wander through a village on the coast." Imogen turned her back and slipped out of her sweatpants and into sturdy canvas pants that would cut the slice of the wind when she was on deck.

"I don't know how much time I'll have to answer questions before Prince...I mean, Callum, comes along and breaks your door down." Bianca hurried on. "But ask away."

"Prince?" Imogen asked, her tone sharp.

"Whoops. Well, as I said...I don't have much time." A small smile hovered on Bianca's lips. "And this might be a situation where one question leads to hundreds."

"They're not human, are they?" Imogen cut to the quick of it and Bianca leaned back, surprise on her face.

"Well, now. That's interesting. What makes you say that?"

A flush of embarrassment raced through Imogen.

Stupid, she berated herself. Stupid, stupid, stupid. She knew better than to speak of such things.

"Forget it." Imogen opened a cupboard and tossed her sweatpants in and slammed the door. "I need to check our supplies and see where our fuel is at. I'm not sure where we are going or how long we'll be gone."

"I didn't say you were wrong."

The words stopped her, and Imogen just stood, her back to Bianca, and leaned forward until her forehead rested against the cool wood of the door. Her breath hitched as she took in Bianca's words.

"What...what do you mean?" Imogen's voice rasped and she waited. Waited for the words that might, just might, mean she wasn't actually going crazy. That would tell her that all these years she hadn't been imagining the things she saw. That perhaps, there was more to this world than anyone really knew.

"Callum, well, Prince Callum that is...he's the Prince of Fae."

Fae.

The word rocketed through her, a gift and a curse, and Imogen spun to stare wildly at Bianca.

"It's a lot to take in at once. I know it." Bianca held up a hand and laughed. "But also – how cool, right? It's just fascinating to learn that all these myths and legends were based in truth. I mean, an entirely different realm exists still today! Twenty-some years later and I'm still learning new things about their world. I have to tell you, the Fae are exceedingly complex..." Bianca trailed off when Imogen held up her hand to stop her. "Sorry, I get carried away."

"You're...you're saying to me that the Fae are real? And those men..." Imogen lifted her chin to the door, "out there are Fae? Not human? But...magick?"

"Sure, and it sounds a touch silly, doesn't it then?" Bianca laughed. "But, aye, that's the truth of it."

"Fae." Imogen whispered, her eyes darting to the side table that housed her ring.

"Is that surprising though? You already seemed to know they weren't of this world. How does that come to be?" Bianca tilted her head at Imogen.

"I..." Years of keeping her thoughts quiet made it difficult for Imogen to speak.

Bianca waited her out, her eyes warm, an understanding look on her face.

"I just...it's just a sense of things. I don't know how to explain..." Or Imogen wasn't ready to. Though she felt she could believe what this woman was telling her, there was too much about tonight she still needed to process. Now certainly wasn't the time to unload all her deeply buried secrets.

"That's fair. That means you have good instincts. We can talk more about this, but I suspect Nolan is about to lose his mind here shortly if we don't get on with it. Should we be messaging your crew then and getting everything sorted to leave?" Bianca could have been planning a picnic for all the casualness with which she spoke.

"Yes, let's." Imogen put her walls back up, not ready to reveal more about herself.

"Just one thing..." Bianca reached out and touched Imogen's arm, her voice serious. "If you see someone glowing silver, kill them."

"You...wait..." Imogen's eyebrows shot up to her hairline. "You want me to kill someone? I *can't* do that. I didn't think this was...I don't want to get involved in..."

"You're already involved. They'll come after you no matter what now. The silver are the Domnua. The bad Fae.

The Dark Fae. They'll kill you in seconds if they think you stand in the way of what they want. Don't talk to them. Don't trust them. Don't let them close."

"You're serious?" Imogen's mind couldn't get past Bianca speaking about glowing silver men. If the Fae glowed, like the faint sheen of light she'd seen around the men outside tonight, that meant she'd been seeing Fae her whole life. And, the bad ones, at that.

Yeah, it was a lot to process. Had she been in danger all along? Why hadn't she been killed before this?

"I'm serious. I wouldn't usually advocate for violence, however the Dark Fae make it virtually impossible to live in harmony with them. In a situation where it is kill or be killed? You'd better damn well believe I'll kill first."

Imogen tripped over the image of the bubbly blonde killing...well, anything really. She just seemed so soft and maternal.

"Noted," Imogen said. "Except Nolan has my knife."

"We'll get it back for you. And likely a few more weapons. So long as you promise not to use it on us, of course."

"I won't. Not on you or your man at least. I'm withholding judgment on the other two. Technically speaking, this is still a hostage situation and you all have pirated my boat. I'll be making up my own mind as we go along."

"Do I need to warn Nolan to be on guard with you? He'll be the one protecting the prince, that is."

"You might as well. I don't yet trust him, so...yeah, I think it's fair to warn him," Imogen said as she opened her door. She came up short when she saw Nolan blocking the hallway.

"Why would I be giving you your knife back then?"

Nolan asked, his raspy voice sending a shiver through her once more.

"If you're good at your job, then me being armed shouldn't worry you." Imogen raised her chin.

"Being good at my job would mean disarming any threats." Nolan crossed his thick arms over his barrel-like chest.

"She'll need some defense, Nolan. What if we're at sea and a Fae boards while she is on deck? Then we'd be without a captain."

"We'd figure it out." Nolan dismissed her death as though the loss of her would be but a mild annoyance.

"You're a real charmer, aren't you?" Imogen glared at Nolan and pushed past him into the wheelhouse.

"Charm isn't a useful tool."

"You'd be surprised how incredibly helpful charm can be when used at the right times," Imogen shot back, pulling out a notebook and coming to stand in front of her dash.

"Oh, I've been known to use it." Nolan's voice turned husky, and warmth slipped through Imogen's core.

"Nolan. Give her the knife back. You're asking a lot of her right now. Show some faith." Bianca nudged Nolan. "Go on then, be nice."

"We're not asking anything of her. We're telling," Nolan pointed out and when Imogen whirled, ready to tell him just what she thought of him, she stopped when he handed her the knife.

"This isn't my only weapon," Imogen forced herself to look into Nolan's stormy eyes. "Don't underestimate me. This is still my boat and I'm in charge. If you don't want to get hurt, I suggest you stay out of my way."

"Not happening, *mavourneen*."

"I'm not your darling," Imogen all but snarled at his Irish term of endearment. "My name is Imogen. But Captain will suit."

7

"I'M CALLING A TEAM MEETING," Bianca declared, opening the door of the pilothouse and whistling for Callum and Seamus. Nolan followed Imogen through a small doorway and down a few steps into a lounge-type area with a curved seating bunk and a few tables for meals.

"I thought your man outside was in charge." Imogen raised her chin at Nolan and a ripple of awareness flitted through him. He didn't *want* to be aware of this caustic and difficult woman. He didn't want to think about how the weight of her breasts had pressed softly into his arm as he'd held her against him nor how her scent had clouded his mind for a moment. Her hair had smelled like fresh morning dew on rose petals, and he'd had to actively restrain himself from burying his face in her braid and taking a deeper inhale. No, Imogen was most certainly a distraction, and one he couldn't afford when the prince's life was on the line.

And yet... Her eyes, a glacial blue so light they were almost silver, could stop a man at ten paces. Nolan's hands itched to unbraid her hair just to see the fiery mass spread out across his sheets...

Shaking his head, Nolan cursed softly and pulled his mind away from *that* particular image while lust surged in his veins. It had been a while since he'd taken a lover, Nolan reminded himself, which was certainly why he was having such a palpable response to the woman currently spitting daggers at him with her eyes. She could be a trap, Nolan reminded himself. Why had she been wandering the streets earlier and singing a magickal song? She wasn't fully human, that was for sure, but he couldn't quite place his finger on what she was. He wondered if he could get her to tell him.

"Aye, Prince Callum is in charge. But we are a team. And Bianca and Seamus have already proven their worth in Fae battles. I wouldn't be so quick to dismiss her."

"I wasn't dismissing her. I was asking if she was also in charge." Annoyance flashed across Imogen's stunning face, and Nolan found himself caught at the way her emotions rapidly played across her visage. "She's the only one I'm listening to at the moment, actually. I'm surprised a man like you would even bother to give her credit."

Now it was Nolan's turn to be annoyed. His hand hovered at the hilt of the dagger tucked at his waist, a subconscious reaction to being provoked, and he rocked back on his heels.

"Our leader is a woman. Queen Aurelia. She's as fierce as any man in battle, if not stronger for her cunning. I have no qualms with women in power, *mavourneen*. If anything, I often prefer it." Nolan let heat infuse his voice, wanting to see if his words would unsettle Imogen. He was rewarded when a faint blush tinged her porcelain skin. At the very least, it didn't seem like he was the only one affected.

However, it wouldn't do for him to push the limits with this one. As much as it pained him to say, they couldn't magick their way to where Callum thought Lily was imprisoned, which meant they needed Imogen. And her boat.

No, he most definitely should pretend like he didn't see the flush on her skin, nor the way her eyes dilated slightly when she looked at him, or the fact that the air had grown so heavy with desire that he could almost taste it. If he was going to be honest with himself, never had a woman impacted him so. But now was not the time for truths of the heart and Nolan took point by the door when Callum and Seamus joined them in the lounge.

"How soon can we leave?" Callum demanded, and Imogen immediately sighed.

"I need more information," Imogen began, but Bianca held up her hands to stop the conversation.

"First things first. Let's all have a seat, a cup of tea perhaps?" Bianca glanced to the galley. "And, Imogen – do you have a map of the area?"

"Aye, I've a digital one I can pull up on my iPad." Imogen was already moving to the galley where Nolan could just see her turning an electric kettle on to boil.

Callum seared Bianca with a look, but she just shrugged and gave a little wave of her hands.

"Listen, you two in particular," Bianca put her hands on her hips and Nolan wanted to hunch his shoulders when she took on a lecturing tone. "I understand what is at stake here. We love Lily as well. However, this isn't our first time bringing human and Fae together in a manner that requires the human to get caught up to speed. And fast, at that. If you don't take a quick moment to fill in some background and give the human a chance to understand what and why they should be helping you, you're going to have problems down the road. Understood? She's not dumb, from what I can see. She'll be quick on the uptake, but sure and you need to be giving her some information."

"Thanks, Bianca. I appreciate that." Imogen strode back into the room with a tray full of teacups and biscuits. "She's not wrong. If I'm to put my life and livelihood on the line, I deserve to know what for. What you need to understand about me is that this boat is all I have in the world. If it gets damaged, or worse, destroyed, I'll be left with nothing but a hefty debt to the bank. Particularly if I can't explain to my insurance what happened. I'll really be needing to know just what is happening and what the dangers are. You're demanding a lot of me and it's only fair."

"We don't need to tell you anything," Nolan said, unsure why she grated at him so. "We took your boat from you, and the only motivation you should need is the wish to stay alive."

"Now, Nolan." Bianca whirled on him. "That's not very nice."

"It's the truth." Nolan shrugged. This wasn't his first battle, and with any battle, there were always going to be people who got the short end of the stick when it came to contributing to the greater good. In this case, that would be Imogen.

"I'd sink this boat rather than let you captain it." Imogen's icy eyes were on his, and he could feel the heat of her anger in his core.

"Well, now, that would be a bit tough to explain to this insurance place now, wouldn't it?" Nolan made a mental note to ask Bianca what insurance was, as it wasn't a thing in the Fae realm.

Imogen's lip curled but before she could shoot a response back, Bianca held up her hand again.

"Right, that's enough out of both of you. Yes, technically we've commandeered a boat. However, Imogen has agreed to help because she has a good heart and knows a woman is in danger. Therefore, we owe it to her to explain some of what is going on. Well, the parts we know so far, that is. First of all, Imogen, we need your boat because if we use too much of our magick to get us to Lily, it's basically like a tracking sensor for the bad Fae to find us."

"You're not human." Nolan's eyes were drawn back to Imogen as she wrapped her braid nervously around her hand. Though she was looking at Callum when she spoke, Nolan could feel in her words the tremor of nervousness and something else...fear was it?

"No, I'm not." Callum had decided to follow Bianca's lead, and this time his tone was soft as he studied Imogen across the table. "I'm Prince of the Danula Fae – also known as the good Fae."

"And your mother is Queen Aurelia?" Imogen asked, surprising Nolan with her quick memory.

"Correct, you've heard of her?" Callum asked, surprise lighting his eyes. He leaned back against the booth, his head tilting at Imogen.

"No, this one mentioned it." Imogen wouldn't look at Nolan but gestured with a hand to where he stood. For some reason, it angered him that she wouldn't say his name.

"Aye, she is queen and has full ruling rights. The throne will pass to me when she sees it is time. But first, I needed to find my fated mate."

"Lily?" Imogen asked.

"Correct. A human, at that. Not improbable for a fated mate of royalty to be human, but also not usual."

"And how does one know they are fated?" Imogen asked, and then pressed her lips together as though she hadn't meant to ask. The move drew Nolan's eyes to her mouth, and he found himself running his tongue over his own lips, wanting a taste of her.

Aye, he had a problem on his hands. Nolan tore his gaze away and scanned the dark windows, opening his senses to see if any threats were near. When nothing signaled, he turned his attention back to the conversation. Was this woman meant to be an enchantress that would lead him astray? Or was it just her heart-stopping beauty that was already distracting him?

"A fated mate is something that is taken very seriously in the Fae world," Callum explained. Nolan was surprised at his patience in this moment, but he'd clearly decided they needed Imogen as an ally. Nolan wasn't sure why – couldn't she just drive the boat and stay in the background? "It starts when they begin to sing each other's heartsong. It will grow louder and more persistent through the years, almost to the point of annoyance – or distraction – and you can't think of anything else until you find your person. Or, in some cases, you can run magicks to actively cut the cord to your fated mate. Not many choose this route, but some who aren't willing to take a chance on love do so."

"A song?" Imogen's face had gone whiter, if that was possible. Nolan's interest piqued. He already knew that she was capable of wielding power with her voice.

"Yes, a heartsong. You'll hear it at the damndest times," Callum laughed and ran a hand over his face. "Across the water. During work. In battle. While you're sleeping. You can't get away from it. The heart wants what the heart wants. And if you have a fated mate, the day will come when you'll need to choose."

Imogen took a few deep breaths before continuing to

speak. Annoyance flashed through Nolan at his preoccupation with this woman.

"And what happens when you meet your fated mate?"

"Ideally? Love. Instant connection. A knowing. A reckoning. You'd be aware of this person in ways you've never been with others. You can read their emotions, feel their presence, and it's...it's just a knowing. A rightness."

Nolan's eyes locked on Imogen as his heart picked up speed. She continued to twist her long braid around her hand, and his eyes were riveted on the way the light danced across the strands of her hair, pulling out deeper tones of gold and honey mixed with the red. For a brief moment, he considered the fact that she might be his fated mate. Immediately dismissing the idea, Nolan mentally rolled his eyes. He'd been very clear with the Fates that he wasn't interested in being matched with a fated mate. Surely, the goddesses would have listened to his requests.

"So, Lily is human. You found her here? In Grace's Cove? And she's your fated mate?" Imogen said, her voice sounding tense.

"She is. And she's been abducted by the Water Fae. Or so we think. We've only a small clue to go on."

"Water Fae. Right." Another tug on the braid and Bianca leaned forward.

"Listen, I'll spend some time with you on the journey explaining all the intricacies of the Fae world. But essentially the good Fae? They're the ones glowing faintly purple. They oversee the Elemental Fae. They keep our natural world in order and make it so us humans can rely on things like...water, fire, seasons and so-on. The bad Fae? Well, they want to be more powerful than the good. They want to control the Elementals."

"Why?" Imogen blinked at Bianca.

"Because their end-goal is to leave the dark realm and inhabit Ireland."

"Wait...like Ireland now? Among humans? Just...take over?" Imogen's eyes widened.

"Yes. It would be catastrophic, and that's me stating it lightly." Bianca reached out and patted Imogen's hand. "I can't stress this enough – the bad Fae will kill you in an instant if they think it will get to Prince Callum or it will help their end goal. You cannot hesitate."

"That's...that's a lot to take in. What would Ireland even do? What would the world do? It's just...I'm still wrapping my head around the existence of any Fae, let alone bad ones that want to take over the world." Imogen shook her head, her nose wrinkling in distaste.

"Yet it didn't seem such a surprise..." Bianca smiled gently at Imogen. "You're the one who said the men weren't human. So there had to be something there that you knew of their world?"

A flash of sheer panic raced across Imogen's face before she shuttered her emotions with a wall. Interesting, Nolan thought. She knew more than she was letting on. The question was why? When Bianca glanced at him, he realized she'd come to the same conclusion as well, but when he opened his mouth to speak, she gave him a subtle shake of her head.

"I mean...I'm Irish, aren't I? And a sailor, at that. You'd be hard-pressed to meet a sailor that doesn't believe in myths of some sort, no?" Imogen said. She was lying, Nolan realized. He could feel it. Well, not entirely, but this wasn't the whole truth.

"What are you hiding?" Nolan bit out. If they had a traitor in their midst, he needed to know.

"My secrets are my own, servant." Imogen glared across

the table at him and crossed her arms over her chest. Nolan tried to ignore the way her breasts shifted beneath her sweater and instead focused on her words.

"Hardly a servant." Nolan's lip curled in distaste.

"You're in service to the prince, no? I'd say that makes you a servant." Imogen shrugged, a hint of glee turning her eyes a deeper blue.

"Careful, *mavourneen*. You don't know what game you're playing." Nolan's voice was low, but he pushed a wave of magick through them so she could feel his power.

"Just because I didn't volunteer to play doesn't mean I won't compete." Imogen shocked Nolan by remaining unruffled by his wave of magick. Had she not felt it? It was as though it had hit a wall and bounced back to him.

"Children. Enough." Callum broke the tension. "We only have so much time and my patience is running thin. Imogen, do you understand the stakes?"

"Aye. Bad Fae are bad. Good Fae...are questionable," Imogen raised an eyebrow mockingly at him and Nolan wanted to throttle her. Or kiss her senseless, he couldn't quite decide. Which infuriated him even further. "Trust nobody. Find Lily and get her home safely."

"Basically, yes. But you can trust me." Bianca tapped a finger to her chest. "And Seamus. He's a good sort."

Seamus, who had remained quiet this entire time, leaned in and pressed a kiss to Bianca's cheek.

"Aye, I'll protect you the best I can, Imogen."

"Well, thank you," Imogen smiled at him and jealousy flared low in Nolan's gut. Why did Seamus get a smile, while he was treated with bitterness? Didn't the woman understand he'd kill anyone who tried to harm her?

"Her song comes to me..." Callum brought Imogen's attention back to him. "I can take you in the direction and I did get an image of a cave of sorts. But I don't have a lot to go on. However, I'll be able to sense the wards the Fae have set when I'm closer. I'll be able to read their magick. Can you help?"

"Well, sure and we can take a look now, can't we? Not that I know what wards are. But I do know of some caves along the cliffs here. And some I'd earmarked to explore at some point to see if they would make for good spots for my tours." Imogen swiped her hand over the iPad and turned it to show a map. The four bent their heads over the table as they began to plan.

Unsettled and unaccountably frustrated, Nolan ducked outside, wanting the cold air on his skin. Too many thoughts were causing his focus to stray, and that wasn't something he could allow. Did the prince have doubts about Nolan's loyalty or that he'd somehow colluded with the Water Fae? What did Imogen really know of the Fae? Would the Water Fae harm Lily? When would the Domnua attack next?

And most importantly, why had Imogen's eyes flashed in recognition when Callum had spoken of the heartsong?

Had a Fae already claimed her or did she know more than she was claiming to?

8

"I DON'T LIKE HIM."

Imogen and Bianca were taking stock of the contents of the kitchen cupboards, as Imogen wasn't in charge of that department and had no idea just what exactly was stocked.

"Callum? I mean, he's a prince. He's used to barking commands." Bianca shrugged and marked down something in her notebook as she pulled her head from a cupboard.

"Not him. I can understand why he's upset. I would be, too, I suppose, if I knew what that kind of love was like."

"It'll drop you to your knees, and that's the truth of it," Bianca said. "I couldn't imagine if it was my Seamus that had been taken. I'd be raging."

"He doesn't strike me as someone who could get taken easily," Imogen shrugged and scanned the cans of beans on a shelf.

"He's not at that. One of Seamus's strengths is that people underestimate him. Mine as well."

"Sure, and I reckon I can understand that, too." Imogen nodded, thinking of how many times she was dismissed as ship captain because she was a woman.

"It's Nolan, then? The one bothering you?" Bianca angled her head at Imogen in question. Annoyed with herself, Imogen shrugged and ducked her head into another cupboard.

"I wouldn't say he's bothering me then. I just don't like him."

"He's a touch on edge right now. I'd give him a break," Bianca said.

"Give him a break?" Imogen pulled her head out and narrowed her eyes at Bianca. "He held me against my will and stole my ship. Excuse me if I'm not feeling all warm and fuzzy toward him. Not to mention his attitude could use some adjustments."

"In all fairness, you did throw a knife at his head," Bianca held up her hands when Imogen whirled on her. "Not that I'm blaming you, of course. I'd have done the same."

"Well," Imogen rolled her shoulders, trying to ease the tension that gathered there. "I don't like him. And I'm certain the feeling is mutual."

"I…" Bianca looked like she was about to say more and then pressed her lips together.

"What?" Imogen demanded.

"You don't have to like him. But we're on the same team, so just remember he'll protect you with his life if need be."

"Why? I'm nothing to this quest or whatever. As he's reminded me. Sure, and it would be wiser to protect his own life, no?"

"He'll do that as well," Bianca said with a small smile. Closing the cupboard door, she held up her notepad. "I think I've got what I need. I'd say we're fairly well-stocked. I can cook, and enjoy doing so, so am happy to take my shifts here."

"If you don't mind? I'm passable at best. You won't be starving with my food, but it's nothing fancy," Imogen said, closing her cupboard door as well. She looked around the brightly lit galley, where everything was precisely put in its place. Cillian, her chef/engineer, was going to be mad when he found out someone else had used his kitchen. She'd cross that bridge when she got to it.

"Are you ladies done gossiping?" Nolan stuck his head into the galley, immediately putting Imogen's back up. Did the man need to be so abrasive all the time? Would it kill him to be polite? However, she was used to crude men, what with having worked the docks for years, so she didn't even pause in her response.

"Aww, we were just going to get the nail polish out and talk about the best shag we've had."

"I doubt you've had your best yet." Nolan's voice held a husky undertone, and the timbre of it warmed Imogen's core. Why was she responding so strongly to this man? It annoyed her, which only made her want to be bitchy.

"And how would you be knowing that, then? You Fae like to spy on us humans, too? You've been peeking in my window at night? I didn't take you for a voyeur."

"I don't need to resort to sneaking around to get my needs met, *mavourneen*. I know it because you haven't been with a Fae yet."

"Oh well now, you're so sure of your entire race then? That you speak for all of them as being some sort of supreme lovers that are better than humans?"

"If you know, you know…" Nolan winked at Bianca and ducked back out into the inky darkness of night.

"Can you believe that man?" Imogen griped.

"Well, in my limited experience…seeing as I've only been with *my* sexy hunk of a Fae…he's not wrong."

"I don't care to know if Fae are good lovers or not. Why is this even a conversation right now?" Imogen tugged on her braid in exasperation. "Aren't we getting ready for a battle or something? This is not the time to be discussing sexual prowess."

"You brought it up." Bianca shrugged one shoulder.

"Oh...I did not..." Wait, had she? "Well, yes, I did but it was just meant to be bitchy. He thinks we're in here fluffing about with nonsense. He has no idea what it takes to ready a boat for an expedition like this. Even now, I'm nervous to be leaving without my crew."

"Have you driven this on your own before?" Bianca tensed.

"Aye, of course I have. It's my boat, isn't it? But still. Having an engineer along is mighty helpful when things go wrong with the engines."

"We'll have to be relying on magicks for that, I guess."

"You say that so easily." Imogen turned and grabbed Bianca's shoulders, surprising the woman. "But have you been in rough seas with no engine power? No way to steer into the waves? Or with loss of radio signal? It's not fun, I'll be telling you that. And even less so if you've got supposedly murdering Fae ready to take you down."

"No, I can't say I've been in that exact predicament." Bianca gently removed Imogen's hands from her shoulders. "But I can tell you I've been in some incredibly intense and terrifying battles. With...things you wouldn't even begin to believe. Dragons, come to mind. Shapeshifters. Selkies. You have no idea what's out there, Imogen. But we do. We may not be your engineers, but we *will* be the ones who save your life until you get up to speed."

Her comments rankled, and Imogen did what she always did when she was upset – she went to the sea. The bite of crisp wind cooled her heated cheeks as she padded down the deck to where Seamus stood, keeping watch.

"We're cleared to go on my end. I'm assuming you'll be able to handle the lines while I get the engines started?"

"Of course. Just say the word."

"I'll signal. The other men?"

"At the bow," Seamus nodded to the front of the ship. "Keeping watch. Talking strategy. That kind of thing."

"Strategy," Imogen laughed, despite her deep anxiety at their expedition. "It doesn't sound like there is much."

"No, it's hard to plan when you're flying blind. I find that keeping your head up and your heart open is the best way to handle much of what life throws at you."

Imogen wasn't sure what to make of the cheerful-Fae-turned-philosopher so she just nodded to him before skirting the edge of the small bar that was tucked near the benches at the stern of the boat. Crossing to the other side, Imogen refused to look down into the dark water, worried what she might see there. No, she'd had enough stress for the evening, she'd decided.

She still couldn't quite understand how she'd gone from dead sleep to planning an expedition to rescue the Prince of Fae's fated mate. Even now, her mind whirled with so many questions, while unease for the journey ahead rippled through her. Tonight had been one of those moments – the ones you could never come back from – and Imogen wasn't sure she was ready to be thrust into a whole new world that she didn't understand. She'd finally found her footing in her own world and wasn't really all that interested in rocking the boat. She *liked* her life.

Speaking of which...Imogen caught a small motion out of the corner of her eye as the boat dipped lightly under her feet. Nerves skittered up her spine as a softly glowing silvery shape slipped up the side of the *Mystic Pirate* and over the guardrail.

Domnua.

Don't hesitate.

Bianca's words came back to her, and Imogen reached for her dagger. Palming it, she slipped soundlessly forward, walking as naturally with the rhythm of her ship as she would on land. The bad Fae stalked forward, his back to Imogen, clearly making his way toward where Nolan stood at the bow, looking out over the water.

Realizing she had little time, Imogen shouted a warning as she raced forward, and Nolan turned, surprise in his eyes and a sword in his hand. But Imogen was faster.

The Domnua fell, a dagger in his neck, and dissipated in a puddle of slimy silver goo. Imogen gaped down at the mess on her deck, her pulse hammering in her throat. She'd killed someone. *Something.* Either way...sickness roiled in her stomach. Nolan knelt and pulled her dagger from the silver sludge, wiping it on his pants before handing it to her. His face, well, if looks could kill...

"I owe you," Nolan said. Imogen wondered what those words cost him.

"Some watch you are," Imogen said, her anxiety and feelings of vulnerability making her lash out.

"My wards should have sounded." A look of confusion slipped through Nolan's eyes, causing Imogen to pause.

"Maybe you need help in setting them. Whatever they are."

"I don't need help. It is child's play to set a ward." Nolan glared down at Imogen. "And wards are powerful magick. They alert us when someone crosses their line. Depending on the magick, the wards can also tell you what type of person has broken through the wards. Even more so? If the wards are done well, they can also prevent certain types from crossing them."

"Then maybe you're not as strong as you seem. Because...didn't a Domnua just dance past this magickal security system of yours?" Imogen raised a hand to stop whatever retort Nolan was about to make. "Either way...I'd take care of your business before more of those bad guys come on board."

"It won't happen again." Light from the docks glanced off Nolan's eyes and his words were thick with promise.

"See that it doesn't. I like to keep my deck clean."

"Aye, Captain. We'll make sure to take care of the mess." Nolan gave her a mock salute that just annoyed her further.

"I expect that you will. We're ready to leave...and not soon enough I can see. Prepare for departure."

"Yes, Ma'am." His tone sent shivers through her body and Imogen turned, racing back to the wheelhouse before she ran into any other Fae.

"We need to leave." Nolan had followed her to the wheelhouse.

"Sure, and that's what I'm working on, isn't it then?" Imogen didn't spare him a glance, though his very presence seemed to cause a ripple in the energy of her wheelhouse.

Imogen finished her checklist and then glanced to the window where Seamus waved at them from the bow. Given the all-clear, Imogen flipped another switch and Nolan started as music flooded the wheelhouse. Seamus turned as well, which meant the music must be playing over the speakers outside.

"Sure, and that's not the most stealthy way to leave a dock, no? Turn it off," Nolan ordered, clearly annoyed with Imogen.

"No," Imogen said simply, and the boat rocked under their feet as she reversed into the bay.

"Imogen. You can't..." Nolan trailed off when her icy eyes pierced his.

"Oh, but I can. This is *my* ship. I never leave harbor without this song playing. Consider it a good luck charm."

He opened his mouth to protest again when she pointed to the door.

"Get out."

"I think I'll be staying."

"I'm the captain. Get out of my wheelhouse. You're breaking my concentration, and this is crucial, particularly without my running lights. Go."

Imogen looked out to the village as the melancholy Celtic song wove its notes across her ship. More lights dotted the dark hills, the fishermen, bakers, and farmers already readying themselves for work. Rolling from beds warmed by their loved ones, putting coffee on, going about their daily routine with nothing but a thought for the day's work ahead of them. And here, they drifted into the dark sea – and likely battle – duty-bound to protect both the Elemental Fae and the humans of Ireland.

Our love was but a song,
Our dreams could not be wrong,
But it's so lonely round the sea of Innisfail.

9

THE OCEAN'S surface was as smooth as glass when Imogen steered the *Mystic Pirate* from the harbor at Grace's Cove. Once she'd rounded the first rocky outcropping that would conceal them from view of the villagers, Imogen flipped on her running lights and studied the water ahead. It was eerily calm, if she had to admit it, for there weren't many mornings that the water was *this* still. It wasn't unheard of, of course, but after having just killed her first Fae, Imogen was naturally suspicious. Not that she'd necessarily know what to do if she saw a threat out in the ocean, but at the very least she could sound a warning.

Imogen nibbled at her bottom lip, her gaze straying to where Nolan now stood at the bow. He held one line in his large hand and braced his foot against a lower rung on the railing. He looked out to the sea, motionless, his broad shoulders straight, and Imogen wondered what he was thinking about.

Did he think of her?

Quickly pushing that thought aside, Imogen took the moment of calm to try and piece together all of the new information she'd gathered in such a short time. The Fae *were* real. This was important, Imogen *knew* this was important, because that singular truth had seared through her very soul. In time, it might even explain all the odd things she'd seen over her life. Or not. Imogen shook her braid over her shoulder in frustration. If she had been seeing the Fae her whole life, then why was this the first time she was meeting any? And why did she have the ability to see them? If that was even what she had been seeing?

Too many questions and not enough answers. It wasn't a comfortable space for Imogen to rest in. She liked to be in control, and, well, this whole quest they were on with other-worldly beings was so far out of her control that Imogen was surprised to see the sun still rising in the east that morning. She could've been well on her way to another planet for all she knew of the world now.

Her heart shivered in her chest, and caught once again by Nolan's presence, Imogen studied the man on her deck. The Fae, that is. *He wasn't human*, Imogen reminded herself, which was maybe why she had weird feelings for him? Bianca had suggested that the Fae were excellent lovers, so perhaps they were just more charismatic or had more pheromones than humans? Because no matter how she tried to force her thoughts away from Nolan and her response to his nearness, her brain just kept cheerfully bouncing back to thoughts of him. Under her. Over her. Pressing her against the wall and his lips descending upon hers...

Groaning in frustration, Imogen tore her eyes away from his broad shoulders and down to her console. She blinked in confusion when the little screen with their navigation on it went black. What the...? Tapping the screen, Imogen murmured to herself as she opened the small door beneath and checked the wiring. Lovely, she thought. Just another thing to have to fix. Which is why having her crew around would be beneficial. Straightening, Imogen blinked in surprise at the ocean in front of her. While the water was as still and smooth as glass, the angry dark cloud on the horizon that was currently barreling in their direction was most certainly not. Where had that come from? There had been nothing in the forecast nor had there been any other indication that there would be nasty weather today. Grabbing the microphone, Imogen spoke.

"Storm...or something ahead. All eyes forward. Hands on deck. Whatever it is you do to prepare for an attack. Because something is up." Before she'd even started speaking, Nolan had already jumped into action, racing across the deck and out of her sight. She could hear shouts outside, but there wasn't much that Imogen could do other than stay the course. She'd never gone to battle before. Hell, she barely liked watching scary movies. No, she was about as useless as a lifeguard on an Olympic swim team.

The storm thundered across the water toward them, far faster than any normal storm, and fear slid down Imogen's spine. Immediately regretting not putting up more of a fight when Nolan had seized her ship, Imogen's eyes widened as the surface of the ocean rose up – as though it was a mouth opening to swallow them whole – and a massive wave crashed across the bow. The shock slammed through Imogen as the *Mystic Pirate* seemed to shudder heavily in mid-air before it slammed down onto the now-roiling waters beneath it. The impact sent Imogen skidding across the wheelhouse where she bounced into the wall. Catching the door handle in her side, she gasped and ran a hand over her ribs, praying she hadn't cracked anything. The ship tilted, and without anyone at the helm they'd capsize.

Imogen reared up and raced to the console, bracing her feet against the cupboard, and gripped the wheel with all her might.

The ship tilted once more, and Imogen steered into the waves, trying to force the boat to stay on point and directed into the onslaught. Once the boat turned and one too many waves hit them from the side, well, their journey would be over long before they started. Another massive wave hit the bow and washed over the deck, and Imogen almost went skidding across the room again as the entire boat shuddered beneath the onslaught. With one hand on the wheel, she reached for the harness she'd fashioned during a particularly difficult storm a few years back. She'd only had to use it twice, because, well, this was a charter boat. If bad weather was afoot, they simply didn't leave the harbor. However, Imogen was grateful she'd designed the harness, and now she buckled it around her waist. Essentially, it would keep her locked at the wheel while also allowing her to steer. Feeling more secure now, Imogen held steady through the next crash of waves before reaching for her life-jacket. She'd briefed the others on where their basic safety equipment was stowed, but now she was kicking herself for not requiring everyone to wear a lifejacket.

Now that she was steady, and as protected as she could be in the moment, Imogen blinked out into the darkness. The storm had surrounded the boat, shrouding them from the first light of dawn, and it was almost impossible to see which direction the next wave would come from. The rain came down in thick sheets, and Imogen could just make out Seamus grappling with something on the deck. Panic lanced through her. Not Seamus. He'd been nothing but kind to her.

Blinking down at her console, she forced herself to

think. How could she help? First up, she could light this bad-boy up, Imogen realized. The boat was equipped with industrial-sized lamps that would flood both decks and the waters ahead of them with brilliant bright light when flipped on. Imogen turned on every light she could, and the *Mystic Pirate* blazed to life in a brilliant glow.

For a moment, Imogen almost wished she hadn't. Her boat was positively teaming with Fae. Or...other magickal beings? She had to assume they were Fae as she'd never seen anything like them before.

Actually...maybe she had. Imogen grunted as another wave slammed into the bow, but she kept the wheel steady, her triceps screaming in pain as the wheel tried to wrench itself from her grip. She had seen these faces before. In the water. These were the people who grinned at her from the water. They'd waved at her when she was but a small child. Night after night, when she was alone on deck and gazing into the murky depths they'd flit just below the surface of the water while she pretended not to see them.

But here they were. Out of the water, straight out of her visions, out of her dreams – and Imogen found herself caught. On one hand, these Water Fae were terrifying in their approach. They moved almost sinuously across the boat, as though they were still in water, and they all but rippled across the deck as they tried to reach where Nolan held his ground at the bow. Their skin was translucent, like the soft glow of the moon's surface, and they shimmered iridescent in the lights she'd turned on. For a moment, one of them turned and locked eyes with her and the moment drew out as Imogen blinked at eyes that looked like opals, reflecting out flashes of brilliant pinks and deep turquoise green. What did he see when he looked at her? Imogen's gaze was torn away and back to the waves that continued to

batter her boat. As much as she wanted to go out into the
storm and help, Imogen was certain she was a better asset in
the wheelhouse. There would be no battle to fight if the ship
capsized.

Gritting her teeth, Imogen held on as sweat trickled
beneath her sweater and chilled her clammy skin. Her heart
raced in her chest, and she coughed out a laugh when
Bianca raced onto the deck and felled a Domnua before
promptly gripping the railing and emptying the contents of
her stomach overboard. Sure and they hadn't found their
sea legs yet, Imogen realized. How could the lovely blonde
still go to battle while seasick? It spoke volumes about her
heart, Imogen realized. Seamus ran to Bianca's side and ran
his hands over her body, and Imogen just caught a small
flash of light before Bianca straightened and smiled up at
Seamus, pointing to her stomach with a smile. Seamus must
have worked some magick on Bianca, Imogen realized.
What a handy trick to have up one's sleeve. When Bianca
instinctively moved forward to kiss Seamus, Imogen found
herself huffing out a laugh when he held out his hand to
stop her and pointed to her mouth and then the ocean. He
wasn't wrong – who wanted to be kissed after a bout of
vomiting? Seeming to realize her error, Bianca gave her love
a quick squeeze before turning back to the battle.

Something interesting was happening. Imogen gritted
her teeth and held on as the boat reared up and slammed
down after another almost-impossible wave. Nolan wasn't
killing the Water Fae, from what she could tell. Instead he
was tossing them over the railing and back into the ocean.
He'd even sent out a wave of magick – or so it looked like –
that ripped an entire group of Water Fae from the deck and
flung them back into the teeming waters.

He wasn't killing the Water Fae.

So, was it just the Domnua that they were meant to kill? That could be a bad situation if someone didn't give her the rules, Imogen realized. Because those silvery Fae bastards were here as well, and Imogen gasped as one took Nolan by surprise from behind, launching itself onto Nolan's back. Without thinking, Imogen hit the button for the ship's horn – fully knowing how loud it was – and blared it into the storm. Everybody on deck jumped, but it was enough of a distraction for Nolan to fling the Domnua from his back and drive his sword through its heart. Imogen grimaced at the silver goo that exploded from it – like a blueberry that had gotten squished.

Nolan's eyes locked on hers across the deck and he raised his hand in a mock salute. Imogen felt her lips twitch and gave him a small nod of acknowledgement. His eyes widened just as a cool breeze hit her neck. She didn't have to turn around to know what that meant. Someone had entered her wheelhouse. Nolan was already running, but Imogen knew he was too far away. Refusing to look behind her, Imogen trained her eyes on the raging ocean ahead of them. She'd captain this boat until her last breath.

"Sister."

The Domnua's voice slithered over her skin both warming her and repulsing her in the same moment. Imogen wanted to glance back, wanted to speak to him, wanted to ask what he'd meant by his comment – but she refused to be distracted from her duties. Maybe this weird band of people who had commandeered her boat weren't her crew, but she'd grown to like at least some of them. No, Imogen wouldn't let them down, nor would she allow herself to look back at the Domnua who hovered behind her. For all she knew, it could be like looking into a Vampyre's eyes and the Dark Fae would coerce her into doing some weird shite. No, nope, no. She would *not* make eye contact.

Imogen waited for the blow, knowing death was near, and time seemed to slow down as her mind began to comprehend that these were her last moments of life. The bow sprang up once again, this time maddeningly slow, as a two-story wave bore down on the *Mystic Pirate*. Shouts sounded, and lightning flashed through the frenetic dark clouds that cocooned the boat. The moment hung suspended, and Imogen felt like her heart would explode out of her chest.

"You're safe?"

Relief crashed through Imogen, much like the wave that now spilled across the deck, and Imogen blinked at the tears that had jumped unbidden to her eyes.

"Aye, I'm doing my best to keep us alive." Imogen's breath shuddered, but she refused to look back at Nolan or where there was likely a puddle of silver goo on her wheel-house floor.

"He didn't try to hurt you?" Nolan asked, coming to stand briefly at her side. His nearness warmed her, and Imogen tried to focus on his words and not the urge to turn to him for a hug. After being absolutely convinced she was about to die, tiny shudders now worked their way through Imogen's body. Sure, and she could use a cuddle right now.

"No, but I didn't take my eyes off the water. Too danger-ous." Imogen swore as another massive wave shook the ship. She wondered how much longer the *Mystic Pirate* would hold. She was sturdy, but there was only so much battering a boat could take. "We can't go on like this much longer. We need to seek refuge."

"There." Nolan pointed ahead and Imogen tilted her head in question. Was her mind playing tricks on her? Or was there a brilliant blue-ish light shining through the storm?

"What is that?"

"It's the cove." Bianca burst into the wheelhouse in a flurry of rain and panting breaths. "It's the cove. Grace's Cove. She's calling to us. Can you get us there?"

"Weren't we just in Grace's Cove?" Imogen was already increasing the speed of her engines.

"Aye, but the village is named for the cove that's found further down the way, tucked between two massive cliffs. It's enchanted, and where Grace O'Malley sought her final resting place."

"*The* Grace O'Malley?" Excitement slipped through Imogen. She'd named her ship, well the pirate part, after the famous Irish pirate, Grace O'Malley. She was a legend to Irish sailors.

"The one and only. The cove's telling us to come. Don't you see? She's calling us home." Bianca's fingers squeezed her shoulder as another wave tossed the boat like a child throwing its toys during a tantrum. Nolan and Bianca steadied themselves as Imogen kept a steely grip on the wheel and the blue light in her sights.

The *Mystic Pirate* was about to meet her namesake.

10

As soon as the *Mystic Pirate* passed through the place where the cliffs almost touched – like some sort of mythological gate to an ancient fortress – the storm abated. Inside the rocky cliff walls of the cove, the water lapped gently and a brilliant light shone from its depths.

"We're safe here," Bianca promised.

"I need to drop anchor or we'll damage the hull on the rocks." Imogen nodded to the shore. "But my instruments aren't working. I'll need to go by sound. Can you hold the wheel while I go release the anchor?"

"I can do it," Nolan said, already moving toward the door.

"Do you know what you're doing?" Imogen called, worried about tangling her anchor line. There were many things that could go wrong when releasing an anchor, and getting it caught in its own chain was not something Imogen wanted to deal with right now.

Nolan just waved at her and crossed to the bow where the anchor was wrapped. He examined it for a moment, and Seamus joined him.

"Sure and I'm glad to see my sweetie is safe." Bianca sighed from where she stood next to Imogen, absent-mindedly running a hand across her stomach.

"I am, too. I was worried about you both."

"I can't say that I wasn't either. That was...intense. Plus, it was tricky because we weren't meant to kill the Water Fae."

"I wondered about that." Imogen raised a hand in acknowledgement when both men turned to her. Bianca stayed quiet as the anchor clanked its way down until the men waved once more. Feeling it catch, Imogen shut down the engines. They'd need to conserve as much fuel as possible.

"It was at Nolan's directive. He oversees the Water Fae as part of his role within the Royal Court, and because of that, he has an affinity for them. Well, and, technically it is his job to make sure no harm comes to them. Sure and it wouldn't look so good if he was killing them now, would it?"

"Even if they tried to kill him first? I mean, certainly one could see why that would be an issue, no?" Imogen finished switching things off and noted various measurements in her notebook. Taking note of their coordinates, she jotted that down as well and a few notes in her Captain's log. Finally, she unhooked herself from the harness that had kept her steady and stepped shakily back.

"I think he is trying to be as honorable as possible," Bianca said as she leaned against the counter and tapped a finger to her lips. "Because if my suspicions are correct and the Water Fae are being misled by the Domnua, well, it's not entirely their fault. The Domnua are creating this problem and they are using the Elemental Fae to lash out. No, I think Nolan has the right of it as much as it is tough not to try to defend myself in battle."

Imogen bent over at the waist, stretching, and rocked

backwards and forwards on her heels. Tension from gripping the wheel so tightly knotted her shoulders and all the way down her body. Rolling back up, she lifted her hands to the air, trying to ease the ache in her back.

"Did any of the Water Fae actually hurt you? Wait, where's Callum? I haven't seen him..." Imogen trailed off as Nolan ducked back inside the wheelhouse. His large body seemed to fill the room, making the tiny space feel smaller, and Imogen tore her eyes away from him to bend over into a stretch once more.

"He was protecting the stern. We've captured one of the Water Fae and are about to question him if you'd like to be joining us."

"Of course. I'm just going to get us some water or perhaps a whiskey?" Bianca squinched her nose. "Actually, just water for me."

"I saw you get sick. Are you better now?" Imogen stretched her arms above her head again, rolling her head on her neck.

"Sure and my sexy hunk of a man gave me some magick to help. Isn't that grand? I thought for sure I was done for. Do you know how hard it is to fight when you're about to blow chunks? Granted, I suppose that would be its own worthwhile defense."

"I wouldn't get near someone who was projectile vomiting at me," Imogen agreed with a laugh.

"Okay, I'll get us drinks. Where are we meeting, Nolan?"

"At the stern. We can't keep him above water too long or he'll be hurt."

"On it." Bianca disappeared to the galley and Imogen continued to work the kinks out of her shoulders. She stilled when Nolan's hands came to her neck.

"You're in pain."

"It's not easy holding the wheel through a storm like that. I wrenched my back a bit is all."

"Let me." It wasn't a question so much as an order, and Imogen swallowed against her suddenly dry mouth as Nolan's hands worked their way down her back. A groan escaped her when he hit a particularly sensitive spot, and he cooed to her. "There now, *mavourneen*. Hush. I'll make it better."

Imogen wanted to collapse in a puddle of need at this man's feet as he massaged her neck and her back, the tension slowly rolling from her muscles, replaced by a new ache that settled in her core. Realizing where her thoughts were straying, Imogen hastily stepped forward.

"Thanks for that. Much better. Would you like me to stay away during this interrogation? I'm not sure how much you want to share with the human here, after all."

"You're part of the team now." Nolan's words caressed her and did their job. Imogen, innately, had a deep-rooted need to belong somewhere. It was why she was so tight with her crew. She'd never really known family or close friends growing up, so belonging to anything was a huge deal for her. Being a part of this team – even though it had been against her will – still managed to warm her heart.

"Right, I'll just be down in a second. I need to..." Imogen gestured vaguely at her cabin and Nolan seemed to understand what she was saying. Ducking inside her cabin, Imogen closed the door and dove into her little bathroom. Sure and she needed to use the facilities, but she also just needed a moment.

She needed more than a minute, if she was honest, but a moment was all she'd get. Hurriedly using the toilet, Imogen washed her hands and stopped, caught by her reflection in the mirror. Her hair had half-escaped its braid and curled wildly around her head – a tempestuous medusa of curls – and her eyes were wide in her face. A faint blush tinged her cheeks and she looked...dare she say savage? But in a beautiful way?

Imogen so rarely took time to study her appearance other than to check if something was in her teeth, that she was caught for a second as she reached up and tamed her hair back into its braid. Now that the adrenaline rush had passed, a bone-deep exhaustion worked its way through her. Well, perhaps it was also the way Nolan's hands had soothed the aches in her back. Granted, they'd created other aches that demanded attention, but Imogen promised herself she'd take care of her own needs later – if it meant tamping down on this lust that had suddenly appeared inside her. Sure and all these emotions could be a bit distracting, no?

The wind was calmer in the cove. Buffeted by the two large cliffs hugging the gentle water, the air here seemed a touch warmer, and the sun's rays shifted gently through the clouds that dotted the sky. Had they not just gone through a battle, Imogen would have stopped to admire the pretty beach or tilt her head up to the sun. Instead, she hurried back to the stern where the group was clustered around one of the Water Fae. The Fae stood, his shoulders slumped, the sun shimmering across his almost translucent skin. He was different than the man who had followed her through the years, though Imogen could see the similarities. He struggled for breath, and Imogen wondered if this was what Nolan had meant about the Water Fae hurting if they were in the air too long. She supposed it was much like a fish out of water, though to call this miraculous shimmering being a fish seemed such an unfortunate way to describe him. The man was both beautiful and grotesque, and yet his uniqueness made him even more enchanting. Imogen found she wasn't even bothered by the fact that he was unclothed, for it seemed normal to her. Nobody could swim freely in the water in their clothes, right?

The Water Fae's eerie opal eyes met hers, and Imogen felt a shock of understanding. She drew in a shaky breath. Okay, then. So, she wasn't delusional and she *had* been seeing Fae her whole life. They were a real thing. A real race. And humans just had no idea of them or only spoke of them in fairytales. Struggling to realign her thoughts to change essentially everything she knew of the world, Imogen blinked rapidly when the Water Fae's eyes widened when he saw her.

He bowed his head.

Imogen glanced behind her, wondering who he was bowing to, and realized nobody was behind her. Both Callum and Nolan turned, two impossibly handsome men, and both studied her with calculating looks on their faces.

Another raspy breath from the Water Fae drew their attention back.

"He doesn't have long. This is torture at this point," Nolan said, worry crossing his face.

"Fae. Tell us – why are you after us?" Callum demanded.

"You've stolen our talisman. Our leader suffers greatly. The power...it wanes by the day. We need you to return it to us."

"You need to tell your people that we didn't steal anything. It is the Domnua who are doing this," Callum insisted.

The Fae's eyes flitted to Nolan.

"He was in our sacred space. After? The talisman was gone."

"I am here to protect you," Nolan said, leaning close so the Fae was forced to meet his eyes. "If you noticed...I ordered that none of your people were harmed during your attack. I would have been well within my rights to do so. I don't want to see your people harmed – or hurting. This isn't the answer, brother."

"We have no choice." The Fae began gasping more deeply for air. Well, for water, Imogen supposed. She started when he turned his eyes back to hers. "I didn't know you were here. I'm sorry."

"Me?" Imogen pointed a finger at her chest. "I mean, I'll accept your apology as you shouldn't have attacked my boat – she's my livelihood. But otherwise, I'm not sure what you mean."

The Fae just blinked his opal eyes at her while his whole body shook with the effort to breathe.

"I'm sorry, *mo bhanríon.*"

"Into the water now," Nolan cast a worried glance at Callum and reached out to lift the Water Fae. "Tell your people it's not us they want. It's the Domnua. I don't have your talisman."

The Water Fae said nothing as he hung limply in Nolan's arms, and Nolan strode to the back platform where he kneeled and gently slid the Fae into the water. As soon as he was back in the sea, the man flitted away, clearly needing to distance himself from the boat. Nolan stayed kneeling a moment, watching the water, and Imogen wondered what he was thinking.

"What did he call you?" Bianca piped in. "My Irish still isn't the best."

"My Queen." Nolan's hard stare almost made Imogen want to follow the Fae into the water.

11

THERE WASN'T much to say after that – though Bianca looked like she wanted to unpack everything at once. Instead, Seamus nudged her inside, reminding her not-too-kindly that she smelled of vomit, and the rest of the group had agreed to return to their cabins for rest. As much as it probably annoyed Callum, even he drooped with exhaustion. A tired crew was a reckless one, Imogen had learned through the years, so she'd agreed wholeheartedly with the decision. Now, though, sleep eluded her as she lay on her bunk and stared at the ceiling.

One thought kept making its way to the surface.

She *wasn't* crazy.

And perhaps that meant her mother wasn't either. Imogen had spent so long thinking that her mother's delusions had finally gotten the best of her – when in reality the woman had been fighting against a truth that she couldn't come to grips with. Shauna had turned to drink and drugs to manage that – escaping into a world where she didn't have to face a reality that she didn't want to accept. Imogen still held a lot of bitterness where her mother was concerned, but for the first time, she did feel a softening toward the woman. She hadn't been a good mother, *nope*, but for once Imogen considered the thought that it hadn't been because Imogen was unlovable.

It was the refrain that had ended up defining her life, after all. Her mother had pushed her out of the house when she was but a teenager. Before that, Shauna had told her that she was different – as in mentally different – and that she shouldn't speak of her visions. Because of this, Imogen had been left in serious doubt to her own mental acumen. It had taken years to fight that stigma in her mind, to build a career for herself, and to studiously ignore the "odd" things that she often couldn't account for. Never once had Imogen confided in another soul, though she'd come close to telling her crew about it one night when they'd had a touch too much whiskey on the boat. She'd never taken a chance on love, had barely allowed herself to make friends, and instead had operated on the belief that if she worked hard and kept quiet, she could escape the whisp of otherness that clung to her.

And now?

All of this was real. Unless she was on some intensely extended dream voyage? It would be one hell of a dream if that was the case, but Imogen's gut told her she was very much awake. Which meant the Fae were real. Her mother *had* known of them. And Imogen was somehow tied to their existence. She wasn't sure in what way or how, but the mere fact that other people could see the same "delusions" that she could was like a cool balm to her soul. Pulling a pillow over her head, Imogen allowed herself to cry, the pillow muffling the sounds.

A knock sounded.

"I'm sleeping," Imogen said from beneath the pillow.

"You're not." Nolan entered her cabin without asking and Imogen squeaked. Pulling the pillow off her head, she grabbed for the blanket and pulled it over her bare legs. She'd shed her pants and sweater and had crawled onto her bed in a simple tank and panties.

"What can I help you with, Nolan? There's food in the galley. Bianca's in charge of that." Imogen looked away, knowing that her cheeks would be flaming red as they usually were when she cried. She didn't cry often – but when she did, she wasn't the dainty sort who had a single crystalline tear slide down her porcelain skin. No, pink splotches would cover her face, and her eyes would immediately go bloodshot. It wasn't pretty, that was certain, and Imogen resented Nolan seeing her like this.

"You're crying."

"Sure and you're an observant one, aren't you then? I *am* crying. Is that such a big deal? It's been a tough night for me, okay? I'm not used to all of this." Imogen waved her hand in the air before dashing the back of her hand against her cheeks.

"How can I help?" Nolan hovered over the bed, his hands half-raised, as though he wasn't sure what to do.

"Help? Oh sure, now himself wants to help me." Imogen barked out a laugh. "You could start by not having stolen my ship."

"It was a necessary choice."

"There were other boats." Imogen glared at him and pulled the wool blanket further up her chest. How did he look so handsome even though he was likely as tired as she was? If not more so? He'd certainly battled hard with the Dark Fae and Imogen had to imagine such strenuous activity would wear him out. Perhaps it worked differently with Fae. Maybe they recharged more quickly.

Which then had her mind gleefully dancing over to thoughts of *other* ways that he could likely recharge quickly.

"None with a captain on them."

"Lovely for you then," Imogen griped.

"In this case, yes." Nolan's eyes grew stormier – if that was even possible – as he looked down at Imogen. The silence drew out, and Imogen's heart picked up speed. Nolan reached out and traced one hand down her cheek, his touch impossibly soft, and came away with a teardrop on his finger.

"Why did the Water Fae call you his queen?" Nolan asked, and Imogen stilled.

"I can't say..." Imogen pulled her head back slightly to remove herself from Nolan's touch.

"You can't or you won't?" Nolan's brow furrowed.

"I don't know, okay? I'm weird! Is that what you want to hear? Something must be wrong with me." Imogen punched the pillow she'd pulled across her lap with a clenched fist.

"There's nothing wrong with you. That I can figure out... yet." Nolan crossed his arms over his chest and rocked back on his heels.

"Gee...thanks." Annoyance flashed through Imogen. Why was she getting blamed for something the Fae had said?

"Are you fearful of the Fae?" Nolan asked. "We'll protect you on this journey. I've sworn it to you. Is that why you cry?"

"No...I just." Imogen bit her lower lip and tried to decide how much she wanted to say to this man. He annoyed her. She wasn't sure if she even liked Nolan. And in the same breath, he deeply fascinated her. The confusing mix of emotions left her uncertain how to proceed when it came to revealing her own secrets. "I suppose I am scared of the things that I don't know. And the Fae world, well, it's all new to me. I have no idea the dangers that await. I have no idea how to prepare for any of this. I like to be prepared. I need to..."

"You need to what?"

"I need to be able to take care of myself." Imogen's chin rose and she met his eyes. "And I'm not sure I know how to in this instance."

"I'll take care of you, Imogen." Nolan's voice warmed her, though the sentiment made her bristle.

"You're not hearing me. *I* need to take care of myself. I can't rely upon anyone else."

"Why is that?" Nolan tilted his head at her in question, and Imogen wanted to scream in frustration. Couldn't a body have a crying jag in peace without having to go into a deep and introspective conversation?

"That's my own business, Nolan. Why are you even here? Shouldn't you be sleeping?"

"I was. And then I wasn't." Confusion crossed his face, and Nolan reached up to rub a hand across his chest. He'd changed into denim pants and a simple gray Henley shirt, and he looked positively normal aside from the energy that seemed to crackle around him. Whether it was confidence, prowess, or strong Fae magick, Imogen had to wonder how humans didn't immediately register him as something different. Perhaps he cloaked his presence in the human world? Making a note to ask Bianca how the Fae passed through the human world undetected, she waited for Nolan to explain. "I just knew you needed me."

"I don't need you," Imogen exclaimed. Embarrassment raced through her. She didn't need anyone! Imogen handled her own business and had been doing so since she was a child.

"Seeing as how you're the one sitting here crying, I'd say you're in the wrong on that." Nolan shrugged one muscular shoulder and sent her a lazy smile that immediately made her want to get on her knees and show Nolan just what she needed. Yeesh, Imogen thought, and tugged at her braid. When had she turned into such a hussy? Her internal monologue was becoming downright dirty these days.

"Can't a body cry in peace? We all have different ways of blowing off steam."

"I'm sure there's more enjoyable ways to do that." Again, a lazy smile which put Imogen's back up. Did the man know where her thoughts had gone? Oh, she hated the type of man who was so certain he knew of his effect on women. Those types usually had an ego wider than the *Mystic Pirate*, and Imogen had enjoyed taking some of them down a peg or two over the years.

"Sure and I could go for a swim like I usually do, but that seems to be off limits at the moment." Imogen raised an eyebrow at Nolan, waiting to see if he would make another insinuation.

"It is at that. You were very brave today, Imogen. Sounding the horn like that was right brilliant."

Imogen hadn't been expecting a compliment, at least one that wasn't related to anything sexual, and it threw her momentarily off balance just as much as it warmed her.

"Oh, well, I didn't think it was smart to leave the wheelhouse."

"No, you would have hampered the battle and likely lost us the ship."

"Lost myself the ship, you mean." Imogen pointed to her chest. "It's my ship. My life. I'd save my ship before I'd save you, remember that, Nolan." Now she was just being bitchy, but Imogen was done with his larger-than-life presence filling her cabin and interrupting her emotional moment. "I hardly know you, but my ship has been the one constant in my life. She's the only thing I can rely on, so, no, I won't be leaving the helm during a battle. I owe it to her."

"You speak as if she's alive..." Nolan said, his voice soft, but not mocking.

"To me – she is. She's my freedom. My joy. My livelihood. And, yes, oftentimes a pain in the arse. But most things worthwhile are, aren't they?" Imogen shot Nolan a challenging look. He surprised her by reaching out and tugging once on her braid, and she bristled at his touch.

"Aye, the most important things are challenging." His eyes held hers and for a second, Imogen thought he might kiss her. Nerves scrambled in her stomach, and she sank fractionally back into her pillows.

"You can see yourself out now, Nolan. I'm not in need."

"You'll let me know if you are?" Nolan was already at the door, and she had to appreciate a man that followed a directive and didn't try to overstay when he wasn't welcome.

"You'll likely be the last to know," Imogen grinned cheerfully at him, and Nolan chuckled.

"Challenging," Nolan said and ducked from her cabin, seeming to pull all the air with him when he left.

Sure, she wasn't crying anymore, so if that had been Nolan's intention – he'd achieved his desired outcome. Imogen plopped her head back on the pillows, staring once more at the ceiling while a very different problem presented itself. Closing her eyes, she let her hand drift under the blanket and skimmed it over her stomach, lower, to where she ached with need. It had been a while since she'd allowed herself such a release, and clearly her unmet needs were messing with her head. Distraction was not what she needed at the moment, not when she'd been tossed into warring factions of Fae. Of course, a handsome man would catch her eye – hell, it had been so long since she'd known a man's touch that any man would likely stir something within her at this time. Allowing herself to indulge, Imogen stroked her hand over where she pulsed with need, and with the other she pulled the pillow over her head, gasping into it when she found a sharply sweet release. Sure, and that hadn't taken long, had it? Imogen laughed at herself, but finally her mind quieted, and she dropped into a dreamless sleep.

12

It took everything in Nolan's power not to storm back into Imogen's cabin and give her the pleasure she currently sought. Nolan's hands gripped the railing so tightly that he was surprised it didn't just snap in half. Sweat broke out on his brow as lust rippled through him, causing his pants to grow tight, and his willpower to strain. How was he able to feel her presence so deeply? Nolan schooled his breathing as he thought back to when he woke from his rest, knowing full well that Imogen needed him. He hadn't hesitated then, thinking she might be in danger, and had raced up to her cabin only to find her in tears.

Goddess above, but tears on a woman's face were something that brought out a deeply protective instinct inside of him. Nolan had wanted to smash his fist through whatever was causing Imogen distress, but she'd closed herself off from him, hadn't she then? No, the beautiful ship captain had her secrets, and she clearly wasn't ready to share them with Nolan. Which rankled a bit, if he was to be honest, but as another wave of lust rolled over him, he couldn't quite remember what he was bothered about.

The lass was going to kill him if she didn't finish soon. Grinding his teeth together, he all but panted as another pulse of pleasure rocked through him. He wondered what she would look like in this moment? Her eyes clouded with lust, porcelain skin flushed pink, and her hair spread wildly across the sheets. Maybe he should go back in...

Not unless he wanted to be decapitated, Nolan bit back a grin. Because if he'd learned anything about his fierce little captain, it was that she wouldn't allow anyone to cross her boundaries. He'd learned that the hard way last night when he'd very nearly taken a knife to the face because of her. He had to admire Imogen's skill, even if it annoyed him that she'd taken him off guard twice now. The first time being the knife-throwing, and the second when she'd felled a Domnua to save him. Och, that one rankled a bit now, too, didn't it? Nolan scrubbed a hand over his face and pulled himself together.

He was also going to ignore his brain thinking of Imogen as "his" fierce ship captain. There were much bigger issues at play here than scratching an itch, though Nolan wrinkled his nose at that term. He'd always been a generous and joyful lover, and, like most Fae, roundly celebrated the pleasures of the flesh. Much like anything with the Fae – his people loved extremes. Big celebrations, dancing, lovemaking, battles...all of it. His people were not ones to sit back and let life flash by. No, the Fae loved it all, which is why the human realm was endlessly fascinating to them. His people admired the tenacity of humans, as well as how they managed to continue to evolve even without magick to help them.

Nolan released his vise-like grip on the railing and took a shaky breath. Sure, and it seemed Imogen was finished now for no other bursts of pleasure came through...well, whatever was linking him to her. He studied his hands, thinking about his own powers and trying to understand this link he felt for Imogen.

From a small child, Nolan had known he was more powerful than the other Fae in his family. It worked like that sometimes, and children like him were identified and pulled aside to be put into special programs to hone their skills. It was through one such program, a course in metallurgy – more specifically infusing tools with magick – that he had met Callum. Well, all metals but iron, of course. The Fae hated iron. But, silver and gold? Creating tools or jewelry and infusing them with magicks had been something that both Callum and Nolan had excelled at. From that time on, Nolan and Callum had been almost inseparable – even though he was Prince of the Danula. As children, they were allowed to play and form bonds and no royal protocols governed their interactions. It was only when Prince Callum had become a teenager that they had been forced to follow the rules, and Callum's interactions were more widely monitored. It was a given that Callum would have to pull back from their friendship, and something that Nolan had easily accepted because the young Royal had certain responsibilities and expectations placed upon him.

Nolan still remembered the day that Queen Aurelia had visited his family home. His parents were simple beings, hardworking, joyful, and easy to love. He'd never felt like his needs weren't met or that he wasn't loved. In reality, they had very little to their name, but the Fae were a community that supported each other. Sometimes he'd felt his mother's love was overpowering, but he'd been lucky to have two sisters to balance out some of her attentions. Still, the day the queen had visited changed everything for his family.

The queen, with her violet eyes and luscious pink hair,

had sat easily at their garden table and enjoyed a cup of tea while observing where Nolan had been quietly working on a golden circlet for one of his sisters to wear in her hair. Well, he'd have to make two, of course, because when one saw it, the other would want it. It was the way of things with sisters, but Nolan didn't mind. It would just give him more practice with his magicks.

"Nolan." His mother, her gray eyes shining, had called him over to the table. Nolan bowed when he approached. He'd met the queen many times and had found her to be warm – and just a bit terrifying. Likely the perfect blend in a strong ruler, he'd thought.

"Nolan, I'm delighted to see you're doing well. Callum speaks of you often. He misses you, you know."

"I miss him, too." Nolan had smiled easily. He wasn't embarrassed to share his feelings about Callum, as the Fae were fairly open with their emotions. Nolan had often wondered if life would be easier for the humans if they followed suit.

"We've been watching your studies, Nolan. As well as your strength with magicks. We believe you'd be fit to join the Royal Court if you've interest in doing so? That way you could spend more time with Callum. It would require you moving into the castle, as well as starting to focus on a path toward a higher role within the court."

Nolan's mother had clapped her hands to her mouth, tears in her eyes, and he knew her emotions were mixed. As were his.

"Will I still be able to see my family?" Nolan asked, looking between his mother and the queen. The sunlight filtered down, highlighting the lavender undertones in the queen's hair, and at the time he'd thought her to be the most beautiful woman he'd ever seen.

"Of course, we would encourage that. Perhaps there is an option for them to move to the castle as well if that is of interest to them," Queen Aurelia smiled.

"And you're not just doing this because I'm mates with Callum?" Nolan asked the other question bothering him and his mother gasped.

"Nolan! That's a rude thing to ask. My apologies, my queen."

"None needed. It's a fair question. You're wanting to be chosen on your own merits and not out of favoritism, correct?" The queen had raised an eyebrow at him.

"Yes," Nolan shrugged.

"We've spoken with your teachers, as well as other students who have worked with you. Everyone speaks very highly of both you and your work. You're a credit to your mother." Queen Aurelia squeezed his mother's hand. "It's what we do with any of the children we select to continue on tracks that will lead them into the Royal Court. As you know, we don't believe that our court of advisors needs to be blood-related to our family line. We think it is best to pull in people who exhibit the strengths and leadership skills we are looking for. A curious and open mind makes for a better leader. I try to be both, as much as possible. And you, my dear Nolan, will make a courageous advisor someday – should you choose to take that path."

"And if I don't?" Nolan scuffed the toe of his foot in the dirt. "Will I be in trouble? Or not get to see Callum anymore?"

"Of course not." Queen Aurelia's laugh was like the tinkle of wind chimes. "This isn't a request made with consequences attached. You can still see our darling Callum, though his time to socialize will become less as he takes on more duties. It's your decision, Nolan. And I'll leave you to it. Think on it – as your life will change if you accept." With that, the queen had left their little house and Nolan with a big decision to make. He'd spent the next few days talking it over with his family, and in the end, he'd gone with his heart. That choice had benefited his family in ways that he could never have seen at the time, and Nolan was indebted to the royal family. To this day, he bore the weight of that responsibility – for he loved his family deeply and would never do anything to jeopardize the life they now enjoyed.

That decision had led him here – to this moment – where he solely oversaw an entire faction of Elemental Fae that were rebelling, and his once strong magicks seemed to be diminishing. Where Prince Callum, his best friend, was being stand-offish and accusatory, and the Domnua were rising up once again even though they'd been banished to their dark realm after the curse of the four treasures had been destroyed. Where his mind was distracted by a woman as soft as steel wool with an attitude to match. This wasn't his first time being put in a difficult position as a leader, but it was certainly one of the most deeply conflicting for him. His mind refused to focus on one problem to solve, instead bouncing between worries for Lily, concern about his relationship with Callum, and what their next step should be. Because Imogen *hadn't* been wrong when she'd pointed out they were basically flying blind. They were, and that didn't sit well with him either. Hearing voices, Nolan raised his head and moved toward the stern where he found Callum and Seamus sitting on the benches and looking down at a dagger on the table in front of them.

"So, you're saying this can shoot lightning bolts?" Seamus asked, his eyes bright with laughter. "Like...well, kind of like in Star Wars?"

"I don't know why the stars would war with each other?"

Callum crinkled his forehead in confusion. "Even lightning can't hit the stars."

"No, it's just..." Seamus laughed. "It's a popular movie franchise in the human world."

"Ah, their movie stories. So, the stars go to battle then?"

"No, it's humans, and well, magickal beings, and...you know what? I'll show you one night when this is over. We'll have a movie night. That might explain it a bit better."

"It's worth a watch," Nolan said, and Callum glanced at him, his eyes guarded.

"He's just showing me the things that my Royal Dagger can do. It was a gift at Christmas." Seamus held up the intricately carved dagger and it gleamed in the light. It was Callum's own work, Nolan could tell by the style, and it held strong magick.

"It's a beauty. He does great work," Nolan nodded to Callum as he took a seat on the bench and stretched his legs out in front of him. Though it was cold outside, the sun had won the battle with the clouds, and they were protected from the breeze in the cove. Nolan wasn't as affected by extreme cold or warmth, so he was comfortable without a coat.

"It's one of your own then? I didn't know that." Seamus beamed and turned the dagger in his palm. "I'll treasure it always."

"Well-deserved."

"Did you rest?" Nolan asked Callum, worry for his prince and the state of his mind, pressing through.

"A bit." Callum shrugged and looked away out over the water. "Did you?"

"A bit. I, uh, stopped by to see Imogen."

"Is that the way of it?" Callum slid his gaze back to Nolan.

"Not in the way you're thinking, no. I just woke up and knew she needed help." Again, Nolan rubbed a hand over his chest where he'd felt the dull ache of her pain.

"She was in trouble?" Seamus asked, his eyes full of concern.

"She was crying. Being a woman, I couldn't get a straight answer from her on why, but at the very least she'd stopped by the time I'd left."

"You made love to her?" Callum asked.

"What? No. No," Nolan laughed and scrubbed a hand over his face. "She is not the distraction I need right now. I'm...really worried, Callum. I don't want to see the Water Fae hurt. And I'm afraid of what the Domnua will do to get to you. If they'll..." He couldn't bring himself to say the rest.

For the first time, the usual warmth that Callum held for Nolan bloomed in his eyes.

"Aye, I'm worried sick, too. We've got to figure this out. I respect your wishes to not hurt the Water Fae, but my leniency will only go so far. We need to find Lily. And soon." Callum looked out to the beach. "But first, we need to go to the beach."

"The beach? Why would we do that?"

"Because there is a woman with a puppy waving to us."

13

Imogen stared down at the gently glowing water, searching for any indication of what would cause the light, and glanced over to Bianca.

"So, just magick, then?"

"Aye, it's Grace O'Malley's magick. She enchanted this cove and her own bloodline the night she died here."

"I can't believe this is her final resting place." Reverence laced Imogen's voice. "She was an incredible woman."

"She's still with us today."

"Of course," Imogen nodded down to the glowing light. "Her spirit resides here."

"No." Amusement slid into Bianca's eyes. "She's reincarnated. In her own bloodline. Gracie lives in the cottage that our great Fiona once did. I'll introduce you sometime. Well, if you can see ghosts that is. But Grace has found her greatest love from another lifetime and married him. In the now."

Imogen's mouth dropped open. That was certainly a lot to wrap her head around.

"I have *so* many questions. I mean...just wow. The lives

she's lived. And what do you mean if I can see ghosts? I thought you said Grace was alive?"

"Grace is. Fiona is her bloodline. She's passed on, but still is with us in her spirit form." Bianca said this incredible fact like she was telling Imogen it was going to rain later that day.

"Um, right. So, we've got a reincarnated famous Irish pirate who is currently alive and living in Grace's Cove, and her dead descendant who hangs out in ghost form?"

"Pretty much," Bianca said cheerfully.

"And here I thought I was the crazy one," Imogen muttered, her eyes on the gently glowing water. "Either way...I've always loved Grace O'Malley's history."

"She's pretty incredible, I'll say that much," Bianca nodded down at the brilliant blue water. "But that's not why the light is glowing. Well, I mean, it *is* because of her own magick here. But the cove is known to light up in the presence of true love."

"Awww," Imogen said, grinning at Bianca. She nudged the woman with her elbow. "You and Seamus are too cute."

"Or..." Bianca narrowed her dancing blue eyes but then pressed her lips together. With a little shake of her head, she looked back out to the water. "It's a lovely sight, isn't it then? I can't tell you how much I've loved finding out that magick was real. It's forever changed my life, and sure, there's been some difficult moments, I won't lie. But I wouldn't change a thing."

"Difficult moments, she says." Imogen laughed again. She didn't have any female friends but found herself warming to Bianca's unique blend of humor, nurturing, and courageousness. She'd seen Bianca deliver killing blows to more than one Domnua, all while being violently seasick. Women were, in general, largely underestimated in

Imogen's opinion. "Sure and a few epic battles with dragons and the like were some of those then?"

"That would be the moments I speak of," Bianca chuckled. "But the dragons were on our side, so that was pretty cool."

"Okay, while I'm intensely jealous on one hand, I'm still struggling to wrap my head around all of this."

"Sure, and it's a steep learning curve, isn't it then? If you need to talk about any of it, I'm here for you." Bianca wrapped an arm around Imogen, pulling her into a half-hug of sorts and Imogen stiffened. She couldn't remember the last time anyone had hugged her – let alone with an easy affection. It just wasn't something she did. Was that odd? It *was* odd, Imogen decided, as her throat went dry. It was normal for people to hug and be intimate with each other. She just wasn't normal was all it came down to.

"Ladies." Seamus joined them at the railing. "We are going on a little trip."

"So soon?" Bianca automatically leaned into Seamus, round and short to his tall lankiness, and his arm came around her shoulders.

"I believe Fiona is here and inviting us to the beach." Seamus nodded to the pristine stretch of sand where a softly glowing person waved.

"Is that..." Imogen tilted her head in confusion. She had great eyesight, but she squinted, nonetheless. It almost looked like the woman was lightly transparent.

"Aye, that's the Fiona I spoke of. While she's not in this realm anymore...you'd hardly know it for all the meddling she does," Bianca said, winking at Imogen. "Let's go see what she has to say."

"So, a ghost. Not a Fae?" Imogen asked, letting out a deep breath. What if Pirate Grace O'Malley had actually been Fae? There was a lot to be catching up on, and Imogen had this strange feeling like time was running out.

"No, Fiona isn't Fae. But she was, well is, a great healer and her magick comes from the bloodline that Grace O'Malley enchanted in this very cove as I was saying."

"I..." Imogen trailed off and shook her head helplessly.

"Sure, and it's a lot. I'll do my best to get you up to speed. But, for now – let's go have a wee chat with Fiona and see if she's to be offering us any help."

"I don't have a dinghy," Imogen protested, looking down at the glowing blue water and knowing it would be icy cold. "It's a touch cold for a swim, no?"

"No problem with that."

Imogen jumped at the voice at her ear and whirled around, fists up, to find Nolan grinning at her. Oh, but his smile just about took her breath away, Imogen thought, as awareness rippled through her. She hadn't expected a smile from him, as she was so used to seeing him with his face set in angry lines. He'd changed back into those leather pants that had her mind thinking about him riding a motorcycle out on the open road. Riding her...

"Sure, and you're going to swim in those pants then?" Imogen asked, hands on her hips. "Leather isn't the best for swimming, I'd say."

"Nobody's getting wet." Nolan's grin widened, and for a moment Imogen saw a flash of heat in his eyes. Remembering what she'd just been doing prior to coming out on deck, Imogen almost squirmed beneath his gaze. It was as though the man could read her very thoughts, and she didn't quite like it.

"I'm not, that's for sure. It's too cold for..." Imogen trailed off and gasped when Nolan stepped forward and wrapped his arms around her, pulling her tightly to his chest. Before she could even register what was happening, there was a tiny whoosh of air, a sensation of falling, and then her feet sunk into the soft sand of the beach. Nolan immediately released her, likely sensing she was about to have a fit about him touching her, and stepped away. Imogen staggered back and turned a full circle, looking up at cliff walls that she could now reach out and touch. The *Mystic Pirate* rocked gently out in the still-glowing cove, and she was...well...*they* had just been on the boat. And now they were here. Which meant...

"You can transport?" Imogen screeched. She stomped forward to Nolan, not caring that the others appeared out of thin air and watched her warily. "You can fecking transport across the air like a fecking magickal airplane?"

"Erm, well...I suppose it's something like that." Nolan closed his hand around her finger, stopping her from stabbing him in the chest again. Furious, Imogen reeled back and kicked him hard in the shin with her boots. Nolan winced, but to his credit, he didn't step back.

"I should've aimed higher." Imogen almost spit at him – *almost* – but even that was a touch too unladylike for her.

"What seems to be the problem?" Callum approached cautiously.

"You all!" Imogen screamed. Tendrils of rage wrapped around her. "You could've just fecking transported to Lily. You didn't need a stupid boat. You're fecking magick! *Magick!* Instead, with no thought to me or my life – you just fecking steal my boat and pull me on some stupid fecking quest when you could've just used your own damn magick to get you where you need to go. And you could've left me the hell alone." With one last searing glance, Imogen stomped away through the sand, her rage propelling her blindly forward.

It was only when she reached the edge of the beach,

where she had nowhere to go unless she wanted to scale a cliff wall or swim her arse back to the boat that Imogen allowed herself to stop. Clambering onto a boulder, she turned her back to the beach and wrapped her arms around her legs, staring out at the glowing water. When tears threatened once more, Imogen pushed them down with the same sheer force of will that had led her to where she was today. She was a fighter, that was for sure, and this little ragtag band of magickals would need to respect her. Her emotions churned in her stomach, like a pit of venomous snakes, and she struggled to pull them apart and understand why she was so angry.

She'd spent so much of her life putting walls up and keeping people out, Imogen realized, her eyes trained on the water – always on the water, for the ocean soothed. She'd kept people at arm's length for fear they'd think she was crazy if she told them the things she saw. Or hell, not to mention the things she could make happen with her mind if she was so inclined to try. *So* much time had been lost to her second-guessing herself. On top of that, Nolan was impossibly attractive and it irked Imogen just how much she was aware of him. Him – the man who stole her boat, forced her on this quest, and then had the nerve to try and soothe her when she was crying. She groaned again, thinking about how he'd seen her at a vulnerable point, and she wanted to kick him in the shins all over again.

Imogen almost toppled off the rock and into the water when a puppy ran up to her – and she realized she could faintly see through it. Well, that sounded gross, Imogen thought. But, honestly – she *could* see through it. Not its intestines or anything, but it was there – a regular bouncing fluff-ball of a dog – but it was like the printer had run out of ink or something. A ghost puppy. How odd. The dog sat in front of her, its tongue lolling out in a smile, and Imogen softened. She'd always wanted a dog, but a life at sea wasn't suited for pets.

"Having a bad day?"

Imogen dragged her eyes from the ghost puppy to the ghost woman and just...laughed. The laugh bubbled up through her and rolled out, as though it wanted to explode, and she found herself doubled over, laughing so hard that tears did roll from her eyes this time.

"Well now, that's a new one. Usually people are scared or annoyed when they see me. I'm Fiona, by the way."

"Sure, and I'm sorry to be rude," Imogen wiped at her eyes, as small giggles still erupted from her. "It's just..."

"Overwhelming?"

"That's one word for it." Imogen wiped her tears and finally took a moment to study the woman. Ghost. Spirit woman. Whatever you'd call her. She had white hair that curled around her face and was pulled back in a complicated half-up style. A thick tangle of necklaces wrapped her neck, and she wore a simple white tunic. Her wrists were coated in bracelets as well, and her eyes radiated kindness. Instantly, Imogen felt the tension ease from her shoulders.

"Yesterday, I was normal. Today? Ghost puppies." Imogen gestured to the dog.

"*Were* you normal?" Fiona asked, her tone direct.

"I..." Okay, so she wasn't entirely normal she supposed. But she wasn't all Fae and dragons either.

"Your man won't let you sit here long. He already approaches..." Fiona glanced over her shoulder to where Nolan was striding across the beach.

"He's not my man," Imogen promised hastily.

"Either way...while we have this moment, Imogen, I'll leave you with this..."

Imogen briefly wondered how the woman knew her name but shook the thought away and focused.

"Everything you need? You already have." Fiona tapped her own chest, her bracelets tinkling gently with the movement. "Understood?"

"Not in the slightest." Imogen blew out a breath and looked up at her. "Could you be a bit more explanatory, perhaps?"

"No, I can't." A smile hovered on Fiona's lips. "Just remember my words. Trust yourself, Imogen."

"Sure and that's easy to be saying..." Imogen trailed off as Nolan reached her rock.

"Are you done with your temper tantrum now? Because in case you hadn't noticed, a woman is in mortal danger. A human woman, at that. You could, at the very least, put your drama aside to help her."

"Oh..." Imogen's eyes went wide, and rage whiplashed back through her. But before she could do anything, Fiona turned on Nolan.

"Well, now, I see politeness isn't part of your toolkit as a leader, is it?"

"There's no time for being polite. We need action." Nolan ran a hand through his dark hair in frustration.

"You should know better," Fiona chided Nolan and his shoulders hunched. It made Imogen want to grin, as though he was being scolded by his grandmother. But the fact he'd just said she was having a temper tantrum also made her want to unleash great physical pain upon the man. The Fae. Whatever he was.

"We really don't have time for this," Nolan insisted.

"There's always time for kindness, Nolan." With that Fiona disappeared, leaving Imogen and Nolan staring at each other.

"I'm..." Nolan began, but Imogen cut him off. She wasn't interested in his apology or anything he had to say. Frankly, the sooner this little mission was over – the better. Imogen could treat this just like a work charter if she had to. She couldn't begin to count the number of times she'd had to paste a smile on her face and deal with difficult customers over the years. Nolan was just another difficult person – and Imogen was a master at putting on a façade.

"No need to say anything. I totally understand." Imogen beamed at him and scrambled down from the rock, patting him on the arm as she passed him. "You're right – we need to stay focused and get Lily home. Let's see what Fiona has to say." With that, Imogen crossed the beach, holding onto one absolute truth that she'd known for years.

It didn't matter how much she moaned about life circumstances – nothing ever changed if she didn't change first. Accept the facts. Assess the situation. Move forward.

And leave smoking-hot and surly men behind her.

14

"You okay?" Bianca asked, coming to Imogen as soon as she drew close, surprising her once again with a hug.

"Um, yeah. No, I'm good." Imogen extracted herself from the hug and pasted her customer service smile on her face.

"Uh-huh," Bianca nodded, raising an eyebrow. "Sure, and you think I don't know a furious woman when I see one?"

"Well, there's no time for temper tantrums in the middle of a mission, now is there?" Imogen continued to smile.

"You're looking a little manic there," Bianca whispered as the others came closer to form a little circle. "I'd tone that smile down a bit. Also – did he really say you had a temper tantrum?"

"He did at that."

"Oof, that's not a good look for him, is it now?"

"Sure isn't," Imogen agreed, but felt some of the tension easing in her chest. Was this what it was like having girl-friends? Because within seconds, Bianca had shown her allegiance and had helped her to feel a little better. Taking her advice, Imogen toned her smile down.

"Everything sorted?" Prince Callum asked. He stood, a touch detached from the group, his face haggard in the soft light of day. Despite her own emotional turmoil, Imogen felt bad for him.

"Yes, sir. Let's keep moving," Imogen said, fake cheer in her voice.

Prince Callum studied her for a moment, but deciding to take her at her word – or perhaps he just wasn't willing to unpack what had just happened – he nodded and turned to where Fiona had reappeared.

"You summoned us?"

"Well, that's a fancy way of phrasing it, isn't it?" Fiona put her hands on her hips and looked around at the group. "You've not eaten."

"Surely you didn't bring us here to discuss our dietary needs?" Prince Callum raised an eyebrow.

"No, but now that you're here, I see you need to be fed. I know you're chomping at the bit, Prince Callum, but the Irish in me refuses to let anyone be hungry on my watch. Could you arrange…?" Fiona tilted her head at Callum in question and then beamed when he pinched his nose and then waved his hand out in the air. Imogen started as two large beach blankets appeared with a veritable feast of food laid out.

"Wait…why was I arranging for supplies if you could just do…that?" Imogen lost her grip on her cheerful façade again as rage began to boil.

"It's not a convenient thing, though it seems so." For the first time, Callum smiled softly at her through the weariness etched in the lines on his face. "When you use magick like this, you are pulling energy from other forces in the world. Too much use and it can grow disruptive or reduce our powers. It's sort of a built-in safety catch for Fae not to become *too* powerful."

"Because then you'd all just be lazy and magicking up everything you need at any given moment?" Imogen asked.

"Precisely. It's good for a body to put some effort into the things they want or need."

Despite herself, Imogen glanced to Nolan and found his stormy eyes on her. Annoyed, she glanced away and, deciding not to act on ceremony, she walked to the blanket and plopped down, delighted to see one of her comfort foods there. Grabbing a cheese toastie, she settled in and waited for the others to join. When Nolan sat next to her on the blanket, Imogen deliberately turned the other direction and was about to speak to Bianca when Fiona joined the picnic.

"You're welcome here, at this cove, because your intentions are pure and your quest is important," Fiona began, sweeping her arms out to encompass the stunning cove behind her. "The cove is particular with who she allows in, so I'm happy to welcome you to these waters that hold great power."

Imogen's eyebrows rose, but she said nothing, instead opting for another bite of her sandwich.

"Thank you for providing a safe spot from the attack on the boat," Prince Callum said. Fiona inclined her head in acknowledgement – just as regal as any prince, Imogen thought.

"I'm sorry that Lily has been taken. I've only met her briefly, but she's a lovely soul, Callum. You're lucky there."

"I am." Prince Callum's voice was hoarse.

"You're worried she's gone?" Fiona's tone was gentle.

"I...I can't hear her song," Prince Callum admitted, burying his face in his hands. "I'd heard it until just after the battle this morning. But...she's gone silent. I'm terrified of what that means."

Imogen opened her mouth to speak – to offer some sort of reassurance – though what she could offer was likely minimal she realized. Nolan stood and crossed to Callum, dropping down beside the man and throwing his arm over his shoulders while whispering something in his ear. The move spoke of years of intimacy and a brotherhood that Imogen longed for. Well, she had that with her crew, she supposed, but nothing like this. No, this movement spoke of family, of a deep bond, and it made her heart thaw just a bit toward Nolan.

"She's still with us, Prince."

Callum glanced up at Fiona's words, his eyes burning in his face.

"You're certain?" Prince Callum rasped.

"I'm certain. She hasn't yet crossed to this realm, or I'd know of it. No, I think after the battle, the Domnua have figured out a way to silence her. They realized you were using her song as a tracking device of sorts."

"Bastards...I'll dance on their graves, I will at that..." Callum promised, a mixture of relief and anger crossing his features.

"I don't doubt that you would..." Fiona said. "Yet you didn't harm any of the Water Fae when they boarded your ship. When they tried to cause you harm. Your team harm. You dispatched them, but you didn't hurt them. Why is that, Callum? Am I correct in saying that they almost killed you? The very first night you came to Grace's Cove to find Lily just months ago? It was the Water Fae who had hurt you, no?"

"Aye, it was."

Imogen's eyes bounced between Callum and Fiona, trying to soak up as much information as she could.

"I helped her that night, you know that right? Because true love's calling demanded it be so." Fiona's eyes all but glowed with their intensity.

"I know you did. I'll forever be grateful for that," Callum grimaced.

"Be grateful to yourself as well. You carried a strong and potent elixir with you. Without it, I'm not sure either of us could have saved you."

"It's smart to be prepared," Callum shrugged it away.

"It is at that. And yet, here we are again – in battle with the same Fae who almost claimed your life once before – and you didn't hurt them. Why?"

"Ah, it was my decision." Nolan cleared his throat and dropped his arm from Callum's shoulders. "The Water Fae are my faction to oversee. I believe they're acting upon misinformation, and I'd like to do my best to not hurt them until this all gets sorted out. There's no need for more suffering. Every one of those Fae likely have family at home."

Wow, Imogen thought, the man did have a conscience. Just not when it came to stealing her boat.

"Kindness gets rewarded," Fiona smiled at Nolan. "Something I'd ask you to think about."

"Didn't you just say I'd been kind to the Water Fae?" Nolan rolled his eyes and Fiona's grin widened.

"Be that as it may, you'll want to let kindness lead your actions, warrior. I won't remind you again. However, our time here is short. Let's just say the Goddesses are watching..."

"Goddesses?" Imogen hissed to Bianca whose eyes widened. The blonde opened her mouth to speak but Fiona shot her a look that had her clamping it shut again.

"And they are willing to reward those who act in pure intent and not out of malice. Your journey thus far has been such. Therefore, I can tell you that Lily is being held on the Aran Islands."

"She is?" Callum jumped up, his face a mask once more. "We must leave, now."

"You have some time," Fiona promised. "Eat, please. You face many troubles along the way, and you'll need your energy."

"But..." Callum said.

"Eat." Fiona's words were so commanding that Imogen automatically reached forward and grabbed an apple from the basket.

"This Shepherd's Pie is divine," Bianca said with a happy sigh, having dug into her own plate. "Compliments to the chef and all that."

For a while, they all ate in silence, each left to their own thoughts. Though how Imogen could eat peacefully when a million questions zinged through her mind was beyond her. Perhaps there was a point that the brain just reached a level of acceptance of whatever new situation it found itself in? She supposed it must – for adaptability was a trait humans could well claim. She wondered if the Fae had to learn to adapt or if they just made the world adapt to them.

Aside from the faint glow around the Fae men, there was nothing untoward that indicated to Imogen that they weren't human. They didn't have pointy ears or wickedly sharp teeth like some of the myths she'd read. No, they could pass for human men – albeit highly charismatic human men – as power all but rippled around them. Imogen wondered how anyone could remain unaffected when these men walked into a room. Surely people would be able to sense their otherness.

"Imogen...tell me about yourself. Are you close with your family?" Fiona's words were like a shock of ice water to Imogen's face, and she flinched.

"Ah," Fiona said, measuring the expression on her face.

"I don't speak with my mam. Never knew my father." Imogen fiercely hoped that would be the end of that line of questioning. The apple she'd been enjoying suddenly grew unappetizing.

"Is that right? Your mother never spoke to you about your father?" Fiona pressed, and Imogen felt her back go up.

"Sure, and that's not a fun conversation for a child, is it? Your da doesn't want you, child. He's gone on his merry way. You're useless to him."

"Is that what she said?" Bianca gasped, her hand to her heart and sadness in her eyes.

"More or less. Not much to say is there? Sometimes the absence of words speaks more, no?" Imogen shrugged, picking at a loose thread on the blanket.

"Nothing else that you can think of? His name, perhaps?" Fiona asked, and Imogen really began to dislike this ghost.

Prionsa.

The name flashed into her mind so fast that Imogen almost didn't grasp it. The name felt heavy with meaning, and yet Imogen couldn't begin to guess what. It was an odd name, that was for sure, but still an Irish one at that. If she'd stayed in school longer, perhaps she'd have been better able to understand the meaning.

"Nope, nothing." Imogen shrugged and looked away from Fiona's knowing gaze.

"Ah, more's the pity then. I'm sorry to press. It's not easy growing up with a difficult family life."

"What family? I've more-or-less been on my own since I

was ten. Just more formally once she kicked me out a few years later." Imogen's mouth dropped open. She never spoke of her childhood. Even with her crew, she'd let them fill in the gaps with only providing the bare minimum of information. Imogen glanced down at the apple in her hand. Was there some kind of truth-serum magick in this thing?

Seeming to sense that Imogen didn't need or want sympathy, Bianca instead handed her a cookie. Grateful that nobody pressed, Imogen took the sweet, and bit into it. When she glanced up again, she found Nolan studying her, his moody eyes unreadable.

No, a cookie wasn't going to fix this, Imogen thought, but sugar always helped. She waved at Bianca for another, and the blonde smiled.

"I've said it before and I'll say it again...cookies always make things better."

15

"IT'S GOING to be at least a ten-hour passage, if not longer depending on the weather."

They'd been transported neatly back to the *Mystic Pirate*, in the same dizzying manner, and Imogen now studied a map in her wheelhouse.

"Surely it won't take so long?" Prince Callum was the only one who had joined Imogen, while the rest presumably were getting ready to leave.

"Well, straight line I'd say it's sixty nautical miles or so. But that's not taking into account we've got to round the head of Grace's Cove. See how the peninsula juts out here? Then we can hug the coastline as we head north." Imogen traced the passage with her finger. "If all goes smoothly, we'd arrive in the middle of the night. Which could be tricky as well, depending on if there is an available slip for us to dock at. Granted, you could transport us there with that magick of yours if you wanted..."

"I wish. It's too much for our powers, unfortunately. Small bursts of people movement, but large ships and armies? It disrupts the flow of natural energy to move that many things at once. It's a Fae no-no, really."

"Ah," Imogen said, as though it made perfect sense. Magick, as a rule, still didn't quite click for her.

"Have you been to this place before?"

"Inis Mór, I have. It's the largest of the three islands. But it's hard to say which island they'll be keeping her at."

"Do they welcome visitors?"

"Sure, and it's a small community that lives out there. This time of year isn't as popular with tourists, so my hope is I'll be getting an easy spot to dock my boat. That's on Inis Mór, though. I can't say for the other two islands, as I've only ever docked at the main one. There's a pub or two and a place to sleep – but otherwise it's largely undeveloped. A lot of old ruins and stone circles though."

"There's great power in stone circles." Prince Callum tapped a finger on her steering wheel, lost in thought. "I wonder if there's a portal there."

"I'm sorry...a what?" Imogen glanced at the prince.

"There's several portals between the Fae and human realm."

"You mean you can't just bounce between them whenever you want?" Imogen asked.

"No." A faint smile crossed Callum's face. "Could imagine? The Fae love the human world. They'd be playing here all day long if they could. The portals allow us some control of who goes back and forth between the realms."

Imogen wondered if there would come a point when her brain became overly-saturated with new information and would just break.

"Right, and since you're a prince, you'd know if there was a portal there, correct?"

"Unless the Domnua managed to create one of their own. But in theory, I should be made aware of all portals. If it's an unsanctioned one, well, I should still be able to sense it."

"Any chance you could just sense it now? You know, put out those magick feelers? It would make my life a lot easier," Imogen pointed out.

"Aye, mine as well. No, unfortunately my magick does have some limits. I'll need to be a bit closer to get a better read. I'd rather wait so I'm not leading you astray. While I know we've stolen your boat and forced you on this journey with us, I'd ideally like to not see you or your boat come to harm."

"Gee, thanks," Imogen shook her head. But because she knew the man was hurting, she also bumped his shoulder with hers. "I do appreciate that though. This is a lot for me, but I'm going to do my best to try and bring your Lily home. From what Bianca says, she sounds really wonderful."

"She's...she's like when the clouds pull away from the night sky and reveal the sparkle of stars. Her presence brings light to even the deepest of darkness. Someday, I'll tell you the story of how we met. She saved my life that night – and captured my heart forever. I don't deserve her and will spend my days proving that to her. If I get her back."

"*When* you get her back," Imogen said, her throat having grown tight at Callum's words.

"She'd be a good friend for you," Callum turned to Imogen. "She takes everyone in. Nurtures. She was a teacher, you know. And I don't think she could harm a mouse. If you're looking for family – you've no further to look than Bianca and Lily."

"Um..." Imogen wasn't sure what to make of this conversation. She'd never really had one like it before. In her world, people just didn't offer up family. If anything, the concept of family was something to be withheld – or earned – like in the case of her crew. Being offered such a thing so easily made her feel a bit itchy in her skin.

"Scars linger. But wounds heal. Will you define your life by a pain you felt as a child?"

"Well, this navigational charting meeting has taken a turn for deep thoughts, hasn't it now?" Imogen angled her head to meet Callum's knowing look. She never spoke of family or childhood wounds and now she found herself stuck once again in uncomfortable territory.

"When would be a better time for deep thoughts than before a body goes into battle?" Prince Callum parried.

"You think we'll have more battles?" Nervousness churned in Imogen's stomach, sending a shiver across her skin.

"Of course. It's to be expected. We'd be unwise to think it will be smooth sailing."

Imogen pressed her lips together and looked out to the bow where Nolan and Seamus were huddled together on the deck.

"He's a good man."

"Aye, Seamus is delightful," Imogen agreed, deliberately ignoring the prince's meaning. Her words were met with a chuckle.

"Seamus is at that. But I'm speaking of Nolan. In every way but blood, he's my brother. We grew up together, you know."

"Two rich kids frolicking on the palace grounds?" Imogen kept her tone light as to not insult the prince. It wasn't his fault he was born into royalty.

"For me, yes. Nolan? No. His family lived a quaint but happy life in the village. However, as a child his powers were noticed, and he was brought into the Royal Court to train for his future. His abilities gifted his family with a more affluent life and have given his sisters opportunities for jobs and marriages they might not have had before."

"Well, good for him. Sounds like a lovely Cinderella tale for him."

"Cinderella?" Callum squinted at her.

"Um, it's just a..." Imogen laughed and tugged at her braid. "A children's fairytale of sorts. A story. A rags-to-riches story. Poor Cinderella is treated horribly by her family until the prince chooses her and she falls in love and becomes a princess."

"Well, Nolan wasn't treated horribly. He's very close with his family. With our family as well. The falling in love part... well, he's stubborn."

"Oh? Turned down a few women, has he?" Imogen kept her eyes carefully on her notebook as she wrote down information for their journey. She did not care about this answer, no she most certainly did not.

"Not turned down. He's had many lovers."

Of course he had. A man who looked like that? Imogen rolled her eyes.

"Delightful for him, I'm sure."

Prince Callum's lips curved. "But never for love. He's intensely loyal. To me. To the Royal Court. To his family. I think, almost to a fault. There is a part of him that thinks that finding love would mean he would be taking away from his duties. Which, to him, is almost sacrilegious. He carries the weight of his responsibilities with pride."

"Well, that's just stupid. Does nobody else in your Royal Court fall in love? Is it a requirement to stay single?" Imogen shook her head at Callum. The Fae were weird if that was the case.

"Of course not. The Fae are romantics at heart. We place finding our Fated Mates as one of the utmost important journeys in our lives. I worry for Nolan that he doesn't recognize this."

"That sounds like a him-problem, not a you-problem," Imogen bit out, annoyed at this conversation. Why was her heart softening for Nolan? She shouldn't care if he found love or not.

"Ah, but I want my brother to find love. He holds himself back because he thinks his role as advisor will be enough to always secure his family's happiness. He's so focused on his duties that he doesn't see that the rest of us will be happy when he is happy. Instead, he carries his job like that is the sole thing that will define him in this world."

Imogen actually *could* understand that. Without the *Mystic Pirate*, she'd be absolutely lost. Her life was intimately entwined with the career she'd made for herself, and it gave her great comfort.

"You've seemed cold with him." Imogen neatly changed the subject because, no, she was not interested in hearing more about Nolan's love life. Or lack thereof. Though it didn't sound like finding partners to share his bed was an issue, which didn't surprise Imogen in the least. Despite herself, she glanced to where he had reached overhead to tie a knot, and his shirt lifted at the waist revealing well-defined muscles.

"You pay attention." Prince Callum didn't deny her words.

"It's part of my job. A distracted captain is a dangerous one."

"I might have been misdirecting some of my anger toward him as he oversees the Water Fae, and this is their doing."

"And yet he's risking his life to help you." Imogen wasn't sure why she was coming to Nolan's defense, but fair was fair in her book, she supposed.

"He is at that. It's his duty."

"It's more than that." Imogen glanced to the prince. "You can't call him a brother in one breath and claim he's only following his royal duties in the next."

"No...I don't suppose I can." Prince Callum took a deep breath. "I'll speak with him."

"What I need from you is to take care of your team," Imogen said. "I'll captain the boat and do my damndest to get us there safely. But your team needs to be working as a unit. Every good crew functions that way. If there's a breakdown in communication or a misunderstanding, I suggest you go fix it now before we leave."

"Yes, Captain." Callum's lips quirked as he left the wheelhouse, clearly amused at being ordered around. Imogen didn't care what kind of royalty he was. The boat was hers which made her in charge. Even if she didn't fully understand the scope of what she was dealing with, the one thing she did know was how to run a successful ship. Which meant Callum better shore up any cracks in his foundation or they'd be in for a bumpier ride than expected.

Imogen stopped, caught by the image of Callum approaching Nolan and pulling him into a hug. There was something so...just...*appealing* about the way they freely expressed their emotions for each other. It was rare to see the men in her world be affectionate with each other in ways other than rude banter and scathing insults. A pat on the back here and there? Sure. But never had Imogen seen any of her crew hug each other. She found it didn't diminish the men's attractiveness at all. In fact, it just made them seem more powerful to her. A contrast in study, the two men spoke earnestly with each other, and Imogen was hard-pressed to decide which of the two was more handsome.

Well, there was something intriguing about Nolan's dark looks and searing smiles. Oh, but his smile. Her heart fluttered a moment as she remembered when he'd grinned easily at her earlier that day. It was as though she'd been given a rare gift, and the warmth of it had overloaded her system. Which is why he'd been able to pick her up and transport her so easily, Imogen reminded herself. She'd been caught off-guard. Something she'd do well not to repeat during this journey. But still, her eyes lingered. As though sensing her gaze, Nolan turned abruptly and met her eyes through the window.

The moment held, and nerves shot through Imogen. She was the first to break contact, though it annoyed her to do so. She had work to do though, didn't she? Flipping a page in her notebook, she pushed thoughts of sexy Nolan from her mind and finished charting their course.

16

IT HAD BEEN A SURPRISINGLY smooth passage, Imogen reflected, as she rubbed her tired eyes. True to her estimation, they were nearing the ten-hour mark and she'd been on her feet for much of it. At various points, people had popped into her wheelhouse and offered to relieve her from her post, but Imogen held strong. There was no one she trusted to handle her ship if another battle arose. Now, she found herself bone-deep tired as she was operating on only a few hours of sleep in two days. Soon enough they'd arrive to Inis Mór and there Imogen hoped to seek a safe spot for her boat and a few hours shut-eye for herself.

Everyone else had decided to take shifts for the watch, which would allow them to get some sleep, but still protect the ship. Each person on watch had stopped in to have a chat with Imogen at some point, and she'd had an enjoyable time learning more about the Fae world from both Seamus and Bianca. Callum hadn't been as chatty, but she didn't blame the fellow – his heart was currently breaking.

Only Nolan had avoided the wheelhouse on his watch, instead prowling the deck like a restless cat, and Imogen couldn't help but wonder what was going on in his thoughts. He'd seemed somewhat happier after his conversation with Callum earlier, but it was hard to gauge the difference in annoyed Nolan and happy Nolan as both moods were hidden behind the stern mask he wore. She wondered if that mask helped him to be a better ruler to the Water Fae.

Imogen checked their course and made a minor adjustment. They were entering Foul Sound, which would take them around the island Inis Meáin, and into the bay at Inis Mór. She'd heard the waters could be tricky there and needed to pay close attention. Perhaps that was how this area had gotten its name, Imogen mused, as she stared out into the night, keeping her eyes trained on the water lit up by the running lights in front of the boat. It wasn't typical for her to run the boat at night with this much light, but she'd figured the bad Fae likely already knew where they were, as the Water Fae certainly did. The light would only serve to benefit them, for at the very least they'd be able to see if anyone tried to attack again.

A few shapes had slipped below the surface of the water, tracking them, but none had made a move to board again. Had the Water Fae decided to deal more softly with them? Was Nolan's decision not to harm them causing the Fae to reevaluate their position?

Or were they just waiting, lulling them into complacency? Imogen worried that the latter was the case. Movement on her little television screen caught her eye. She'd installed the security cameras when she'd first started overnight charters, wanting to make sure if a tipsy guest fell overboard, one of the crew would see it. Luckily, they'd never had that issue, but now Imogen was grateful for the cameras as it gave her eyes on every corner of the boat.

She watched Nolan prowl the side deck, his shoulders

broad beneath the light sweater he wore, those leather pants showcasing his muscular legs. The man was built—what could she say? She had eyes, didn't she? But a good-looking man did not automatically a partner make, Imogen gently chided herself. Their worlds were too far apart – and frankly she could barely get through a conversation with him without wanting to throw him overboard – so no, she really didn't need to be paying attention to how he filled out his pants.

Imogen's eyes bounced to another screen as a flurry of movement drew her attention. She gasped, seeing Prince Callum being dragged by several dark beings toward the loading platform at the stern. Nolan continued prowling, clearly unaware they'd been breached.

"Nolan! Attack! At the stern!" Imogen shouted into the microphone and watched as his head whipped up and he sprinted to the back of the boat. Imogen's eyes widened and sweat pricked her brow as she watched Nolan unleash his ferocity upon the Domnua. Well, at least she thought they were Domnua. Her security cameras were in black and white, so Imogen could only see the faint glow surrounding the Fae, but not the colors. Briefly, she wondered if other people would be able to see the glow of the Fae through video – kind of like when ghost hunters tried to capture images on film. Would video pick it up more? Or was the ability to discern who was Fae and who was human relegated solely to certain people touched with...well whatever it was that she had in her.

"Oh shite," Imogen breathed, her eyes bouncing between the little screen and the water ahead of her. Worry about the bad Fae coming over the front of the boat almost eclipsed the concern she had for Callum.

But Nolan? He was...in a word...incredible. He flew into

the pack of Domnua, whirling and striking as though he had little thought for where his blows landed. Imogen gasped as he tossed one Domnua straight overboard.

One-handed.

She gulped as he ripped his dagger through another one, the Domnua instantly popping and dissolving into that little puddle of silver goo that Imogen had seen before.

"Behind you!" Imogen screeched into the microphone, just as five more bad Fae scurried over the railing and launched themselves at Nolan. There were too many. How was he going to survive this? They needed more help. Imogen reached out and flipped the fire alarms, hoping to rouse Seamus and Bianca from their beds. Helplessness coursed through her as the waves picked up in a frenzy and the boat began to pitch heavily from side to side. Bracing herself, Imogen held the wheel steady, hoping that the sudden appearance of waves hadn't thrown the men off their feet. Her eyes darted to the small screen again where she saw Callum on his back on the deck, a Domnua raising a knife over his head.

"No!" Imogen gasped.

At that moment, Nolan dove forward and tackled the Domnua, punching him mercilessly in face until the Fae crumpled to a heap on the deck. Picking up the knife, Nolan used it on its owner, and another little puddle of goo slid across her once clean deck. Nolan wiped the knife on his pants and tucked it in his waistband before turning to survey the back deck. The fire alarms had worked, Imogen noted, as Seamus skidded to a stop by Nolan and Bianca blew into the wheelhouse, her hair wild around her head.

"Are you okay?" Bianca shouted.

"Aye, I'm fine. It's Callum that was in trouble."

"Be back in a few." Bianca had already disappeared, and

in seconds Imogen saw her enter the frame and bend to kneel where Callum sat, rubbing his head.

The door to her wheelhouse swung open and Nolan stalked inside, fury his cloak, and his gaze pierced hers. The air hummed between them, heavy with tension.

"You're safe?"

"Yes, I'm safe." Imogen drew her gaze back to the water where the waves continued to hammer the hull. "So long as I can keep us on course."

"See that you do. I'll be back."

"See that you do..." Imogen mimicked to the now-empty wheelhouse. Who even spoke like that? Could the man get any more annoying?

A soft tap on the other door to her right dragged her attention away from the rocky waters ahead of the boat. Imogen grasped the wheel tightly and slid a glance over to see opal eyes glowing at her in the darkness. It was the man from her dreams. The same one she saw flitting beneath the water all these years. They measured each other through the glass, the reflection of the light in the cabin making it difficult for Imogen to fully see the Fae. Her heart hammered in her chest as the boat hit another tough wave, but she held strong to the wheel.

"What do you want?" Imogen asked, wondering if the Fae could hear her.

The Water Fae tapped again, and Imogen found herself suddenly compelled to reach over and flip the latch on the door. Hypnotized, Imogen couldn't tear her eyes away as he slipped inside the wheelhouse with her. The Fae's chest rose and fell steadily, and he didn't seem to struggle for breath like the other Water Fae had when he'd been held out of water for too long.

He smiled. As he always did. And Imogen gasped as he

reached out and wrapped his icy cold arms around her. So shocked was she that the Water Fae had almost pulled her through the door before she was able to react. Panic gripped her, and Imogen went with her first instinct. Slamming her head backwards, she heard the Fae's sharp hiss as the back of her head connected with his face. Using the moment to her advantage, Imogen twisted and brought her knee up between his legs, and he doubled forward. Following the motion, she grabbed his slimy head and connected her knee to his nose, satisfaction racing through her as he squealed in pain and threw himself over the side of the boat. A loud splash assured Imogen he'd hit the water and she darted back inside to grab the wheel before the boat capsized.

In seconds, the ocean went from teeming with nasty currents and waves to flat and smooth as glass once more.

"Suspicious," Imogen whispered. The ocean didn't work like that, which meant more magick had been afoot. Perhaps the Water Fae had pushed the Domnua back? Or were they still working together? Impossible to know, Imogen thought with a toss of her head. There were just too many things to consider. No wonder the Royal Fae were finding this battle difficult to navigate. It seemed the Fae were tricky in general, no matter whether they ran to dark or light.

"Everything okay in here?" Seamus popped his head in, his red hair sticking up every which way from his head.

"Yup, all good," Imogen said, though she was certain the strain carried through to her voice. She wasn't ready to talk about what had just happened, as her brain was still scrambling to process it. Adrenaline coursed through her veins, making her vibrate like a plucked guitar string. She wondered if Nolan would punish her for hurting a Water

Fae. "How could the bad Fae overpower Callum like that? I thought he was, like, the strongest of the Fae?"

"His powers have lessened because they kidnapped his fated mate," Seamus explained.

"For real?" Imogen eyed Seamus in disbelief.

"Yes, the longer he's away from her, the more his power wanes. Love is...it's everything in our world."

"So...right, then. Okay." Imogen adjusted her thoughts of the prince as being all-powerful. "Understood. I guess."

"You ready for a nap yet?"

"I will be when we dock. It's not much farther now. I see the Straw Island lighthouse which means the bay is just beyond. There, see the light?" Imogen pointed, deliberately distracting Seamus from asking her any other questions about what she'd seen.

"It's quite dark out. Will you be able to dock?"

"Aye, I contacted the harbormaster before we left. They should be aware of our arrival, though you'll need to pay the docking fees."

"No problem with that. The Fae coffers run deep," Seamus assured her.

"I'll need everyone on deck and ready to throw lines. Once we're safely docked, I'm going directly to my cabin and don't want to be disturbed unless we are under attack again. You hear that?" Imogen raised her voice as Nolan stopped behind Seamus.

"What's that?" Nolan asked.

"Once we are docked, I am going to sleep and I do not want to be disturbed. I don't care what kind of bug's up your arse – my cabin is off limits. Understood?"

"Yes, Captain," Nolan said, tapping his finger to his head in a mock salute.

"Don't give me that tone," Imogen snapped, fatigue and

anxiety driving her annoyance with him. "You're the one who doesn't understand boundaries."

"This may be your ship, but it's my quest. Boundaries mean nothing to me."

Och, the man was infuriating. Imogen turned to say something scathing but it was just Seamus standing in the open doorway.

"Surely, he has to have some redeeming qualities, no? I'm trying here, Seamus. But the man makes me want to pull my hair out," Imogen fumed, reducing the speed of their engines as they bypassed the rocky island holding the lighthouse. The light was a welcome sight, lancing its beam into the night, and anticipation of sleep made Imogen antsy to be docked so she could disappear for a while.

"Was that you trying? It sounded more like you were looking to rile him up," Seamus said. Imogen shot him a narrowed look and he grinned at her, rocking back on his heels, all affability and ease.

"Maybe we have different definitions of trying."

"Ah, sure and that's it. How's that trying going for you? Working out all right then?"

"Seamus, I'm trying really hard to like you, as well," Imogen warned, and Seamus laughed.

"Sorry, boss-lady. Just calling it as I see it. Seems to me you're both finding ways to pick at each other. Which usually means one thing in my mind..."

"That there's a mutual dislike, and we're stuck working together because neither of us has much interest in dying at the moment?" Imogen chirruped as she motored past the lighthouse and saw the welcome sight of the brightly lit docks.

"Or..." Seamus began but Imogen cut him off.

"Ever have a co-worker you hated, Seamus? Wait...have you ever had a real job?"

"Sure I did. I worked in the IT department at the University when I was working for the Danula for the first quest during the curse of the Four Treasures."

"That's where he met me," Bianca said, joining Seamus in the doorway and automatically winding her arms around his waist. "Lucky for him, that is."

"She was too busy dating every other man on campus to give me the time of day. It took an epic Irish curse and Fae battles before she batted those baby-blues at me."

"Oh hush, I'd always been aware of you. It's your own fault you didn't ask me out sooner." Bianca poked Seamus in the ribs and he squirmed.

"When? In the hour between your breakup and the next man in your queue?"

"Oh, you're going to make me sound like a right hussy, you are."

"How so? There's nothing wrong with enjoying yourself." Seamus bent down and pressed a kiss to Bianca's lips. "But now it's just with me, isn't it?"

"Sure thing, cutie. Unless, of course, you wanted to start adding others into our relationship?" Bianca tapped a finger on her lips.

This was too much for Imogen.

"Don't even look at me. I have enough to worry about without involving myself with a single man, let alone with several people. Could you imagine? No, thank you. Now, please get to your spots on the deck as we'll be docking soon."

"I don't think I'd like an open relationship," Bianca agreed, as they left the wheelhouse. "I want to be the only one you focus on."

"You're the only one I've got eyes for...forever and always, my love."

Imogen might have let out a little sigh at their endearments, though she'd never admit it to anyone. Maybe she'd find a partner like that one day, but who was to say? It just wasn't a priority of hers. Now, or ever. Having a partner meant having to share, well, everything – and Imogen had learned long ago to take care of herself. On all levels, really. No, having a partner just wasn't in the cards for someone like her. Which was just fine, really. Right now, the only thing she cared about was successfully docking her ship.

Which went as smoothly as it could possibly go in the middle of the night, Imogen thought, pleased that nothing had happened to her boat in the docking process. After a quick conversation with the harbormaster, who was paid handsomely by Callum, Imogen had slipped away to her cabin, giving strict orders to be left alone. Unless her boat was on fire, she *needed* her alone time. Not even caring about anything but sleep, Imogen stripped and glanced down to see the light glowing from her drawer. After the day she'd had, Imogen was not in the mood for more weirdness. For the first time, she didn't put the ring on before bed but instead, slipped beneath her covers and sank into a dreamless sleep.

17

IMOGEN BLINKED AWAKE, her fuzzy gaze sliding immediately to the alarm clock on her bedside table. She'd slept longer than she'd planned as it was early afternoon, but since nobody had come to wake her, she had to assume they were still safe.

Or everyone had been murdered while she slept, and the Fae hadn't thought to come check her cabin. Great, Imogen thought, as she dashed from the bed to use her bathroom and take a hasty shower. Now all she could think about was the weird team of people that she was slowly coming to care for. She hoped they'd made it safely through to the morning. She toweled off quickly, ran a wide-toothed comb through her mass of dripping hair, and wrapped it in a towel to soak up excess water while she pulled out clean clothes to wear. Her hand hesitated by the drawer to her nightstand and, glancing guiltily over her shoulder, she slid the drawer open.

Quickly, she opened the lid of the box and the ring immediately started glowing – a soft blue light emanating gently from the depths of the aquamarine stone. Great, just great, Imogen thought and slammed the top of the box closed again. If she was reading this correctly, her ring might well belong to the Water Fae.

Which meant...what, exactly?

Is that how she'd been able to see all these otherworldly beings her whole life? She had no idea how long her mother had held the aquamarine ring in her possession. Caught on the thought, Imogen paused as she pulled the towel off and her hair tumbled to her shoulders. She studied her reflection in the mirror, her eyes huge and worried in her face, her skin even more pale than usual. At least sleep had helped with removing the dark circles beneath her eyes.

If she'd been carrying a magickal item of sorts all these years, then perhaps it wasn't Imogen that was abnormal. Maybe it had everything to do with the ring and nothing to do with her. Nibbling her lip, as she thought it over, Imogen walked out into the wheelhouse, her mind switching over to her need for a strong cup of coffee. Sure, she'd just had a good sleep, but coffee was her life's blood, and she never started her day without it.

"Oof!" Imogen exclaimed as she walked right into what felt like a wall but turned out to be the hard chest of an even harder-headed male.

"Steady as she goes there, Captain." Nolan grabbed her shoulders. Imogen's mind scrambled and it took her a moment to think of something to say. His nearness almost overwhelmed her, and she barely resisted leaning up to sniff at his neck. Was that Irish Spring soap he'd washed with? "You're looking a bit better then. Did you sleep well?"

"Aye, I did." Grateful her words had returned, Imogen pushed past him and made her way down the small staircase to the kitchen and lounge area. There she found Bianca reading an aged leather-bound book and her stomach cheered at the platter of French toast she saw on the table. "How's Callum?"

"He's well," Nolan said.

"Did you make that? I could kiss you," Imogen said, shooting a bright smile at Bianca. Bianca glanced up with her own smile. Today the pretty blonde wore a cheerful red sweater and dark denim pants and had her hair pulled into two pigtails.

"You'll have to save your kisses for Nolan, as he's today's chef," Bianca nodded to where Nolan had followed her into the galley. Imogen grimaced and then put a polite smile on her face.

"Thank you for cooking, Nolan."

"What? No kisses for the chef? Although I'll happily watch you and Bianca kiss if that's the way you swing."

"How is it that every time you speak, you just annoy me further?" Imogen wondered out loud, turning to grab a coffee cup and pouring her own life elixir. She'd wanted to ask Callum what Fiona had meant about the life-saving elixir he'd had on him that had saved him from near-death, but she hadn't worked up the courage to do so yet.

"That's just how I charm all the ladies," Nolan said. Imogen was glad her back was to him because she couldn't help but grin.

"And... that explains the lack of ladies I see lining up for you," Imogen quipped, schooling her expression into a bland look of indifference before she turned with her coffee and moved to grab a plate.

"Maybe I don't like to keep the ladies waiting...so there's no line to speak of."

"Och, and see? There you did it again," Imogen shook her head and blew out a breath. "Bianca, can you teach this man why he is insufferable?"

"Who has the time, really?" Bianca grinned from her table, winking at Nolan.

"I'm certainly open to anything you want to teach me, Imogen." Nolan's words were like a warm slide of silk against her skin and Bianca fanned her face.

"I should probably just be on my way..." Bianca made to stand, and Imogen pointed a fork at her.

"You. Stay. You..." Imogen swiveled to Nolan. "Go away."

"But I wanted some food."

"Take it with you to the deck. There are tables out there."

"But the view's nicer in here." Nolan shot her a lazy grin that about melted her insides. Imogen countered by narrowing her eyes.

"Do you remember how quickly I can throw sharp instruments?" She gestured with her fork.

"Fine, fine. I'll be going then. Clearly someone wakes up in a temper."

"I don't like to talk before coffee." It wasn't entirely true, but it was an easy out for Imogen and she waited while Nolan piled food on his plate and left with a put-out expression on his face causing Bianca to chuckle.

"Well, now, *that* was interesting." Bianca fluttered her eyelashes at Imogen.

"No, it was not." Imogen sat and took a healthy gulp of her coffee, her senses perking up at the first hit of caffeine.

"You sure about that? I found it fascinating, really." Bianca had a lilting sing-songy tone to her voice.

"You know something, Bianca?" Imogen neatly cut off a bite of the toast and stabbed it with her fork. "I was starting to think I might enjoy having female friends."

"Och, now go on with that nonsense." Bianca slapped her hand on the table and let out a peal of laughter. "That's what female friends do, you know. We confide in each other. And I'm not going to lie to you when I say that I see something's boiling between you and Grumpy McFaeFace."

Imogen choked on her bite, and Bianca leaned over, gamely slapping her shoulder as Imogen gasped for air. Once she cleared her throat, she blinked at Bianca through the tears that had sprung to her eyes.

"I'm sorry...but did you call him Grumpy McFaeFace?"

"I mean...it just came to me. It fits though, no? Or should we give him a different name?"

"No, no, I like it." Imogen was surprised when a giggle escaped. "It's just so...oh he'll *hate* it."

"Even better. I can't decide who is more uptight – you or him."

"Me? What happened to being understanding that I was on a steep learning curve and trying to roll with punches about all this Fae and magick shite? Now I'm the one who is uptight? That's hardly fair," Imogen complained and took another bite of the toast. Damn it, but the man could also cook.

"Of course, I totally understand this is a lot for you to process." Bianca leaned over and patted her arm softly. "But...that doesn't make you any less uptight."

"I'm not..." Imogen spied a water ring from Bianca's glass on the table. "Excuse me...have you not heard of coasters?"

"See?" Bianca beamed at her and hastily wiped up the water.

"I'm not...it's just..." Imogen blew out a breath. "I don't have a lot in this world. And the bank still owns a chunk of this boat. It matters. To me at least, okay?"

"I can totally understand that. I wasn't raised with much, either. That's not what I'm talking about. If you're wound too tightly, you'll shatter, Imogen. You're going to need to blow off some steam."

"How though?" Imogen honestly couldn't understand why Bianca wasn't more uptight. What with the Dark Fae trying to murder them and all. "Are we not seeing the same things here? You know...Fae trying to kill us every day and all that?"

"Sure, and that's a bother, isn't it? But you still have to learn to have fun, too."

"A bother, she says." Imogen widened her eyes as she carefully assessed the woman across from her. Maybe she'd grossly miscalculated her opinion of Bianca. Perhaps the woman was just a straight-up nutter? "Magickal beings with nasty knives and silver goo for blood are just...a bother? What do you call midgies then? Mates? Best friends? Cuddle-buddies?"

Bianca chuckled and took a sip of her coffee.

"Okay, I'll allow that what my normal has become is wildly different than someone else's normal. And no, I'm not discounting the serious nature of what we're doing here. But, also, you know...you have to relax a bit. Between the murdering Fae bits."

"I wouldn't even know where to begin." Imogen blew out a breath. "What, like yoga?"

"I was thinking hot sex with Grumpy McFaeFace would be the best for the both of you."

"Bianca!" Imogen's mouth dropped open just as a throat cleared behind her.

"Did you just call me Grumpy McFaeFace?" Nolan asked and Imogen's face flushed with embarrassment. She would have preferred to turn around and face a Dark Fae than Nolan right then.

"If the nickname fits…" Bianca shrugged a shoulder, an impish expression on her face.

"Women." Nolan slammed his way back out of the galley, grumbling under his breath.

"Bianca," Imogen hissed, certain she would die of embarrassment.

"See? You both need to relax. And I was just suggesting one surefire way to do so."

"Pick another idea," Imogen gritted out.

"Okay, fine. Let's go for a walk."

"A walk?" Imogen asked.

"Sure. The men can watch the boat. Don't you think we should get the lay of the land a bit? See if we can pick up any clues or see any Domnua slinking about?"

"And this is what you consider soothing?"

"No, but I'm already relaxed because my Seamus loved on me like the goddess I am this morning." Bianca grinned cheerfully when Imogen clapped her hands over her face.

"I do not need to know this."

"You know…you didn't strike me as a prude."

"I'm not a…oh for feck's sake."

18

Nolan glowered down at the water from the back of the boat, trying to pull his mind away from thoughts of sliding Imogen over his body and filling her deeply. Need for her pounded in his blood, which made him even more furious. The closer they drew to finding Lily, the more imperative it became that he not become distracted. And Imogen was one big fat distraction with a capital "D."

She'd looked...Nolan's fist clenched the coffee cup so tightly he was surprised it didn't shatter in his hands. When she'd wandered out of her cabin, her wet hair in a riot of curls around her head and her skin freshly scrubbed clean, he'd almost reached for her right there. He'd wanted so desperately to back her up against the door to her cabin and take a taste of her sweet lips. Well, not that she ever had sweet words for him. But he'd imagined her kiss would taste sweet. Cursing long and low, Nolan narrowed his eyes at a movement in the water.

Just a fish, coming to pluck a piece of seaweed floating at the surface. He'd been ready to unleash magick on the poor thing. Nolan blew out a breath and turned, taking in the view of Kilronan Harbour. Grumpy McFaeFace she'd called him. Was he grumpy? Sure, and he was a bit tightly wound at the moment, but who wouldn't be? One of the sweetest women he knew was being held captive, and it was his job to help find her. It was normal to be tense under these circumstances...Nolan glanced up when a cheerful whistle caught his attention.

Seamus strolled to the back, a navy knit cap pulled over his red hair, his eyes dancing when he saw Nolan.

"That was some fantastic French toast, mate. Thanks for cooking."

"What are you so cheerful about?" Nolan all but growled.

"I'm just..." Seamus narrowed his eyes at Nolan's face. "Sun is out. Had a good meal. I'm feeling positive we can make headway on finding Lily today. It's all good, right?"

"And your needs were met by your woman," Nolan clarified.

"Also that, but I'd like to think I had a good hand in meeting her needs as well." Seamus smiled and wandered to the edge of the boat to peer into the water.

"This is why couples shouldn't go on quests. They ruin the vibe."

"Is that right? Seems we were pretty successful on the most important quest in all of Fae history. In case you forgot?" Seamus turned and raised an eyebrow at Nolan.

Nolan grimaced. The man had a point.

"I'm just..."

"Grouchy? I heard."

"Grumpy, I believe was their word. Listen, should we go have a look around? See what's what?"

"I believe that's what the ladies were planning to do. Ah, here they are now." Seamus beamed as the women joined them on the deck and dropped a kiss on Bianca's lips. Nolan averted his eyes, annoyed for some reason with their easy affection, and instead looked out to the quiet harbor.

"We're going for a walk," Imogen said. "I'll trust you to protect my boat?"

"Of course. With my life," Seamus half-bowed to her.

"He will at that," Bianca nodded to Imogen. "He knows how important this is to you."

"You can't just...you're not going with them?" Nolan demanded, whirling on Seamus. Anger rocketed through him. "You'll leave them unprotected?"

"We can protect ourselves, can't we?" Bianca demanded, her hands on her hips. With her pigtails and bright sweater, she looked barely old enough to drive a car.

"You're not going alone. I won't have it."

"I'll..." Seamus began but stopped when Nolan stomped forward.

"I'll go."

"Oh, will you? I don't recall inviting you," Imogen hissed at him. She'd pulled on an emerald-green sweater over the thin white shirt she'd been wearing earlier, but had left her hair down, presumably to dry, and now it stood out like a beacon against the color of her sweater. Her hair was wild, like a fire out of control, and the wind whipped tendrils around her face. Nolan wanted to dive his hands into her hair and feel its warmth, for surely a hair that red couldn't be cold to the touch.

"Maybe it will be good for him to walk a bit," Bianca decided. "He doesn't strike me as a man used to being caged up on a boat."

"It's hardly being caged up," Imogen said with a scowl. "The boat moves and it takes you all over the place."

"You know what I mean," Bianca said, gently. "Nolan,

you're welcome to join us. We were just going to stretch our legs a bit and get the lay of the land."

"I'm not sure that this is exactly the recipe for relaxing that I was looking for," Imogen muttered under her breath. She stopped in front of Seamus. "You'll watch over her?"

"Like she's my own, Captain!" Seamus saluted, and Imogen rolled her eyes, but smiled anyway.

"It's a nice day, isn't it?" Bianca said, her tone bright as they wandered down the main pier. Their worry over finding a spot to dock was unfounded, for only the ferry was currently tied up to the long dock, and a few passengers milled around on board waiting for it to depart. As it wasn't yet high season, it was likely the island reduced the ferry crossings over to Galway Bay.

"Aye, it's not bad for early spring. Nice not to have it pissing rain," Imogen agreed. "Do you get seasons in the Fae realm?"

Pulled from his thoughts, Nolan glanced over at her in question.

"Seasons?"

"You know…autumn…winter…"

"Oh, right then. Sorry, my mind was elsewhere." They reached the end of the dock and turned left, following a road that wound into a small village – much smaller than Grace's Cove – with a few charming stone buildings. "Yes, we experience much of the natural world the same as you do. Which is why we rule the Elemental Fae."

"Of course. Sorry." Imogen flushed.

"Don't be. I can imagine there are many questions you have, just as the Fae do about humans."

"Like what?" Imogen raised an eyebrow at him as they crested a hill and came to the front of a cheerful-looking pub where an old man in a newsboy cap sat on a bench by the door.

"Like television, for example. I don't understand these shows you watch all the time. Or why you go home and watch shows about people interacting instead of going out in the world and interacting with people."

"Um..." Imogen scrunched her nose in an adorable manner when she was thinking about something deeply. It made Nolan want to bend over and kiss her. "I suppose because sometimes we get tired of talking to people all day in our career, so we like to be entertained without any requirements on our energy?"

"But if you're around people all day, then why watch more people?" Nolan asked.

"I've never really thought of that," Bianca laughed and turned her smile to the old man who was tamping tobacco down into a carved wood pipe he held in his gnarled hand. "Good day."

"Lá maith." The man nodded his head to them.

"Do you understand English or Irish only?" Bianca asked the man.

"Both." A smile creased the old man's wrinkled face. "Though I prefer speaking in Irish to tourists as it preserves the old language."

"An bhfaca tú aon rud aisteach?" Nolan asked. Imogen looked surprised at his words, but he wondered why. He was Irish Fae, wasn't he?

"Sea, tá agam." The man nodded and struck a match on the stone of the pub wall and puffed his pipe for a moment. The sweet smell of tobacco wound through the air, reminding Nolan of his grandfather.

"Cá háit?"

The man launched into a flurry of words mixed with

gesticulations, and Nolan nodded as he followed along. He glanced up as Imogen turned away to study the pub. Simply named, "The Bar," it looked like a nice gathering place when the weather was warmer. With a courtyard full of picnic tables, window boxes that would bloom with flowers soon enough, and pretty windows to let in the view of the water, it was likely a lovely place for a pint.

Nolan dug in his pocket and handed over some coins. The old man glanced at him and then gestured with his thumb toward the back of the pub.

"Let's go."

"What's happening?" Imogen asked, and Bianca shrugged.

"My Irish isn't strong enough to fully translate that conversation. But I think we might be getting bicycles."

"Why?" Imogen skidded to a stop by where Nolan was pulling bicycles from a long rack.

"It's a touch chilly for a ride, isn't it?" Bianca asked, her eyes trailing hopefully to the pub.

"You can stay behind if you want."

"Well, now. Sure, and that's not how this works, is it? We go as a team or not at all," Bianca said, moving forward to adjust the height of the seat for her short legs.

"What's going on, Nolan?" Imogen didn't move, uncertainty lacing her words.

"I asked the man out front if he'd seen anything strange lately. It's always good to ask the old timers. Or children. They see everything."

"And what did he say?" Imogen still didn't move.

"He'd seen some folks he thought to be a touch odd. Moved weird, he says."

"That could be anything really, right?" Imogen asked.

"No, it's likely Fae he saw." Bianca shrugged one shoulder. "It's typical for humans who do see the Fae to think they move quickly or oddly. It's because they are more fluid in their movements. Fae are very agile where humans can be clumsy or clunky in their motions. It makes sense to me."

"What she said." Nolan waited by a bike, narrowing his stormy eyes at Imogen. The wind kicked up, blowing her hair across her face, and she reached for her hair tie to bustle it back in a messy bun. His fingers itched once more to touch her.

"Don't you think we should at least alert the others? Or have them come with us?"

"It's just a scouting mission," Nolan said. "There are several stone circles on the island. I just want to go past and see if I can feel any magick."

"And if we get jumped?" Imogen asked. "Then what? I'm sure Seamus and Callum wouldn't be all that happy."

"My man knows I can handle myself. See?" Bianca held up her phone to show kissy-face texts from Seamus. "They're fine with us going to scout things out, but Callum asked us not to go into any of the circles."

"That's fine then. Well, what's it going to be, *mavourneen?*"

He couldn't help but enjoy the flash of fire that came into her eyes when he called her that.

"I think that I might just wait here and see if anything odd happens out front of the pub."

"Maybe we could have a pint at the pub tonight if we don't go on a rescue mission..." Bianca's voice held a note of longing.

"It'll all depend on what we find. It's already mid-afternoon, so we'll have to see if Callum wants to make his moves in darkness or not. If she's close, it's going to be tough to keep him from searching for her."

"I can't say I blame him," Bianca admitted, swinging her leg over the bar of the bike and easing herself onto the seat. "Well, then, Imogen. On we go. We aren't leaving you behind."

Imogen glanced down at the bike and then back up. Her cheeks tinged pink, and Nolan wondered just what the issue was.

"I would rather just wait here. Hang with the old man or wander back to the boat. I can scope things out by foot."

"Don't tell me you're scared of riding a bike?" Nolan cocked an eyebrow and deliberately provoked her. Scared? A ship's captain was many things, but a scaredy-cat was not one of them.

"Oh, of course." Understanding dawned on Bianca's face. "Come now, Nolan. You heard she had a rough upbringing. You can't assume everybody knows how to ride a bike."

Instantly apologetic, Nolan stepped forward and took the bike away from Imogen. Grabbing her hand, he tugged her over to his bike.

"I'm sorry, I wasn't thinking. Here, see these two posts?" Nolan pointed down to where little posts poked out on either side of the back wheel.

"Yes." Imogen said, a nervous lilt to her voice.

"I'll drive the bicycle. You'll stand on those and put your arms around my shoulders and hang on tightly. That way you can come along for the ride. Does that suit?"

"Perfect," Bianca beamed.

"Um. Sure, I guess we can…" Imogen trailed off as Nolan straddled the bike and sat on the seat, his back facing her.

"Go on then. Climb on up and give it a feel, yeah?"

Imogen cleared her throat, and then reached out to put her hands on Nolan's shoulders. Instantly, a feeling of… rightness flooded through him. Imogen snatched her hands back and Nolan couldn't bring himself to turn around and look at her while his stomach tied itself in knots from the smallest touch.

"You can do it, Imogen." Bianca sent her an encouraging smile.

"Right, sure thing." Imogen took a shaky breath and then put her hands on his shoulders once more, and that little hum of energy zipped between them again, before she climbed onto the posts. "Just give me a moment before you start."

"Just say the word," Nolan said, his throat catching. She leaned forward, so that she was all but plastered against Nolan's back and wrapped her arms around his shoulders. Though she was standing, he was still so much taller than her that even when he was seated, her head wasn't much above his. Nolan caught that sweet scent of her – like dried flowers mixed with soap – and his stomach twisted once more. He had to deliberately focus on the road ahead of him and not on the soft press of her breasts at his back. He wouldn't be able to live with himself if he crashed this damn bicycle and hurt her in the process.

"Well, team? All sorted? Which way then?" Bianca asked.

"First one's just down the way about two kilometers the man said," Nolan pointed to where the dirt path joined up with a paved road. "He said the biking should be smooth as most of the main road is paved."

"Even better. I'll just work off some of those calories from the French toast then." With that, Bianca took off, a beacon of bright red on a crisply cold sunny day. Nolan followed suit, quickly adjusting the rhythm of the bike to having the added weight of Imogen at his back. She didn't say a word, though her arms tightened around his shoulders, and he wondered if she'd felt the same zip of energy that he had when she'd first touched him.

Perhaps it was just him then. Which was well and fine, Nolan reminded himself, as they caught up with Bianca and kept an easy pace along the road. For someone who was determined not to be distracted during a mission, he was doing a right shite job of it.

"Is this alright for you then?" Nolan asked, turning his head ever so slightly so Imogen could hear him. The wind had picked up a bit, the bite of it stinging his face, but it also served as a reminder to stay aware of his surroundings.

The blade of a Dark Fae would sting much worse than a spike of cold wind, that was the truth of it.

"It's not as bad as I thought it would be." Imogen's voice was warm at his ears, and Nolan instantly thought about waking up next to her, that sensual voice whispering to him, and lust surged. Annoyance whipped through him. If he couldn't even control his own reactions to a woman, how was he going to control his magick when it came time to battle? He'd need to get his head on straight before he accidently let Callum down.

Instead of answering, Nolan continued in silence, his eyes scanning the landscape around them constantly. Low stone walls, the kind built seemingly haphazardly with various sized stones fitted together, lined the road and on one side, the hills stretched out in a gentle greenish-brown slope. On the other, the world dropped away into the icy waters far below the cliffs, and Nolan wondered if the Water Fae watched them.

"There's a circle," Bianca slowed and pointed to a spot where large stones, several paces from one another, formed a circle. Reaching out with his senses, Nolan scanned over the circle but found only the smallest amount of energy –

and that of a Pagan nature – but nothing to do with the Dark Fae. Shaking his head, he motioned for Bianca to continue.

"How can you be sure?" Imogen asked at his neck.

"Dark Fae magick feels like...tar, I suppose is the best way to describe it. A sticky residue. Whereas our magick flows with universal energy, theirs does not."

"Is it easy for you to feel it?"

"Aye, it is for me. Not others. It also depends on the type of magick. While I can't always detect their immediate presence – like when they snuck onto the boat the other night, I can feel if they have spelled an area. There's not a ton of consistency, which is the way of the Fae both dark and light."

"Mercurial," Imogen murmured.

"Exactly. It helps keep us as undetectable as possible. Predictability is dangerous."

19

IMOGEN'S blood hummed like she'd been plugged into an electrical socket, and she felt...well, she felt like she'd had one too many cups of coffee. It was as though she wanted to bounce up and down on the posts she stood on, almost giddy, and yet she had no release for this energy that churned inside her. If she was being honest with herself, it was wrapping her arms around Nolan that had caused this sudden buzz of energy. But Imogen wasn't in the mood for deep reflections of that nature, so instead she attributed it to the excitement of her first time riding a bicycle. Sure, she wasn't *actually* pedaling, but riding while wrapped around Nolan was thrilling in its own right and Imogen started to hum, happiness dancing through her. Was it weird that she was happy knowing that they could be ambushed any second? Probably.

Imogen had always been a live-in-the-moment type of girl. Frankly, she'd never had enough time to spend worrying for the future because she was too busy making ends meet in the now. An existence such as that made it easier for her to appreciate the small day-to-day moments that brought joy, instead of looking to the future, with some sort of unattainable happiness always hovering on the horizon. She'd read somewhere once that those feelings were similar to how nomadic people felt. The article had said that people like that rarely ever stopped to consider if they were happy or not. They just...were. They existed. They got up and found food and made shelter and moved on to new places. The idea of worrying over happiness just wasn't a concept. Imogen had identified strongly with that article, because that was basically her life. She worked to live and lived to work and stole moments of fun when she could. It wasn't a bad life, but different than most, she supposed.

"What are you singing?" Nolan snapped, tearing Imogen from her thoughts.

"Um..." What had she been singing? A melody floated just out of her grasp, like when she woke up from a dream and was still half-asleep and trying to hold onto the threads of the story. "I...I can't say. I don't know. I'm sorry, I was daydreaming a bit, I suppose."

"You said that love is an ocean both powerful and healing."

"Did I?"

"Yes, you did." Imogen felt his words rumble through his back where her chest was pressed to him. The vibration of it excited her in a way that she couldn't quite explain. "I didn't know you spoke Irish."

"I don't." Imogen laughed.

"You were speaking in Irish just now. Well, singing it."

"Was I? Well, isn't that something?" Imogen looked around, wondering if something was amiss. Had she fallen under a spell of sorts?

"Look!" Bianca called, drawing their attention to a massive stone wall that was shaped in a large circle.

"Well, that's a stone circle if I've ever seen one," Imogen said. "It's almost like a fort of sorts. I mean..."

"They're here." Nolan's voice sent a chill through her as he whistled sharply to Bianca who immediately stopped so that Nolan could catch up to her. Stopping the bicycle, Imogen slid off, immediately missing the warmth of his body as a gust of icy wind slapped her.

"What is this place?" Imogen asked, turning to study the stacked stone wall that formed a massive circle – too tall for Imogen to see over the top from where they were on the road.

"It's called Dún Eochla," Bianca said from where she stood in front of a little roadside plaque. "It's a fort dating back to around 500 A.D. that might have been used as a dwelling for an extended family of sorts or a small village."

"It's stunning," Imogen said, drawing closer. There was something so compelling about the beautiful structure, with the gray stones of the wall juxtaposed against the wintry blue sky. She started walking, needing to see more.

"Wait just a moment..." Nolan snagged the back of her jumper, pulling her up against him. Instantly, the draw to Nolan felt stronger than the pull from the fort and she turned, blinking up at him in confusion. "We'll go look together."

"Just a reminder that the prince has ordered us to stay outside of any stone circles," Bianca said, starting on the path up the hill that led to the fort. "So, this is just a brief exploratory mission."

"What, specifically, should we be looking for?" Imogen fell into step behind Bianca, her pulse picking up as they climbed the somewhat steep hill to where the fort stood. It was a good spot for a fort, Imogen thought, for it would be easy to see any threats from all sides.

"Essentially I want to get a read on the magick here. Because our dark brethren are tricky on a good day and downright maniacal on a bad, I'll need to assess if this could be where they are holding Lily, or..." Nolan's voice trailed off as the wind picked up, slowing their advance.

"Or if it's an ambush?" Bianca asked, her dagger already in hand.

Imogen followed suit, slipping her favorite knife from her pocket, eyes on the break in the wall where people were meant to enter the fort. She could've sworn she saw some sort of light pulse from inside and she quickened her steps, almost mowing Bianca down as she passed her on the path.

"Wait, Imogen. You can't rush ahead," Bianca said, her breath coming out in little pants of air as she rushed to keep up with Imogen's stride. "You don't know what's on the other side of those walls."

"I just need to see," Imogen insisted, feeling as though a rope was physically pulling her closer. She couldn't explain it, not really, but as soon as she'd broken contact with Nolan the fort called to her. It was as though her next breath depended on her getting to the fort and she began to run, taking the rampart steps easily, almost to the walls before Nolan caught up with her and snagged an arm around her waist.

"What the hell are you doing?" Nolan hissed into her ear. "Are you mental then? Have you entirely lost your damn mind? Didn't you hear us shouting?"

"You were shouting?" Imogen said, the pull of the fort dissolving once she was in Nolan's arms again. She blinked wearily up at him as confusion fogged her brain.

"Your eyes," Nolan whispered as Bianca skidded to a stop.

"Whoa, Imogen. What's going on, girl?" Bianca said,

holding her knife in front of her. "Your eyes are looking a little crazy right now. You have something you need to tell us?"

"What do you mean, they're crazy? I don't understand." Imogen looked between Nolan and Bianca, who both regarded her carefully.

"Um, well, they're just glowing a wee bit. Silvery, really," Bianca cleared her throat. "But in all fairness, your eyes run to silver as their natural color anyway, kind of that light bluish gray you have going on."

Nolan took a moment to wordlessly stare at Bianca until she shut her mouth.

"I really don't know what you're talking about," Imogen said, her stomach twisting in knots, the need to get inside the fort almost overpowering all conscious thought. "I have to...there's something inside. We have to go in."

"No, we do not. Callum said we can't. Remember?" Bianca hissed, her hands on her hips like she was scolding a small child.

"The Dark Fae are calling to her. She must be susceptible for some reason." Nolan motioned to Bianca. "Can you hold her here while I go check this out?"

"Sure can. I may be short, but I'm strong," Bianca said cheerfully, looping an arm tightly through Imogen's. "We're just going to stay right here, girlfriend, while Nolan has a wee perimeter check, mmmkay?"

As soon as Nolan walked away from her, the compulsion to follow him into the fort was almost debilitating and Imogen bent at the waist, gasping as she tried to fight it.

"I need..." Imogen said. "I have to..."

"Shite!" Bianca said, and Imogen glanced up just as Nolan shouted. Light flashed and his body was sucked through the entrance of the fort like a piece of lint being sucked up by a vacuum cleaner. Bianca dropped Imogen's arm and raced after Nolan.

Imogen had to give the woman credit – she was fearless.

"Damn it," Bianca screeched, slamming into an invisible wall of sorts so hard that she fell onto her bum on the ground. Rubbing a hand across her head, she glared at the open passageway. "They've magicked it."

"Can you see Nolan?" Imogen asked, bending to help Bianca up, though everything in her wanted to race inside the fort and answer whatever was compelling her to move forward.

"There!" Bianca shouted, pointing to where Nolan vaulted himself onto a smaller stone platform of sorts that was erected in the middle of the circle. Silvery Domnua, three deep, circled the platform. Imogen froze as Nolan fired off some sort of magick...mowing down the first wave of Domnua, but more kept coming. When he raised his hands for his next round of magick, he shook his head and looked down at his hands, confusion on his face.

"Something's not right," Imogen said, the chaos of emotions inside her propelling her forward.

"His magick isn't working. He's only got his knife. Oh... what's happening? Why isn't his magick working? He's a Royal!" Bianca cried next to her.

Imogen barely heard her speak and then she heard nothing at all as she passed easily through the barrier that had stopped Bianca in her tracks. She felt it, almost like diving into water, she supposed, but it didn't hurt her or hold her back. Imogen stalked forward, almost in a daze, Bianca's shouts now muffled behind the magickal barrier that cocooned the fort. Domnua climbed onto the platform, circling Nolan, and he felled one with his knife, turned and knocked another off with a swift kick that swept the legs out and had the Domnua tumbling. Turning in a circle, Nolan's face took on the look of a man who knew he was about to die but wasn't going to go down without a fight. As the crowd of Domnua closed in on the stone platform, they seemed to realize that Nolan no longer had his magick and a cry went through the group of Dark Fae.

Nolan turned toward the entrance and, stepping back, he took a running start and leapt into the air as far as he could, landing almost to the other side of the crowd. Knocking two Domnua's heads together with a sickly crunch, Nolan ran forward.

It was too much. There were too many Domnua. Imogen's heart caught in her throat, and she ran forward to meet Nolan. His eyes widened with surprise when he saw her, and then fury replaced it. Knowing she didn't have time, and not really understanding what she was doing, Imogen grabbed Nolan's hands and ran with him to the entrance, the Domnua hot on their heels.

Turning, Imogen opened her mouth – and the song she'd been humming on the bike flew from her – thundering across the expanse of the circle. Nolan stopped dead in his tracks, pulling her to him, his arms around her as he gaped down at Imogen. The moment hung suspended, before Nolan snapped out of it and they hit the entrance at a dead run. Nolan slammed into the same invisible wall that Bianca had, but Imogen kept moving, pulling him with her through the barrier, refusing to let go of his hands though the force of his impact almost ripped her arms out of their sockets. They tumbled through to the other side, both hitting the ground in a tangle of limbs, Imogen grunting at the impact.

Nolan jumped up, far faster than Imogen and whirled to the entrance of the fort.

"They're gone," Bianca said, her voice shaky, as she crouched by Imogen's side. "Hey there. You okay? Let me see those eyes of yours."

"Yeah, I think so?" Imogen said, moving her body carefully. Nothing seemed to be broken, and the odd compulsion she'd felt earlier from inside the fort had vanished. Nolan towered over her, fury distorting his handsome face.

"What the hell were you thinking?"

"I was thinking I was saving your arse, that's what," Imogen said, hopping up and wiping the dirt from her hands on her pants.

"With what, exactly?" Nolan threw his arms in the air. "You don't have magick."

"Neither do you, it appears," Imogen spat back. Nolan's face tightened and he turned from her, stomping down the path toward the bicycles.

"Stupid woman. Stupid singing," Nolan muttered.

"So, uh, right. A lot to unpack there," Bianca said, glancing back into the fort. Holding out her hand she brushed it against where the invisible barrier had been. Now, nothing stopped her. "Interesting."

"Stupid *man*. Thinks he can save the world. He barely got out of that alive," Imogen muttered, stretching her arms out and making sure nothing had been hurt in that little tumble they just took.

"In all fairness, he was holding his own even without magick," Bianca pointed out and then clamped her mouth shut when Imogen glared at her. "Right, okay, so what's up with the glowy eyes?"

"You tell me. I'm new to this world of magick and mayhem and whatever else is happening right now."

"Why don't we just have a wee chat when we get safely

back to the boat? I'll peek in that book that Callum was so nice to gift me. Perhaps I can find some intel for you."

"You do that. I'll do my best not to throttle Grumpy McFaeFace."

"Sure, and he's going to be even grumpier after this, isn't he?" Bianca said, morosely.

"I'm beginning to think that's just standard operating procedure for him."

"You know what you could do to change that?"

"Shut it..." Imogen paused as Bianca started down the hill. Turning, she looked back into the entrance of the fort and her heart slammed into her chest.

The man...the one she usually saw in the water...stood on top of the stone platform that Nolan had just launched himself from. He grinned at Imogen, and beckoned to her with a finger.

Come to me, my darling.

Much like Imogen had been compelled to race to the fort earlier, now she found herself wanting to take a step forward. To get more information from this man. This Fae. Like...why had he tried to kidnap her? Why had he followed her through her entire life? What did he want from her? The compulsion was so strong that Imogen took two steps forward before Bianca's hand at her wrist snapped her out of it.

"Hey...you okay? You didn't hear me?" Bianca's worried blue eyes searched hers.

"Oh, I'm sorry. I was just..." Imogen gestured to the now-empty platform. "I was just taking a second, I guess. That was pretty intense."

"Well, let's take those moments to process when we're safely back at the boat. We may have won this round, but they'll have hundreds following. There's no time for delays."

"Right, okay. Sorry about that."

Imogen glanced over her shoulder once more as they started down the path, but the fort remained empty except for a single gull that swooped in circles on the icy wind that buffeted the hills.

Alone...just like she'd lived her life, Imogen thought.

20

BY THE TIME they'd made it back to the boat, Callum was pacing with fury. The few people who lingered on the dock kept glancing at him with worry, and Imogen didn't blame them. The Prince of Fae's cool good looks and murderous stare were enough to send even the most bold-hearted scurrying away.

"Didn't I tell you not to go into the circles?" Callum thundered before they'd even made it halfway down the dock.

Imogen was not in the mood for this...no she was *not*. She'd endured a painfully silent bike ride back to town and she wanted nothing more than a whiskey and a hot meal. In that order. What she wasn't interested in was being lectured by somebody who certainly had no ruling over her. It was almost worth Callum's look of surprise when she brushed past him and neatly tossed Nolan under the bus.

"Nolan went in. I just followed after him to save his sorry arse."

"That's absolute shite," Nolan protested. She shot him a one-fingered salute and disappeared into the wheelhouse and then directly into her cabin, flipping the lock on the door behind her. Immediately, she strode to the bathroom and flipped on the lights to peer into the mirror.

Her eyes looked normal to her. Sure, they were very pale – and in certain lights could run more to a grayish silver than blue. But glowing? No, that was just...Imogen straightened and went to her bedside drawer. The only thing she knew of that glowed, other than the weird light around the Fae, was the aquamarine ring she had. Could it be the cause for the glowing eyes? Returning to the bathroom, she leaned over the sink and looked into the mirror once more.

Nope, still no glowing eyes. So, maybe it wasn't the jewelry then? Maybe her life would become more normal if she just got rid of this ring. Mulling it over, Imogen washed the dirt from her hands and face, tamed her hair the best she could, and left her cabin to go dig up some food in the galley.

Nobody was in the lounge area, thank god, and Imogen detoured to the small bar and pulled out a bottle of Jameson's Cask Strength. Grabbing a glass, she poured herself a healthy amount and took it down in one burning swallow. Gasping, Imogen repeated the same maneuver and her throat screamed in protest. Putting the bottle on the table, she poured herself one more before ducking into the kitchen to put together some food lest she fall overboard from the effects of the whiskey on an empty stomach.

Like any sailor, Imogen could hold her drink, but she rarely liked to overdo it. She found she wasn't comfortable with the way alcohol loosened her inhibitions as well as her lips. Some of her secrets were meant to stay her own, and didn't need sharing over a pint at the pub.

Imogen slapped together a ham and cheese sandwich and wandered back out into the lounge area, plopping down on a cushioned bench and pulling her legs up beside her. She was...well, she was scared. Imogen swallowed against the lump that filled her throat and took a small sip of the whiskey. It felt like she was in over her head. It was like being tossed into a game of American Football and not knowing that a football was something you threw and not kicked. Imogen still didn't understand that...the name football clearly explained how the ball was to be used. You kicked the ball with your foot. Why were they throwing it all over the field?

The whiskey began to do its work, and Imogen felt some of the tension slip from her shoulders as she chewed glumly on her sandwich. At some point, she was going to have to accept that in one way or the other she was tied up in the Fae world even if it didn't really make any sense. But, after today, when she'd felt that pull of magick from the fort? It was undeniable that something was going on.

"Pity party of one?" Bianca stuck her head in the door to the lounge.

"Something like that."

"Want to talk about it?" Bianca wandered closer.

"I..." Imogen just shrugged. "I'm not sure."

"The glowy eyes thing?"

"Yeah, it's messing with me a bit. Not to mention..." Imogen looked around and made sure that nobody was coming. "I just...listen, I can't help but wonder what's going on with me? You know? Like...what is happening here? Now I'm wondering if, well, maybe...I am one? Or I'm something? Maybe my mother knew something, that's for sure. And, well, what about my father?" Imogen swallowed. She couldn't bring herself to finish the sentence.

"Maybe your father was Fae? It would make sense." Bianca tapped a finger on her lips. "But if you don't know much of your da? Yeah, that could be a thing. I think we need to talk more about this."

"Do we though? Because I feel like I'm at my limit of what I can absorb at this point." Imogen took another sip of her whiskey.

"If your father is Dark Fae that could be potentially catastrophic for what we're trying to do here. I'm not sure though. Maybe if you weren't raised in their teachings, it wouldn't matter?" Bianca held Imogen's eyes.

"Shite." Imogen breathed.

"Sure, and it is at that. And I know it can't be feeling great to think about these things. But...I mean, the Water Fae did call you their queen. Isn't there...maybe...something there? Sure, and I know we're all in a rush to save Lily, but maybe we're skipping some important parts."

"And you think you'll be able to slow Callum down to delve more deeply into this? Into my past?"

"No, you're right. He's already on a bit of a tear at the moment," Bianca sighed. "I guess we're heading back out right now."

"Really?" Imogen asked.

"We're going to head to the pub. Callum wants to see if he can get any more information from the old man we saw earlier. He's itching to take a cruise about the island as well, see if he can find any other magickal signatures or markers or whatever that might lead him to Lily. You want to come?"

"Nope. Not even in the slightest." Imogen didn't. She just wanted to stay on her boat in peace, well, hopefully in peace and just...zone out for a little bit. This would be her last whiskey, because it wouldn't be a good thing to get drunk and deal with another Fae attack. Or would it? Maybe she wouldn't care so much if she was fighting while drunk? Imogen squinted one eye at the bottle in contemplation.

"I can't say I blame you, but I do think we'll need to talk about some of this stuff, Imogen. There's something more afoot here, and I don't think you can ignore it much longer."

"I'm trying pretty hard right now," Imogen held her glass up to Bianca in a cheers.

"Here's the deal...I'm giving you tonight to mope or whatever this is. Because I get that we all need time like that sometimes. But that's it, okay? We are still a team even if you are a begrudging member of it, and that means we take care of each other. You and I can have a private chit-chat over coffee tomorrow and I'll take a look through my Fae book. Maybe we can come up with some explanations that will help you."

"What if I don't want there to be explanations in your Fae book?" Imogen said, pulling part of the crust of her bread off and rolling it into a tight little bread ball. A crust-ball. A brall? A crumble? Okay, yeah the whiskey was hitting her. Imogen nudged her glass away. "What if I just want to be normal?"

"Whatever for?" Bianca's laughter filled the lounge area. "Why live in a world of the mundane when you can have magick?"

Because what if she was the wrong kind of magick? Imogen didn't say the last thought out loud, but it had been bouncing around in her head since the fort debacle. Her hand went to the ring in her pocket and she wondered if her supposedly lucky charm had been nothing but her own personal curse all these years.

"Have a good night," Imogen said.

"Before I go...can I just get your phone number? So, I can text in case of anything? Or even just to stay in contact? I can't help but worry." Bianca held up her phone.

Imogen pulled out her phone from her pocket. She only

used it to check emails from new charter guests, and the occasional text with her crew. She'd tucked it in her pocket out of habit and now glanced at the screen for the first time in a while.

"I'm at ten percent battery."

"Well, charge it silly."

After Bianca had left for the night, Imogen checked her messages to see a few from Cillian, her engineer, checking in on her. She sent off a message promising that she was okay and that she'd explain soon enough. And yes, he still had a job. It didn't do much to appease him, as a flurry of texts came back in return, but Imogen was at a loss to explain just what, exactly, was happening. Could she really promise him a job on the boat this season when she didn't even know what tomorrow looked like? Guilt filled her stomach, as her crew mattered to her, and she asked him to be patient with her and that she would explain when she could. With that, Imogen slid the phone away and stared out the window where the sun had just dipped below the horizon, leaving the sky a soft navy blue with tinges of rose streaking across. Feeling antsy, Imogen picked up her glass and glanced at the bottle, contemplating topping it off.

Instead, she turned and made her way to the bow, easing down on the deck and considering hanging her legs over the side. However, she realized that she was no longer comfortable with her favorite spot, and even though this was her boat, she should be smart. Needing to remove herself from easy access to the water, Imogen wandered back to the wheelhouse and climbed up the little ladder bolted into the side that led to the roof of the wheelhouse. Sometimes she sat up there, lying back with her head pillowed on her arms and contemplating the stars in the sky. Tonight seemed like such a night, and she sighed as she settled back, the gentle sway of the boat beneath her soothing her like a mother rocking her child.

"You shouldn't drink alone."

"For feck's sake!" Imogen sat up and almost knocked her whiskey glass over. She glared at where Nolan's head peeked over the edge of the roof. "What are you doing here?"

"Did you really think I'd leave you alone on the boat?"

"Yes, I did actually." Imogen brought her hand to her chest and took a deep breath. "Ever heard of not sneaking up on someone?"

"Well, let's just say I'm glad I'm not a Dark Fae, then, or you'd be pretty easy to ambush right now." Nolan finished climbing onto the roof and plopped down next to her. Imogen edged a bit away from him, needing some distance so her thoughts wouldn't scramble as they seemed to in his presence.

"You're annoying, but you're also right. I guess I just wanted to check out for a bit," Imogen admitted.

Nolan didn't say anything. Instead he reached over and tapped his own whiskey glass to hers. Imogen accepted the cheers for what it was – an apology for his earlier behavior – though how she could understand these things about him, she wasn't really sure. The rest of the tension she'd been holding onto slipped away now that he was there, and that was also a thought that she wasn't quite sure what to do with.

The silence drew out for a while, and Imogen enjoyed that he wasn't someone who immediately needed to fill silence with chatter. Instead, she tipped her head back and looked out over the water to the lighthouse on Straw Island. She'd always had an affinity for lighthouses. As a sailor, of course, they played a huge role in safety. But the idea of living in a lighthouse and being a lighthouse keeper had always been a romantic notion for Imogen. Another way for her to live a fairly solitary life, she thought, and laughed softly at herself.

"Care to share?"

"Ah, well," Imogen took another sip of her whiskey and then gestured to the lighthouse. "I was looking over at the lighthouse and thinking how I'd like that job. Living alone on an island, left to my own devices, only responsibility to keep the light burning so that sailors can make it home to port."

"You don't think you'd get lonely?" Nolan asked.

"Not really. I'm used to being alone." Imogen shrugged one shoulder.

"How so? You have a crew you work with on the boat? And you take people on charters, right? Aren't you always around people?"

Caught, Imogen took a moment. How was she to explain that even if she was around other people, she was still alone? Alone with her secrets. Alone with her inability to trust anyone fully. Alone with her knowledge that if her own parents couldn't love her as a child – then who could love her as an adult? Imogen swallowed thickly, shaking her head and looking back out to the lighthouse.

"It's hard to explain, I guess."

"Try."

"Nolan…" Imogen groaned.

"What? We've both had a shite day. And a weird one at that. If we're not ready to talk about that, let's talk about other stuff. Tell me why you are alone."

"I've always been alone," Imogen rushed out, thinking maybe if she just told him about her past, then he'd let the subject die. "I have no father. Well, that I know of, at least. My mother barely took care of me and resented me more than anything. I didn't really have friends in school because I couldn't participate in any activities, and I wasn't allowed to play at other kids' houses. I've never had a birthday gift. Never been to a birthday party. I don't...I just don't fit in, Nolan. Not as a child. And not now. After Mam kicked me out, I made my own way and at the very least, I've been able to build a life for myself where nobody else can tell me what to do. Until you came along, that is."

"Which is why you hated me so much."

"Kind of, yeah. This is more than just a boat to me."

"I see that now," Nolan moved closer, bumping his shoulder against hers. "If it helps, I wouldn't have taken your boat if it hadn't been a really serious situation."

"I get that. I do." There wasn't much else Imogen could say to that. There was no going back to change the situation now.

"So, no birthday parties, huh? I'm sorry for that, I am. Everyone deserves to feel special once in a while. Tell me about your mother. Why do you think she was the way she was? Do you speak to her now?"

"No...we don't have contact. I did try, at least the year after she kicked me out. I guess I felt nostalgic around Christmas and thought maybe she'd answer the phone when I called. But..."

"But what?"

"She'd changed her number. And then I went back. And she wasn't living in the house anymore. Just gone. It's almost like she was a figment of my imagination."

Nolan surprised her by reaching out and squeezing her hand. He seemed to sense that she didn't need or want platitudes. Much like her boat being stolen, there wasn't much she could do about the situation with her mother.

"As for what she was like? Well...I don't think she was a

happy woman." Imogen pulled her knees up and wrapped her arms around her legs, resting her chin on her knees. "I think she was searching for something in her life. And her unhappiness spilled over to me. She resented taking care of me. She resented my presence. She resented my needs. I was merely baggage to her, and she got rid of me as soon as she could. If anything, I only made her angry when I would speak of..." Imogen caught herself.

"Speak of what?"

"I've...I don't really talk about this stuff, Nolan," Imogen proceeded cautiously. The biggest surprise of it all was that she wanted to tell Nolan about her past. As much as the man infuriated her, she felt connected to him in a weird way.

"Trade you a secret for a secret?" Nolan asked, and Imogen turned, lifting her chin at him.

"Okay, you first," Imogen said, and Nolan's smile flashed white in the light from the dock.

"Fair enough. You don't trust easily, do you?"

"Very few people have given me reasons to trust them."

"I find that people can surprise you if you give them a chance," Nolan said, lifting his glass for another sip.

"Your secret, Grumpy McFaeFace?" Imogen surprised herself by laughing at the grimace he made.

"Och, that's not a favorite of mine," Nolan arched an eyebrow at her, and Imogen laughed harder.

"Blame Bianca. That was all her."

"She's hard to stay mad at," Nolan grumbled.

"I like her. She might be my first female friend."

"You can't claim that as your secret, because I still haven't gone yet," Nolan pointed out and Imogen winced. Damn, but that would have been an easier secret to reveal.

"Fine, your secret?"

"My powers are fading, and I don't know why." Nolan's voice went sharp in the night and Imogen straightened, turning slightly toward him. "And I'm worried. I'm scared I won't be able to help in a battle. I don't understand what is happening."

"I saw it," Imogen said, wanting to reach out to him and comfort him, but unsure what to do. Comforting people didn't come naturally to her. Nor did intimate conversations where secrets were revealed. Many of the people she'd met on the docks and on the water kept their secrets tightly held – which suited Imogen. "Today when you were fighting the Dark Fae. It was like your hands misfired or something. It's why I came to help."

"I...I guess I don't know how to explain magick to some-body who doesn't have it. But it's a source inside me that I can tap into. And it just flows, if that makes sense? I've had it my whole life and it's quite strong. This power has defined my life, has led me to the Royal Court, and has changed mine and my family's lives."

"And it's not working anymore?"

"Not like it should, and I don't know why. It hasn't since..." Nolan's eyes met hers.

"Since when?" Imogen whispered.

"Since we boarded this boat."

"Oh." A soft breath of air whooshed out of Imogen. Immediately she wondered if it was because of her and the glowing aquamarine. She wasn't sure why her mind went there, but since it was magickal – maybe they had the ability to drain Nolan's power. "I...I can't begin to understand what that means or why that is happening. I'm sorry I can't be of more help, I just don't...I don't really understand this world. I know it is kind of a shite answer, but I like problems that I have solutions for. Is there any way that, like, the bad Fae could be draining your powers?"

"It depends on how strong their magicks are. Sometimes, they can charm certain items and use them to their will. For example? The amulet the Water Fae are searching for? It holds incredible powers. But, the same works on the other end. The Dark Fae could spell, say a piece of jewelry or a dagger or something and the wearer would then be harmed by that curse."

Imogen's mouth went dry as an image of her glowing aquamarine ring flashed into her mind.

"Basically you're saying that anything can be magicked to work for or against you?"

"Well, not anything. But particular items are more susceptible to holding magick well. Stones, in particular, do a good job of carrying magick."

"Right. Um, this is just a lot to try and understand." Imogen said, as guilt washed through her. What if her ring was the cause of his issues?

"Sure, I can be understanding that. It's driving me a bit mental, if I'm to admit it. Maybe that's why I'm extra grumpy right now?"

"Oh, this isn't your regular mode of operation?" Imogen cocked an eyebrow at him, and a smile ghosted his lips.

"I have my moments. Okay, Imogen. Your turn. Spill."

Although Imogen was grateful they'd moved on from a problem she couldn't solve for him, now nerves twisted in her stomach at telling someone a secret she'd never voiced out loud before. She thought back to earlier that day, when she'd walked through an invisible barrier and held off a herd of Domnua with a look and a song. If she was honest? She needed to talk to someone about all of it, because she didn't know what was happening to her either. Fair was fair.

"I...okay, I've never actually said this out loud before. In fact, I was threatened with punishment if I did. And the few times I did talk about it...well, I *was* punished. If not physically, then my mam would leave. For weeks at a time if not more. This isn't easy for me to speak of."

"Oh, and admitting that my powers don't work and I could be taken from my ruling post in the Royal Court is?" Nolan asked, but his voice was light, cutting through Imogen's tension a bit.

"Fine, right. So, basically, I was an odd kid. Thinking I could see things that weren't there, that kind of stuff," Imogen shrugged, not looking at Nolan. "Mam didn't like me speaking of it."

"What kind of things, Imogen?"

"Um...faces in the water. Glowing people. People disappearing into thin air."

"You can see the Fae."

"I..." Imogen paused. She was at a loss for words because she'd never really been able to put a name to it before.

And I can move water with my mind, too.

Imogen stopped herself from sharing that last bit. She'd discovered that little feat when she was much younger, and rarely put it into practice. Largely because she didn't really know what she was doing and the flow of energy that pulsed through her when she tried that maneuver scared the shite out of her.

"And your mother knew this?" Nolan asked.

"She never *ever* phrased it as such, no."

"But she knew something. She had to. Right? Because humans don't just...listen, Imogen." Nolan leaned over and turned her by the shoulders, so she faced him. He kept his hands on her shoulders and Imogen found herself wanting to lean forward and into his arms. "There's a piece missing here. There is a reason that your mother knew what you were seeing. Otherwise, she would have thought you were sick or delusional. Perhaps taken you to one of those head doctors the humans go to. I don't know. But the fact that she punished you for speaking about it? Well, that means she knew about the Fae. Because what you are describing is normal for Fae children to see those things. It's just... natural. It is what it is. It's expected. We identify different Fae by the colors that surround them. It's not strange to us... at all. It's what you would call auras. We just see them more clearly. The faces in the water? Those are the Water Fae. You can see all of the Elemental Fae if you look hard enough. Did you see any others? In the fire maybe?"

"No," Imogen said, surprised. "No, I really haven't. Just the water faces. Well, just one face, that is."

"The same one?"

"Yes, the same man."

"I wonder..." Nolan squinted.

"What?"

"Is there anything...anything at all that you were told about your father?"

Imogen found she wanted to tell Nolan about the ring her mother had given her, but something caused her to hold back. It wasn't in her nature to share, and she was already far outside her comfort zone.

"As I mentioned, my mother basically hated me...so, no. And I never really could bring up to her the man I saw in the water."

"Did he try to communicate with you?" Nolan asked.

"Um, not really. He would wave at me, I guess? Honestly, I never stuck around long. I thought...I thought I was mental, you know? I was led to believe I was seeing things that weren't there. It doesn't...well, things like that don't sit well with a person, you know? And then, once I was out on my own, I didn't have much time to think about anything but survival."

"And that's why you've been alone." Imogen jolted as Nolan leaned forward and pulled her into him, wrapping his muscular arms around her. She froze, sitting stiffly against his chest, her heart pounding. Imogen didn't know what to do with this kindness – this willingness to soothe – and she felt a crack inside her. It was as though the walls she'd put around her deepest vulnerabilities were bursting open and a part of her wanted to lean into him and bawl her eyes out.

"Aye, that's why I've been alone," Imogen managed, struggling with her words. Nolan's hand came up and he traced lazy circles on her back, heat following the path of his hand, and gradually, Imogen relaxed against him. Hours ago, they'd been shouting at each other, and now...well, they were doing whatever this was. Imogen was much more comfortable with the shouting.

"Well, you're not alone anymore. Whether you like it or not." Nolan released her and Imogen eased back, sucking a breath in to settle the nerves that danced below her skin. "As annoying as we can be, you're one of us now, Imogen."

"I..." Oh god, tears were threatening. She wasn't willing to cry in front of him, no she was not. "I have to go to the bathroom."

"Careful on the ladder." Nolan let her go and didn't follow her down, which Imogen was grateful for. The emotions that were flowing through her were confusing, as though someone had turned on a hot water faucet to full, and now she felt like she was drowning. At least Nolan understood enough not to press her, so she gave him points for that. Imogen slipped down the side of the boat and instead of returning to her cabin, she detoured to the stern. Glancing up, she scanned the dock for people, and once she was certain nobody was around, she reached into her pocket.

While Imogen still didn't know what the glowing meant, she did know one thing – this ring might be the very reason that Nolan was losing his powers. Or it might be linked to the Dark Fae. Maybe she'd been inadvertently sabotaging everyone all along? She'd seen it when his magick misfired at the stone circle. His powers had been fine until he'd boarded her boat. And this was the only magickal item she knew of that could be draining Nolan's power.

He'd hugged her instead of making fun of her secret.

Imogen ran her finger over the ring, feeling its comfortable weight one last time. Taking her ring to the railing, Imogen held her breath.

And then she tossed the aquamarine into the sea.

21

NOLAN SIPPED his whiskey and watched Imogen at the back of the boat. He'd understood that she didn't really need to go to the bathroom but had needed a moment away from him to collect her thoughts. Now, he hoped she wasn't going to do anything stupid, like try to go for a swim, because it was damn cold out and he was trying to enjoy the one peaceful moment he'd had so far that day.

His eyebrows shot up when Imogen took something out of her pocket and then, after a moment of deliberation it seemed, tossed that same something into the water. She stood for a moment, watching the dark surface, before walking out of his view. Nolan heard the wheelhouse door open and then close, so he knew she'd gone to her cabin.

Now *that* made him curious. What had she taken out of her pocket? Finishing his whiskey, Nolan grabbed his glass in one hand and scampered down the ladder. He walked to the stern and peered over the railing, not that he really expected to see anything in the sea. The water remained dark, the surface glinting dully in the light from the docks, and Nolan waited a moment. For what – he wasn't sure. When nothing happened, he turned to leave.

The wards sounded.

Whirling back, Nolan found a Water Fae hanging onto the boarding platform. It made no move to come onto the boat, instead holding its pearlescent body half out of the water, its opal eyes gleaming in the light. The Water Fae weren't his enemies, Nolan reminded himself, even though it was important he proceed with caution right now. He didn't know who they answered to anymore, and he was itching to try and have a meeting with their leaders so he could work this through with them. However, this was not a ruling Water Fae, but simply one of their people. The Fae waited, tilting its head at him, and Nolan drew closer.

"Brother." Nolan bowed his head in respect.

"Hers." The Water Fae placed something on the platform and nudged it closer to Nolan's feet. Nolan looked down to see a faint glow emanating from something gold. It was hard to see clearly in the dull light.

"Hers? Imogen's you mean?"

The Water Fae nodded once before slipping back beneath the surface of ocean. Nolan looked around, hoping this wasn't a trap, and scooped the item off the deck. He hurried backwards, making sure he was well away from the edges of the boat, and then shoved it into his pocket. After another quick perimeter check, he ducked below and went into his cabin. There, he flipped on the light and dug in his pocket to see what the Water Fae had returned. Because one thing he did know was that whatever Imogen had tossed over the railing, the Fae had brought it right back. Which meant they didn't want her to lose it and it was important she keep it.

Nolan's pulse picked up as he held the hammered gold ring to the light. He knew this ring – intimately – because he owned its mate. He didn't always wear the ring and had tucked it away for much of this charter since the potential for warfare always made him evaluate what he carried on his body. Leaning over to the bedside table, Nolan opened the drawer and pulled out his own ring. Holding the two together, he could see the differences immediately. Yes, they were a matched set – but more like a masculine and feminine band. His ring was chunkier with a rounder aquamarine set more deeply in the band. Hers was of a more delicate nature and meant to be worn on a smaller hand. Both stones began to glow when they were close to each other.

Nolan plopped down on the bed and contemplated the rings.

"We're back! Heading to bed!" A knock sounded at his door, shaking him from his thoughts, and Nolan quickly tucked the jewelry away before striding to his door and opening it.

"All good?" Nolan asked Seamus.

"As good as can be, I suppose. Callum's not doing well. He's gone to his cabin, but I'm surprised he didn't just light the whole island on fire. We've convinced him to stand down, but the plan is to ride at dawn."

"Ride at dawn?" Nolan arched a brow.

"It's a saying from the movies. Basically, yeah. First light. Back to the island. Callum's picking up a strong signature in one area and he wants to investigate. We convinced him to wait until dawn, but he's not happy about it."

"Domnua are stronger at night," Nolan said.

"I know it. And they'll know the land here better than us. It puts us at a disadvantage, and we don't want the darkness to be an added impairment."

"This has to be killing Callum," Nolan sighed. "Should I speak with him?"

"No, he asked to be left alone. I think he wants to sulk a bit and then rest, if I'm to be honest. He'll be ready for war first thing, I don't doubt that, so I suggest you rest up as well. We're going in strong in the morning."

"Understood. I'll be up for a bit, so I'll take watch."

"Give me four hours and I'll trade you out?"

"Works for me." Nolan walked back into his cabin, and pocketed the two rings. He needed to ask Imogen where she'd gotten hers, because too many things were beginning to add up for him.

For now, though, Nolan needed to check his magickal wards again and test his powers a bit without anyone watching. He sincerely hoped that what had happened earlier that day had been a fluke, but he couldn't be sure.

After several slow rounds of the deck, Nolan was satisfied that there was no current threat to the *Mystic Pirate*. He'd double-checked his wards, and they all still hummed along merrily – their magick strong. Now, it was on him to see if he could conjure up even the simplest of spells. Nolan dropped down on a cushioned bench in the outdoor lounge area at the stern, the icy wind that rippled across the surface of the ocean barely bothering him, and he held out a hand in front of him. Channeling his power was as easy as breathing for him, and second nature at this point. But, because he was still worried, Nolan took his time and a few deep breaths before he dipped into the river of magick that ran through him.

A small ball of fire appeared – hovering over his palm – and he gently tossed it through the air so that it twirled about before he extinguished it neatly. Okay, so that was a spell taught to very young Fae, and it was a good thing that he still had the basics down. Next up, he pulled out his dagger. Seemingly innocuous, well as daggers went, this was a weapon that most underestimated. See, Nolan had learned alongside the prince, and they'd delighted in crafting cunning magick that they'd charm into the smallest of weapons. Their thoughts had always been that people expected big power from weapons like swords and crossbows, but often underestimated the simple dagger. Because it was usually a close-range weapon, nobody expected that it could offer protection from further away.

Turning the blade in his hand, Nolan ran his finger over the edges of the handle where he'd carved his family emblem into the hilt. He'd even cut a lock of his mother's hair and melded it into the design, so that her love would add strength to his magick when needed. The blade itself was short, thin, and wickedly sharp. One of his favorite spells invoked all of the elements – so when he pointed the dagger at someone, he could choose fire, water, ice, air or a myriad of ways to disarm his opponent. Not wanting to cause too much of a fuss on the boat, he decided on ice and pointed the knife across the deck.

A singular chunk of ice flew from the blade, barely enough to fill a whiskey glass, and bounced across the deck before sliding over the side.

Nolan pursed his lips, a ripple of anxiety causing the hairs at the back of his neck to stand up. Trying again, he was rewarded with two ice cubes this time, both skidding their way haphazardly across the deck.

His pocket warmed, reminding him of the rings, and he paused as a thought slammed into him.

His powers had gone astray when he'd boarded this boat. He'd been fine before that, hadn't he? He'd pulled lightning easily from the sky and had sent it after the

Domnua outside Gallagher's Pub. It was only once he'd arrived to the *Mystic Pirate* that he'd started to experience trouble with his powers.

Imogen clearly had more secrets than she was willing to share, for she'd not mentioned the magickal jewelry to him before she'd tossed it into the ocean. The Water Fae had lovingly returned the piece...which now made him think of the first battle they'd had – just before they'd gone into the cove.

The Water Fae had called Imogen his queen.

Nolan slammed his dagger down on the table. How had he forgotten that tidbit? It was quite an important little bit of information now that he thought about it. And, today? Her eyes had glowed silver when they'd drawn close to the Domnua. Not to mention the missing bit about who her father was? It was all beginning to make sense now. Nolan cursed long and furiously, standing and grabbing his dagger from the table.

Imogen was the trap.

She'd been a set-up all along. The Water Fae were using her to lure them closer to whatever the Domnua had planned for them. They had a traitor in their midst and her name was Imogen. Rage boiled through him as he thought about how he'd comforted her up on the roof earlier that night. He'd actually believed that little sob story of hers about her mother leaving her and being surprised she could see the Fae. Oh, she *was* good, wasn't she? She'd had a magickal ring all along and had never said a word to any of them. This whole time she'd kept telling Bianca how shocked she was by the Fae world and that she was trying to get up to speed to learn about the magickal realm. And yet – she'd seen faces in the water her whole life and casually carried around an incredibly magickal ring as if it was nothing? Why would she have thrown the ring in the water? Nope, none of this was adding up for him. One thing Nolan did know about the Fae is that if something seemed off – it usually was. The Fae loved nothing more than to wield their trickery in all manners.

Steep learning curve, my arse, Nolan thought. They'd been played by a stunning trojan horse of a ship captain, and he'd walked neatly into the trap. Now, his powers were waning and Lily's life was on the line, and he was no closer to solving any of these problems. Nolan paced across the deck, his steps heavy as he considered the best way to handle this. What he wanted to do was to race into Imogen's cabin and reveal her betrayal. But a good leader didn't react on impulse. No, he needed a cooler head before he made his decision on how to punish Imogen.

The thought of betrayal twisted in his stomach. Bile rose in his throat. For a moment tonight, when she'd burrowed into his arms, Nolan had allowed himself to think of her as more than just a woman whom he had a visceral attraction to. He was genuinely coming to like her as a person, and he'd admired how she'd run into battle to help him instead of hiding.

Which was a confusing part, sure enough, for if she was a traitor – wouldn't it have been easier to just let the Domnua kill him? He wondered just what the Fae had promised her. Maybe it was riches? Or was it to finally have a place to belong? They'd gotten to her somehow, hadn't they?

Confusion warred with anger, which was the only reason that Nolan missed the first sounding of the alarms for his wards. It wasn't until movement caught his eye that he realized the magickal wards were screaming and that Domnua had flooded the deck of the boat. Always by night, those bastards, Nolan thought as his mind switched swiftly into warrior mode. He dashed across the deck and pulled the fire alarm, the shrill bell resounding loudly into the stillness of the night, and the two Dark Fae who approached him paused and looked startled at the noise. They weren't the smartest beasts, Nolan thought. It was enough time for him to race forward and slice his dagger through their necks, neatly destroying them, and he kept moving as more flooded the back of the boat. Shouts sounded from below, and pounding feet hit the deck.

Nolan was grateful for any backup, because he didn't think that sputtering ice cubes at the wave of Dark Fae that poured over the side of the boat was going to do much. In moments, he found himself in hand-to-hand combat, blood pounding in his ears and fury driving his moves.

There were just *so* many of them. What they lacked in smarts, they made up for in sheer volume.

Nolan doubled over as a wave of magick hit his stomach, ripping the breath from him for a moment, and he took an uppercut to the face that snapped his head sharply back. The sting of pain shook him out of his fugue, narrowing his vision, and he dove into the fray again with a ferocious bellow.

"Nolan!"

Nolan turned and ducked, narrowly missing taking a sword to his head, and drove his arm up and sunk his dagger into the stomach of the Domnua who'd come up behind him. Glancing up, Nolan cursed as Imogen surged forward, her small knife in her hands, her eyes wide and... yup, they were glowing again. He didn't have much time to dwell on that as he was jumped from behind.

Imogen's eyes widened and she shouted, throwing her arms out, and a wave of magick slammed into him, so powerful that he dropped to his knees on the deck. He looked down at his arm, where blood welled from a slice of her magick, and his suspicions were confirmed. Rage clouded his vision and Nolan bounded to his feet. Stalking across the deck, he grabbed Imogen and wrapped his bleeding arm tightly around her waist. Dragging her down the side of the boat, he ducked downstairs and kicked the door of his cabin open. Tossing her inside, he grabbed a thick leather cord from the top of his bag on the floor.

"Nolan...are you okay?" Imogen darted closer, reaching for his arm. "I don't know what..."

"Shut up," Nolan hissed. Imogen gasped as he grabbed her arms and turned her, pulling both arms behind her. Quickly he wrapped the leather cord around her wrists, binding them so that she couldn't pull her wrists free.

"What are you doing? Are you insane?" Imogen screeched, stumbling back from him when he let her go.

But Nolan didn't care. He could hear the shouts from above and knew the battle raged on. His loyalty was to Callum first, and not to this woman who was betraying them all. Scanning the room, he grabbed the bathrobe that had been tucked into the closet of the cabin when he'd arrived. He ignored Imogen's attempts to kick him and instead picked her up easily and tied her feet with the belt from the robe. Then, he tossed her on her side on the bed.

Bending over, he brought his face close to hers and held up his bleeding arm.

"You almost had me fooled, *mavourneen.*"

"Have you lost your fecking mind?" Imogen seethed. Her eyes still glowed, convincing Nolan that he was right. Silver was the color of the enemy, and Imogen was showing her true colors.

"No, I just think I've finally found it. I'll be back for you, and we'll have a nice long chat. In the meantime, if you even try to leave this cabin or break these bonds? I'll sink this ship in a fecking heartbeat. Understood?"

"You're insane. You bastard," Imogen hissed, hatred roiling across her beautiful face. She panted on the bed, her arms pulled behind her, one cheek pressed into his pillow as she glared at him.

"I might be. But a good woman might die because of your betrayal. My loyalty lies with my prince."

"Nolan...you can't possibly think that I..."

"Don't. Say. Another. Word." Nolan hissed, striding to the door. Turning, he looked down at her and ignored the warning in his gut. "I'll be back to deal with you."

Slamming the door behind him, Nolan stalked down the hallway and grabbed a chair, and brought it back to wedge under the doorknob. Certain the door was secure, he ran back upstairs to join the battle. Instead, he found Callum with his hands in his hair, turning a slow circle while Seamus and Bianca called an all-clear from the bow of the boat.

"You're safe?" Nolan asked, his eyes racing over the prince.

"Aye, but you're bleeding." Callum nodded to Nolan's arm as Bianca and Seamus skidded to a stop next to them.

"Och, that's nasty," Bianca said, grabbing Nolan's arm and studying the wound. "We need to treat this."

"Where's Imogen?" Seamus asked, turning to look around the deck.

"I regret to inform you that she's a traitor," Nolan said, pulling his arm back. Bianca gasped.

"No! That can't possibly be true." Bianca shook her head. Her hair was wild around her head, and she wore simple sleep pants and a thin t-shirt.

"Surely you're wrong," Seamus agreed, coming to stand behind Bianca and wrapping his arms around her.

"I don't believe I am," Nolan said. "I've restrained her in my cabin, and I plan to interrogate her now."

"You may question her, but you will not harm her. Bring her to the lounge so I may speak with her." Callum held his gaze, making sure that Nolan understood that this was a direct order and not a suggestion.

"Yes, my Prince." Nolan left without another word.

22

IMOGEN GLARED at the door when she heard the handle turn. The minutes had felt like hours, with her arms twisted painfully behind her, and fury bubbled low in her gut.

Nolan was dead to her.

As far as she was concerned there was no greater betrayal than having him turn on her after she'd finally revealed herself to him. In fact, he'd just solidified her belief that she'd been correct all along – it really was impossible to trust other people.

Nolan stepped through the door, holding a towel to his arm, and Imogen caught a glimpse of an anxious Bianca hovering in the hallway.

"I'd just like to make sure she is okay," Bianca protested, but Nolan kicked the door closed behind him. For a moment, he stood there, his gray eyes darker than normal, and then he shook his head.

"You really had us fooled, Imogen."

"Sure, and I had myself fooled as well then. I had no idea I was a traitor either." Imogen shot him a syrupy smile.

"There's just too many factors weighing against you."

"So that's it then? Tried and convicted. I don't get a say?" Imogen blinked up at him, furious with herself for still wanting him. Because she did, and it was useless to deny it, but now his betrayal sliced through her, making tears well in her eyes.

"Don't try tears on me, Imogen. It won't work."

"I'm not *trying* anything. I'm just...it's how I feel. Can you take these off, please? I'm going numb." Imogen shifted against the bonds. She felt incredibly vulnerable, tossed like a trussed-up hog on the bed, and if she was going to be accused, at the very least she'd like to be standing on her own two feet. Imogen closed her eyes and tried to stop her tears. The bed dipped as Nolan sat on it and it took everything in Imogen's power not to swing her legs up and kick him in the head. She wanted to – *oh*, but did she ever want to. But she was also tired of fighting, and what was the point really? If she hurt Nolan, the prince would take care of her in seconds. Callum's priority was his love, Lily. He'd get rid of anything that he deemed as a threat to that end goal. If Nolan said she was, Imogen was done for. There was no way around it really.

Imogen eased her legs over the side of the bed when he finished untying her ankles, trying her best to ignore the little zip of energy she felt from him when his hands brushed her ankles. Attraction mattered little if there was no trust. Sitting up, she hunched her shoulders, her arms aching behind her. Nolan sat beside her, and the silence stretched out until the tension was unbearably thick between them.

"How?" Nolan's voice rasped as he finally broke the silence. "How did you pull it off?"

Imogen choked out a laugh that muffled a sob.

"I haven't done anything, Nolan. I don't even know what you're talking about."

"Don't you?" Nolan turned, his eyes hard, his face like granite.

"I don't." Imogen half turned to him, pleading. "Nolan, I thought..."

"You thought what?" Nolan demanded.

"I...we shared...our secrets. I thought we..."

"What? That we were going to hook up? Is that what you wanted?"

"I didn't say that..." Imogen blinked at him, her breath shaky as Nolan leaned dangerously close, his lips hovering near hers.

"Is that what you wanted all along, Imogen? To make me fall for you? Because I'll admit it. You were damn close."

The information both excited and wounded her. Imogen swallowed against her suddenly dry throat. Slowly, she raised her eyes to his. She wanted to spit in his face. But behind the anger that dominated his eyes, she saw something more. Hurt hovered there. He thought she'd betrayed him in some way, and he was hurting because of that. Her heart twisted. She didn't want to feel bad for Nolan, or even forgive him, but there was some unexplainable link between them that pulled her to him.

"The only thing I ever wanted was to get my boat safely home, Nolan," Imogen said quietly. "And to hopefully rescue a woman in need. I never wanted any of this. I was happy with my life as it was."

"Yet you were lonely, weren't you, Imogen?" Nolan's lips hovered closer, almost brushing hers. Confusion warred with sadness inside her.

"I was alone. That didn't mean I was lonely, Nolan.

Please, tell me what's happened? Let me help," Imogen whispered.

"I think the Domnua planted you. To take my powers. To make me lose my mind. To lose sleep while I dreamed about you. To distract me from my mission of protecting Callum. Exactly at a time that I can't afford distraction. Isn't that right, Imogen?"

"No..." Imogen shook her head, tears rolling down her cheeks. "I never would do such a thing."

"Damn you," Nolan hissed, and then his lips were on hers – both a punishment and a gift. Where she'd expected brute force, Nolan offered a gentleness that warred with his words. She whimpered as her entire being seemed to light up, as though little firecrackers were exploding under her skin, and despite her anger with him, she leaned into his lips. Nolan angled his head, deepening the kiss, and Imogen's heart cracked as she felt his pain and anguish wash through her. She wasn't sure how or why she could read him like this, but she just knew that they were connected in a way that she couldn't yet understand.

Imogen pulled away first, certain her heart couldn't handle any more, and dropped her eyes to her lap. Everything ached. Her arms had gone numb from where they were still bound behind her, but the pain paled in comparison to the pain in her heart.

"Care to tell me about this?" Nolan asked, his voice hoarse as he held up his arm and pulled away the towel. Imogen winced at the wound that still seeped blood.

"I don't know what happened." All Imogen had was her truth and she would die before she admitted something that wasn't her fault. "I...I don't know."

"Explain to me. In detail, please." Nolan shifted away

from her on the bed and it felt like a cord was cut between them.

"I..." Imogen cleared her throat and rolled her shoulders, trying to ease the pain. "I came out and saw that the Domnua were overwhelming you. There were like ten of them around you. I don't know...I just...I reacted."

"How did you react? Explain."

"I...just wanted them gone. I...I made it so. I don't know what to say. I've never..." Imogen stopped. Well, she'd never done that type of magick before, but that didn't mean she hadn't done some magick in her life. Her mind flashed back to being a child and redirecting the flow of water in the brook outside their house. She couldn't bring herself to lie – not even if it meant saving her life. "I didn't mean to hurt you. I was trying to help."

A knock sounded at the door and Bianca popped her head in before Nolan could respond.

"Callum has ordered you to bring Imogen to the lounge."

"I will in a bit."

"He says now. Sorry, but those are his orders." Bianca shot Imogen a sympathetic look. "Can we remove the restraints? That looks painful."

"No." Nolan stood and took Imogen's arm, lifting her from the bed and propelling her in front of him. She stumbled, for her legs were asleep, and he caught her before she could fall.

"I don't like this, Nolan. Not one bit. You untie her." Imogen's heart soared at Bianca's championing of her. "Whatever you think you saw, well, you're wrong. I know it in my heart. And you should, too. Didn't this woman save your stupid arse today? I can't believe you're treating her this way."

"Move, Bianca." Nolan ordered, his voice like a whip.

"I won't." Bianca crossed her arms over her chest, looking like a mutinous child, and waited. "Untie her."

"No."

"Yes," Bianca stamped her foot. "There's four of us on this ship. If, for some reason, she did betray us, do you really think that we can't contain her?"

"I have restrained her already. Why do it again?"

"You will not drag her out of here like that." Bianca spread her arms out so that she gripped the frame of the doorway, her face set in stubborn lines and Imogen could have kissed her.

"Stubborn fool…" Nolan hissed and then Imogen felt his hands at her wrists. In seconds, she was freed, and she let out a whoosh of air as she brought her hands forward. Sharp needles of pain ratcheted up her wrists and tears pricked her eyes again.

"There, now. That's better." Bianca immediately stepped forward and wrapped her arms around Imogen and she almost lost it right there. Never had someone, particularly a woman, stood up for her like that before. For all Bianca knew, Imogen could have betrayed them. And yet the woman stood here, facing down a huge and angry Fae warrior, refusing to let him mistreat Imogen. It was the kind of protection she'd always wanted from her mother, Imogen realized. "Let's get you upstairs for a wee chat with Callum and we'll clear everything up."

"A wee chat," Nolan scoffed. "This isn't coffee and gossip with the girls, Bianca."

"Oh, stuff it, Nolan. You're being impossible, as usual, and you'd do well to get your head out of your arse."

Imogen could have cheered. Despite her fears, she

smirked at Nolan over her shoulder. His stormy eyes narrowed, and she whipped her head forward once again.

Once they arrived in the lounge area, Imogen immediately crossed the room to sit at the table across from Callum. The prince looked particularly regal in a black coat and with his blonde hair tied back. He surveyed her, his eyes seeming to see everything, and then he turned to Nolan.

"Explain yourself, Nolan."

"She wounded me." Nolan held up his arm. "With her own magick. She fired off magick at me and hurt me with it, Callum. Her eyes glow silver in battle. The Water Fae called her their queen. She has power. She's even admitted to me that she's been able to see the Fae her whole life. I believe she's been sent here to distract me on this mission. My powers..." Nolan trailed off.

"Yes? Your powers?"

"His powers have stopped working since he's been on the boat," Imogen piped up. If he was going to just throw her secrets out for everyone to hear, she might as well do the same for him. "They stopped working during battle today, too. I saved him, though I'm regretting doing so now."

"You didn't tell me this." Callum's gaze swept from Imogen up to where Nolan stood.

"Hardly stopped working..." Nolan began but Bianca cleared her throat.

"May I?" Bianca asked.

"By all means," Callum swept his hand out and Bianca plopped onto the bench next to Imogen, firmly showing her allegiance. It made Imogen want to cry again.

"Since I was also there during the ambush today, I can clear a few things up for you."

"That would be ideal." Callum's tone was like ice.

"Imogen was clearly being pulled in by the Domnua.

They do have some effect upon her. And her eyes did glow silver when she was close. But," Bianca raised a finger when Nolan began to interject. "This did not seem to be something that was of her own willpower. It was like she was being pulled to the fort. And Nolan was overpowered."

"I was not."

"Oh, hush up. You were." Bianca gave Nolan a scathing look. "There were hundreds of Domnua. He was sucked into the fort and was going to die, and I couldn't get through the barrier to help. Imogen went right on in and pulled his stupid arse out."

"She did not *rescue* me. I was already on my way out..."

"Oh, she did!" Bianca slammed her hand on the table, frustration etching her pretty features. "Sure and she did, Nolan. You hit that barrier just as hard as I did. But for some reason it didn't affect Imogen. And she pulled you right on through to safety. Now, tell me, please – how is that someone who is working to betray you?"

"Maybe this is just the long game. She's playing the role until the end."

"Or maybe you're an idiot," Bianca muttered.

"Fine. Then explain this." Nolan dug in his pocket and tossed some objects on the table. Imogen gaped at her ring as it skittered across the surface, along with another ring she'd never seen before. Her heart skipped a beat. How did he get it? She'd thrown it away, thinking its power was hurting Nolan.

Both pieces of jewelry held aquamarine stones. And the stones were currently glowing gently.

"Do you recognize these pieces?" Callum directed the question to Imogen.

"This ring I do. The other I don't."

"That's your ring, Nolan."

Imogen glanced at Nolan in surprise. He had the matching ring to hers? What could that possibly mean?

"Aye, it is."

"Imogen – what can you tell us about these pieces?" Callum asked. Bianca picked Imogen's ring up and held it to the light.

"It's lovely. The glowing is pretty, too. This doesn't feel bad, does it?" Bianca held the ring out to Callum, who took it and gently cupped it in his palm.

"No, it doesn't feel like bad magick. It's powerful. But not harmful," Callum agreed, and relief washed through Imogen.

"My mother gave me that ring. It's the only thing she's ever given me." Imogen heard a swift inhale from Nolan but refused to look at him. He'd know what her secrets had meant to her, but she needed to close herself off to him. It didn't matter what he thought anymore. "She handed it to me with no explanation right before she booted me out the door. I've kept it ever since."

"And has it glowed for you?" Callum continued to twist the ring in his fingers.

"It has. More recently it's glowed quite a bit. Probably around the time you guys came to Grace's Cove actually."

"And you said nothing? This whole time?" Nolan demanded.

"Which is why, when I thought that I fully understood the ramifications of it, I tossed it into the sea. I don't know how it got back on the boat. I swear to you, Prince Callum." Imogen ignored Nolan's cursing and pleaded to the prince. "When I thought it was doing harm, I got rid of it."

"What made you think it was doing harm?" Callum asked, turning the ring in his hand.

"Because Nolan told me as soon as he got on the boat his

powers waned. I...well, it's the only thing magickal I can think of that would be doing that. Once I understood that was what it could be doing to his powers, I got rid of it."

"You..." Nolan's voice trailed off and Bianca let out a little harumph.

"See, you thick-headed oaf? She tried to help you. And you treat her like this?"

"I'm sorry, Prince. I should have brought the ring to you. I don't understand this world all that much yet. I'm...I'm still learning. And I thought what I was doing was the right choice. I truly didn't mean to hurt Nolan," Imogen said. Turning, she met Nolan's eyes. "Please know that. I didn't mean to hurt you."

"Of course, you didn't," Bianca patted her arm.

"I believe you," Prince Callum said, and he slid the ring back to her. "But is there anything else – anything at all – that you think you should share with us? Now is the time to do so. It might not reflect so well on you in the future if we find out there's more."

"I can move water. I think. I don't know what happened during battle. Well, that whole wave of magick thing was new to me."

"You can move water?" Bianca raised an eyebrow at her. "That's kind of cool. What else can you do? I mean you did, basically, take down all the Dark Fae at the stone circle, too. Isn't that something else?"

"I don't know." Imogen threw her hands in the air. "Truly, I don't know how or why I did...whatever it was that I did. It was instinct, I guess? I've never been in a battle before so I'm not sure why I reacted the way that I did."

"But you know you can move water," Bianca prodded.

"How so? Explain." Callum asked while Nolan began to pace the room. Imogen tried to ignore him.

"I don't know. I try not to do it. But sometimes when there's a particularly rough passage, I can smooth things out with my mind. That's all I know really. I've been so stressed during our travel here that I didn't even think to do it when the Fae attacked."

"Hmm. I need to think about this a bit." Callum turned and handed the other ring to Nolan who pocketed it with a grimace. "Nolan, you owe Imogen an apology."

"I..." Nolan sighed, his shoulders hunching. "I'm sorry, Imogen."

Imogen waited, wondering if he would say anything else, and when he didn't, she just shrugged. It was fine, she lied to herself. They didn't have to be friends to complete this mission.

"If you don't think it's magickal jewelry deflating your powers, what else could it be?" Bianca wondered, picking up Imogen's ring again to examine it.

"It's quite simple, really." A gentle smile hovered on Callum's lips. "The longer Nolan denies his fated mate's call, the more his powers will wane."

Imogen couldn't decide who was more surprised, as both she and Nolan looked to each other with their mouths hanging open in shock.

"I'm certain that I haven't been denying any call," Nolan scoffed.

"Aye, I mentioned it earlier, remember?" Seamus piped up. "Perhaps you've just not been in tune with her call?"

"What does that even mean?" Bianca asked, looking between the men. "How does one get in tune?"

"You can close it off. Or ignore it. Not all Fae want to be mated," Prince Callum explained.

"Well, who is his mate then? Get her on board before he has a stroke," Imogen demanded.

Silence stretched out. Imogen turned to Bianca, but the woman looked steadfastly down at the ring in her hand, refusing to make eye contact. When she looked back up, Nolan stormed out of the room and Imogen's eyes widened. Surely they couldn't think *she* was his mate? They could barely stand each other.

"Anyone for a whiskey?" Bianca piped up.

23

IMOGEN WAS surprised out of a deep sleep when her alarm went off the next morning. She'd been certain that there was no way she'd get any rest after the day she'd had – between the battle with the Fae, well two battles that was – and all the other events, well, her mind was bouncing around like crazy. Yet, as soon as she slipped away to her cabin, half-fearful she'd run into Nolan, she'd all but collapsed on her bed and slipped into a thankfully dreamless sleep due to sheer exhaustion.

Now, Imogen flipped her alarm off and shuffled to the bathroom to take a hot shower. While she didn't particularly prefer waking up this early, Imogen was never one to grumble when there was work to be done. And, oh boy, did they need to get some work done today. After Nolan had stormed from the lounge the night before, Bianca had steered the subject matter away from the topic of fated mates to Callum's plans to rescue Lily. While the topic of fated mates made Imogen want to squirm, because she wasn't really ready to examine what that could potentially mean, it would have been nice to gather a little more information on *that* particular subject. Because, well, what if...

She also really wanted to know why Nolan had a matching ring to hers. The only conclusion she'd been able to reach was that because he was tied with the Water Fae that they must have gifted him with a piece of jewelry as well. At this point, she had to assume her ring was from the Water Fae too. Which...felt a little odd, she had to admit, knowing those faces in the water all those years ago had gifted her with a token. Was it possible...that her father? A shiver went through Imogen at the thought.

What she really needed was answers. She needed to take Bianca aside the first chance she could, grab that book of hers, and start digging. Because Imogen felt like she was in a play where everyone knew the script but her. She didn't like feeling out of her element, and aside from when she'd been captaining the ship, she hadn't felt in control since they'd left Grace's Cove.

Imogen bundled her hair in a tight ball on the top of her head and let the hot water pound her neck. Steam wafted around her, and she leaned her forehead against the wall of the shower, letting the water work on the kinks in her shoulders from having her hands tied behind her back. It had been humiliating to be treated like that, and Imogen's feelings for Nolan were now tied in a nasty ball that she wasn't sure she'd be able to untether. On the one hand, if she looked at the situation objectively, now knowing he'd seen her toss the jewelry in the water and that the Water Fae had returned it to him, she could understand the seeds of his distrust. On the other hand, it was supremely awful of him to make such a leap and not even talk to her about it first. Granted, they had been under attack and she had injured him with magick she didn't know she carried. But *still*. She realized that a part of her wanted Nolan to hold her in high esteem.

Imogen opened and closed her fists, trying to recall the feeling she'd had when she'd used magick the day before. It hadn't been a conscious thought, really. When she had seen that Nolan was going to get hurt, she'd reacted instinctively. Now, she tried to break that moment down in incremental steps in her mind, to see if maybe she could access that power in a more controlled manner. Turning, so that her back was against the shower wall and she was facing the water that poured from the showerhead, Imogen focused on a singular stream of water. She studied it for a moment, thinking about what she would need to do to move the water with her mind, and then she pulled the power from her core. There was really no other way that she could think of it. There was just this little tingling core of energy inside her and Imogen mentally dipped into that and directed the energy at the stream of water. She gasped when it flipped a ninety-degree angle and sprayed her directly in the face.

"Oh!" Well, then, she'd need a touch more control, wouldn't she? Imogen spent the next precious ten minutes, even though she knew time was limited, playing with the water until she began to feel more comfortable with her abilities. She wasn't sure what it meant that she could do such a thing, but she'd just table that for her chat with Bianca.

Bianca was her new best friend – as far as Imogen was concerned. She'd never, *ever* had someone champion for her like that before. Whatever happened today, in this quest to find Lily, Imogen was going to keep her eyes on Bianca and make sure she protected the woman at all costs. Because that was what friends did and if nothing else came of this insane quest she'd been forced into, Imogen would now forever know what it felt like to have a true friend.

Imogen sped through dressing and at the last moment, she slipped on the hammered gold ring that the prince had returned to her. If Prince Callum said it wasn't evil magick, then it might actually help her. She didn't know, but since her only other weapon, aside from her courage, was her dagger, Imogen was taking it with her.

"Did you rest at all?" Bianca asked, hurrying over to Imogen as soon as she stepped into the lounge and pulling her into a hug. Imogen stiffened, still not used to such intimate contact, and then returned the hug fiercely. It felt good, this easy exchange of affection, and she promised herself to be more free with her hugs in the future.

"You know, after last night I thought I wouldn't be able to – but somehow I dropped right off to sleep."

"Exhausted, you poor thing. Sure, and it was a belter of a day, wasn't it?" Bianca leaned back to study Imogen's face. "You're alright then?"

"As well as I can be, I guess. I, uh, tried to practice with my, uh, powers a bit this morning." There. She rushed it out before she could second-guess herself, having promised herself she'd be more open.

"Did you then? And how'd it go?"

"Well, after I doused myself in water, I think I made a pretty good go of it." Imogen crossed the lounge and filled a travel mug with coffee. She didn't think they'd be on the boat much longer, as Callum had been clear he wanted to be on land at first light.

"That's a fine girl, isn't it then?" Seamus dropped a kiss on her cheek as he passed by, almost jolting Imogen out of her damn skin.

Nolan entered the lounge, his eyes scanning quickly and landing on her. Damn it, but Imogen wanted to be unaffected by his presence. And still, her heart seemed to do a little sigh. The man was just too handsome for his own good. That had to be it. He was back in that sexy flannel shirt, and he wore a hunter-green canvas coat on top, along with sturdy steel-toe boots. His hair was tucked under a gray knit cap that highlighted his storm-cloud eyes, and it had been several days since he'd shaved. If Imogen wasn't so hurt by him, she'd enjoy the view. Instead, she turned to finish readying her coffee.

"Can I speak to you?" Nolan asked at her back.

"Sure," Imogen said, reaching for the sugar.

"Alone?" Nolan asked.

"I don't think so, boyo," Bianca said from where she spooned up porridge at the table. "You can say what you need to say in front of us. We're a team, and there shouldn't be secrets. What you did last night fractured our foundation, and I think you need to fix that. For all of us. Imogen isn't the only one mad at you."

Imogen pressed her lips together because Bianca's fierce mothering made her want to smile, and she knew that would only push Nolan further over whatever edge he was already teetering upon.

Nolan muttered something that sounded dangerously like "fecking meddling women" and then turned to address the room.

"Right, so here's the deal. I screwed up."

"You think?" Bianca asked, stabbing her spoon into her bowl.

"Now, my love, let the man speak. It's not easy to grovel if you interrupt him every two seconds," Seamus said.

Imogen beamed at the two of them.

"Imogen." Nolan turned and waited until she looked up and met his eyes. "I know I apologized last night, but that was at Prince Callum's demand. I'm apologizing this morning because I...I really screwed up. I jumped to conclusions, and I acted on them without thought. I think part of it was that I was so scared at my misfiring powers that I was looking for any excuse, and any person, to take my anger out on. As I told you earlier last night, I was scared. Which is not something that is easy for me to admit – to anyone. However, I made poor choices. A better leader would have looked at the situation from all sides instead of making assumptions. Assumptions that in the long run ended up hurting you and damaging our trust. For that, I'm truly sorry. I don't know if you have it in your heart to forgive me, but I'd like to ask that you at least consider it."

Imogen's eyes widened. She was not expecting such an honest and forthright apology, and now she didn't know what to do with all the anger and hurt inside her.

"Well, now, sure and that's a corker of an apology there, Imogen, isn't it? I wasn't expecting that. Nolan, well-done." Bianca nodded her approval.

"I appreciate your apology, Nolan." Imogen tested out her feelings before continuing. "But you've hurt me. You really hurt me. Which is surprising, because since I've known you, well, you've largely annoyed the shite out of me. Yet, I finally thought we were *maybe* building a bond. I shared my secrets with you, and you almost instantly used them against me. I think I'll be able to forgive you, but I'm not sure I'll be able to forget how you made me feel."

"I hope, given time, that I'll be able to change that. If you'll give me a chance to do so..." Nolan's face was set in grim lines, and Imogen could tell he meant his words. The problem was it didn't change the hurt that still lingered inside of her.

"We'll see. I don't know what else to say…"

"That's fair. Isn't it Seamus?" Bianca turned to Seamus, who nodded.

"These things do take time. But, today – we have to be a team. Callum is pretty certain he's got a read on where we're going. We have to have each other's backs today, no matter what." Bianca looked around the room, meeting each person's eyes as Callum walked in.

The prince looked tense, but his eyes were alive with a fire that Imogen hadn't seen since she'd met him. It was that look alone that made her realize that today really was the day.

They were going to bring his Lily home.

"Is everyone better this morning? Will we be able to work as a team?" Callum asked without preamble.

The group nodded their assent and Callum glanced to the window.

"It's time to go. I have a car waiting for us."

"Is there anything that I can do…or bring?" Imogen walked over to Callum and looked up at his haunted eyes. She reached out and touched his arm, sensing he needed a connection of sorts.

"I don't think so. We just…we need to go. I can feel she is close. I'm terrified of losing her." Callum's words were clipped, as though he could barely speak them.

"Then I'll do everything I can to help. I don't know what use I'll be, but I can try."

"You might surprise yourself. You saved me yesterday," Nolan said from behind her, and his words sent a trickle of warmth through her.

"Let's just see what waits for us. Hurry now. I want to get there just as it goes to light."

The group hastened to the car, a compact van, and Seamus took the wheel while Callum directed. In the back, Imogen sat next to Bianca on the first bench seat, and Nolan took the seat behind them. She'd be lying if she said she wasn't aware of his presence looming over her shoulder, but she had enough other thoughts weighing on her at the moment.

"Where are we going, Callum?" Bianca piped up, breaking the silence. It was the darkest part of the night, that moment just before dawn, and the headlights cut a swath of light across the empty road. They were the only car out at the moment, and Imogen wondered if anyone was looking out of their windows and wondering who the crazy folks were driving around at this time of day. Soon, they'd left the small village behind them, and no other lights dotted the landscape. It was eerily empty out this way, but Imogen tried not to take that as a note of warning. She reminded herself that the island was sparsely populated as it was, so this was normal.

"It's known officially as the Serpent's Lair, and locally as the wormhole."

The name sent shivers across Imogen's skin.

"I read about it. It's like a perfect rectangular formation cut in the rock where the ocean surges up. You can look down at it from the cliffs surrounding it."

"A rectangle? Is it man-made? Like a swimming pool?" Imogen asked.

"Nope, it's naturally formed, I guess. I think I saw it on one of those extreme games or whatever on television. Where people were diving off a platform and into the water. It looked pretty intense," Bianca said.

"And we think that Lily is there. In this hole? But how...if there is water?" Imogen looked up and Callum glanced back at her.

"If she is there, it might be likely that they are holding her underneath the water."

"But..." Imogen trailed off. "Right. Magick."

"What's the plan?" Nolan asked, from behind her, jolting Imogen because she'd forgotten about him for a moment.

"We'll need to split up," Callum said, his tone serious. "Due to the nature of the cliffs surrounding the hole, we'll need coverage up high on the cliffs, while I try to get to the Serpent's Lair."

"How will you know if she's there?" Imogen asked, her nerves kicking up as she thought about the group splitting up.

"I'm close enough now that I'll know. The Dark Fae can use their magick all they want, but nothing will mask the heart bond of fated mates. It's how I know she still breathes. When I was further away, their magick worked. But now? I can feel her. We're getting closer now."

"The road won't lead us directly there. We'll need to get out and hike it," Bianca said, studying her phone.

"I thought you guys did your magickal transport thingy?" Imogen asked and Bianca fist-pumped the air.

"Much smarter, Imogen. So, we split up. What are the teams?"

"Callum and I will go to the lair. The three of you take the top coverage," Nolan said.

"No," Callum turned and met Imogen's eyes in the soft light from the dashboard. "Imogen is with me."

"Um, is that really your smartest move?" Imogen gulped. "Nolan is likely a much better..."

"You are coming with me." Callum's tone brooked no

argument and Imogen swallowed thickly. Right, then. She was going to tag along with the Prince of Fae into the Serpent's Lair. No big deal, right?

"Why are you insisting on taking her?" Nolan piped up, his voice holding a dangerous note that brought the prince's chin up.

"Are you challenging my orders?" Prince Callum asked.

"I'm questioning your intent. See...to me? It would be the smartest thing to bring a warrior with you. Such as myself. And yet, you insist on bringing Imogen? Are you going to use her as a barter?"

Imogen gasped, as did Bianca, and both women looked at each other.

"Barter? Like trade me for Lily?" Imogen's fear kicked up. Bianca reached over and squeezed her hand.

"I would do no such thing," Prince Callum promised Imogen.

"But love makes people do crazy things," Nolan continued. "How do I know you won't use her to get what you want most?"

"Why do you even care?" Prince Callum asked. "You think she's a traitor anyway."

"I *thought* she was. I was wrong. So, now I stand for her. She's part of our team and I need to understand why you're splitting us up."

"Is that the only reason?" Prince Callum challenged.

Nolan just shrugged a shoulder and made a noncommittal sound. Imogen let out a shaky breath as her stomach twisted, the raspy timbre of Nolan's voice warming her.

"I'll protect Imogen as if she was my own. I promise you that," Prince Callum said. The moment drew out until Nolan finally nodded once.

"Then we split," Seamus said, trying to get them back on track.

"We'll cover you from the top." Bianca bumped Imogen's arm. "My Seamus is a crack shot with his arrows, aren't you, lover?"

"You're not so bad yourself, baby."

"See? We've got you covered. Plus, Seamus can work some of his spells. He can be quite creative with his magick."

"If you rain poison darts or something, can you just make them, like, not hit me please?" Imogen asked.

"I got you, Imogen. Don't worry," Seamus promised. Nolan turned and his stormy gaze held hers, causing Imogen's nerves to kick up.

"We're here. Pull over," Callum instructed. Seamus pulled the car to a stop on the side of the road. "Silence from here on out. Everyone understands their roles? We'll transport to the cliff side. Imogen. You're with me."

"Um, but what will I do, exactly?" Imogen asked, worry turning her stomach in knots.

"You'll know what to do when you need to do it," Callum promised her and Imogen hoped he was right. Surely, he wouldn't gamble Lily's life on her ineptitude. They piled out of the van, sliding the door quietly closed behind them, and Imogen stepped next to Callum, waiting for him to wrap his arms around her and transport her like Nolan had the other day.

Callum reached for her hand. Before she could take it, Nolan stepped between them. Cupping her face in his hands, he pressed the softest of kisses against her lips, barely a whisper, and yet full of untold promises. Imogen's eyes grew wide in her face as he pulled away. She had a thousand questions, and no answers. Nolan turned, without a word, and disappeared into the darkness with Bianca and Seamus.

Callum grabbed Imogen's hand, and that strange sucking sensation enveloped her, and in seconds they were gone from the side of the road.

When they landed, mayhem erupted.

24

SOMETHING WHIZZED PAST HER HEAD, causing Imogen to duck, as she whirled in a circle and tried to get her bearings after being transported. The sun had just crested the horizon, shooting golden rays across the churning surface of the stormy gray sea. The Serpent's Lair was exactly as Bianca had described it – an almost perfect rectangular pool cut into the sharp rocky ledge surrounded by steep cliffs. Imogen could just make out Seamus and Bianca far up on the cliffs, firing off arrows at the Domnua that raced across the ledges.

Toward them.

Realizing that she was essentially a sitting duck, Imogen squeaked as a Domnua exploded in a silvery spray of goo directly in front of her, and she looked up to where Nolan had his bow trained on her.

Nice shot, she thought, as Nolan took down another Domnua that approached Imogen. She turned to keep pace with Callum who had begun to fight his way across the rocky surface toward the edge of the pool. Imogen's heart skipped a beat.

If arriving at dawn was meant to give them a better fighting chance, Imogen wondered just how bad it would have been in the middle of the night. Because from her estimation? They were *screwed*. Hundreds of Domnua poured over the rock walls like a dark wave of ants when their nest was disrupted. It was like nothing she'd ever seen before, and Imogen didn't know how five people would ever hold their own against such a force. The Domnua had planned their attack well, Imogen realized, luring Prince Callum in and having an army ready to take him down. Lily was just the bait, but the prince was the prize. Imogen watched as the Domnua swerved around her, heading directly for the prince.

It was like they didn't even see her.

Or they just didn't care. She wasn't the high-ticket item today, oh no. If they took down the prince, it would be the next step toward their domination of Ireland. Imogen understood that much from what Bianca had told her.

Callum fought like a man possessed, edging closer to the pool with every step, but he was only one man. Even with the waves of magick that he shot out, mowing down groups of Dark Fae at once, more filled their spots. Silvery blood coated the rocks, making the surface slippery, as Imogen surged forward, her panic making her movements jerky. This was too much – she was in over her head. There was no way she could stop what she already saw happening. Helplessness surged through her, and the moment hung suspended in the air as Imogen's eyes darted to where Domnua scaled the stark cliff walls as easily as if they were climbing ladders. Her eyes landed on Bianca, her fierce friend who had stood for her, and something burst open deep inside her. No, not like this, Imogen vowed. The

Domnua weren't going to take her first female friend from her.

For a second, the ghost Fiona's face flashed through her mind, her words from the day at the beach in Grace's Cove, rising to the surface of Imogen's panic.

Everything you need is inside you.

Imogen's gaze darted to the Serpent's Lair where the water roiled in thick knots like a washing machine tumbling clothes about.

Water.

She could move water.

Imogen stared at the stormy sea in the Serpent's Lair, pulling at that little sparkly ball of energy inside her, allowing her fear and rage to build, and shot her power toward the rectangular pool of water. She slipped on a rock covered in silver Domnua blood as she surged forward, but she didn't stop. The water rose in a massive column, higher and higher, spinning into a massive tornado of water, and Imogen turned, slamming it into the side of the cliffs, and taking down the hundreds of Domnua that were a threat to Bianca. Without stopping, mad with rage, Imogen stalked forward, her hands out, and drew another wave of water from the layer, flicking with one hand so that it crashed across the lower ledge, completely wiping out the immediate threat to Prince Callum in one vicious wave of bad-ass Water Fae magick.

Callum turned, his eyes alight with hope, and cheered for her.

Bianca did the same from high up on the cliff.

They cheered for *her*. Imogen was helping her friends. She could do this.

She reached his side, her eyes scanning for threats, and held the next column of water in the air.

"Can you control it long enough for me to get Lily?" Callum shouted over the thundering noise of the water churning over their heads.

"Go. I'll keep the water out." Imogen didn't know how she could make such a promise, but she just knew that she could do this. She felt lit up, as though she'd been struck by a lightning bolt, and her very veins seemed to vibrate with energy. Imogen sucked more water from the lair, rendering it almost empty, and from this vantage point, she could now see the hole cut into the cliff wall. It was the entrance to the underground cave. Callum saw it too and winked out of sight in front of her before Imogen could even blink. Thank goodness, because now was not the time for hesitation.

A shout carried to her on the wind, and Imogen held one hand in the air, holding the swirling waterspout above her, and glanced over her shoulder.

"Bastards," Imogen seethed, seeing another line of Domnua advancing across the cliffs. Clearly, they weren't all that bright, Imogen thought and she spun around and shot the tunnel of water at the next group, wiping them from the cliff walls. Their screams brought her joy, and she wasn't exactly sure what she thought about this new bloodthirsty side of herself. "Come on, Callum, let's go."

She wasn't sure how long she could hold the water in the air like this, and even as she thought it, the water began to cascade back into the Serpent's Lair. Music thrummed in her veins, and shooting a look to where Nolan shot a stream of arrows from the cliff, she sang for her, no for *their*, lives.

Nolan's head came up, his eyes searing hers, and Imogen's emotions for him intensified, as light and love poured through her as she held the water in the air.

"Love needs to win," Imogen said, narrowing her eyes and digging deep inside her. Sweat broke out on her brow, despite the iciness of the wind that slapped her in the face. The seconds drew out to what could have been hours for all she knew, and Imogen tried not to doubt what she was capable of doing. Because she shouldn't be able to do this, no, not in the slightest, and yet here she was commanding the very ocean while the Prince of Fae rescued his princess.

Imogen jumped when Callum appeared before her, a woman wrapped around him, and before she could even say anything, he grabbed her with one hand, and that weird sucking sensation that meant they were transporting enveloped her. Imogen had one moment to glance at the water shattering down with a huge crash on the flood of Dark Fae that raced across the rocks, before she found herself back by the van, gasping for air. Little dots of light danced across her vision. She bent over, hands on her knees, and drew in deep breaths. Imogen was fairly certain she might embarrass herself by passing out, as the sheer magnitude of what she'd just managed to do threatened to overwhelm her.

"Hell yeah!" Bianca shrieked, dropping to her knees in front of Imogen and grabbing her face. Looking up, her friend beamed her sunshiny smile at Imogen. "Just look at you in all your glory. You, my friend, were magnificent."

"I think I'm going to be sick," Imogen gasped.

"Whoops, let me just get out of firing range then." Bianca bounced up and dragged Imogen around the side of the van, waving the others away. "Here now, go on and be sick if you need to be. Lean on me then."

Imogen leaned into Bianca, grateful for the support, and worked to school her breathing.

"It goes like that sometimes, you know. Big magick can cause a physical reaction. It's not unheard of, at least that I know of."

"I think..." Imogen swallowed and steadied herself. The dancing dots had left her vision, so that was good. "Right. I think...I'm better. I just needed a moment. It was all...that just happened so fast."

"It was pretty fecking incredible is what it was. Oh, and aren't you just something, Imogen? I'm telling you. Just magnificent."

"Are you okay?" A soft voice asked tentatively, and Imogen turned to see a lovely woman with delicate features and soft brown eyes looking at her with concern.

"Lily!" Bianca launched herself at the woman, and the two embraced happily. "Are you hurt?"

"No, I'm perfectly fine. Ravenous, but fine." Lily smiled and then stepped forward. She took both of Imogen's hands and squeezed, her eyes alight with warmth. "You saved me. Thank you."

"I'm happy to help. Your man, well, he really loves you," Imogen said.

"And I him. Thank you for helping to bring us back together."

"Sure, no problem." Imogen shrugged. She was still reeling from what had just happened.

"I hate to break it to you ladies, but we need to go. *Now*. I don't think the Domnua are going to be happy about losing their bait." Seamus hopped in the driver's seat of the van, and they all piled in. Imogen found herself sitting in the back next to Nolan, while Callum and Lily cuddled on the first bench seat and Bianca took shotgun. Callum gazed at Lily, his face tangled with emotion, and the look was so full of yearning and love that Imogen found herself having to look away, not wanting to intrude on such a private moment.

Her eyes locked with Nolan's, and the kiss he'd given her before they'd gone into battle slammed back into the forefront of her mind. Though the hurt from his actions yesterday still lingered, that kiss, well...it had felt pretty damn good.

"I'm so proud of you."

It was not what she'd been expecting him to say, though she wasn't sure exactly what she'd expected from him. But, well, it wasn't that. The statement caused hot tears to spike in her eyes and Imogen turned to look out the window, her emotions conflicted. Nolan didn't say anything else, seeming to understand that she needed space to collect herself.

Imogen pressed her lips together, blinking her eyes rapidly, and a breath shuddered out when Nolan reached over and took one of her hands, squeezing it gently in his. She allowed him to do so, because his touch brought her comfort, though she wasn't quite ready to examine their link more deeply. She wondered if she ever would be. Intimacy was already something that was difficult for Imogen to navigate, let alone some "written in the stars fated link" kind of deal.

"How soon can we leave?" Callum asked over his shoulder to Imogen.

"It takes a bit to fire the engines up, but not all that long. We could be on the way within thirty minutes or so." Imogen did a quick mental calculation.

"Can you make it ten minutes?" Callum asked.

"I...I can try. But..."

"What's that?" Callum asked.

"Why take to the water? Aren't the Domnua just as dangerous there?"

"No, they are far better on land. It's really the Water Fae's playground. And, I'm hoping once they see that we have Lily back and meant them no harm, they'll ease our passage home."

"And if they don't?" Imogen's voice cracked. She wasn't sure she could do another battle. Nope, she was almost certain her adrenaline was all used up for the day.

"Then we're in for rough seas."

"Oh great," Bianca moaned from the front seat. "Does anyone have seasickness pills?"

Despite everything, Imogen found herself laughing out loud with the rest of the group. Because at the end of the day, wasn't taking a moment for laughter what really mattered?

Nolan held her hand the whole ride back to the boat.

25

OUR LOVE WAS BUT A SONG,

> *Our dreams could not be wrong,*
> *But it's so lonely round the sea of Innisfáil.*

"Let's light this place up," Imogen crowed, turning her departure song all the way up and flipping on every light on the boat. Was it a little dramatic? Maybe. Was it kind of a big middle finger to the Dark Fae that likely watched them from shore? Yes, yes it was. And Imogen found that she just didn't care. Her newly discovered confidence sang through her and she drummed her hand against the steering wheel as they blazed away from the port, leaving the quiet island behind them. Imogen zipped the boat past Straw Island, humming as she gave a perfunctory wave to the lighthouse, and turned the boat to Foul Sound. Once they'd made it through this channel, they'd be back to open sea and, she dearly hoped, a smooth passage home.

How did people operate like this? Under constant threat of battle? Imogen checked her navigation and scanned the water ahead of them. It felt like she'd barely had a chance to catch her breath before the next potential threat loomed.

Her fingers continued to drum the steering wheel, and she increased their speed, hoping to barrel them straight through the sound without incident. Her eyes caught on one of her screens. Boats ahead.

"Please be fishing boats. Please be fishing boats." But Imogen knew they were too large to be fishing boats.

"Callum," Imogen spoke into the microphone, hating to interrupt what was likely a very intimate reunion with Lily. "There are boats ahead. Um, looks to be six of them. In formation."

The wheelhouse door flung open, letting in a blast of icy air, and Imogen shivered though she wasn't sure if it was from the wind or the fact that Nolan bent over her to look at the screen. His nearness was deeply unsettling for her, as her emotions were still raw, and she stepped neatly aside.

"How far?" Nolan turned to her. Her eyes caught on his lips, and she remembered their kisses. The first, stolen at the worst time ever. The second, given at the best time ever. Would she ever allow a third?

"Not long out. Ten-fifteen minutes at most?" Imogen pointed. "You can just see them."

Nolan grabbed her binoculars and trained them on the small dots on the horizon. The silence drew out, and anxiety coiled in Imogen's stomach. She loved the *Mystic Pirate*, but her boat could only handle so much. She wouldn't hold up against these massive ships. Seeing the beginning of the end, at least for her life and livelihood, Imogen pressed her lips together, hope deflating like a balloon being popped with a pin.

"It's the queen." Nolan slapped the binoculars down and then pulled a surprised Imogen into a dance. "Queen Aurelia arrives. She's bringing us back-up."

"Wait..." Imogen laughed, and Nolan twirled her around

the small wheelhouse before dipping her in an exaggerated bow and planting a kiss on her lips so quickly that she had no time to protest. Then he pulled her up and planted her in front of the steering wheel before racing from the wheelhouse. Imogen blinked at the horizon, dizzy from the little rollercoaster that Nolan had just taken her on, and held tightly to the wheel. She wasn't sure how she felt about all this kissing Nolan was suddenly doing with her. He'd flipped from one extreme to the other so quickly that Imogen was still struggling to catch up. And, she wasn't sure if she wanted to catch up. Her feelings were still hurt, and she'd barely had any time to process what they meant. Let alone let herself be dragged into the romance of Nolan's kisses.

"My mother comes," Callum said, poking his head through the door. "Please, when you get close, will you be able to slow the boat to ride alongside them? Her army will protect us on our passage home."

"Where's home?" Imogen had to ask. She'd like to go back to Grace's Cove and see if her crew still waited for her there.

"Grace's Cove for Lily and me. We'll split our time between the two realms, of course, but for now we'd like to return there, if that suits?"

"Perfectly fine by me, particularly if we'll have a royal escort to get us there."

"Ah," Callum stepped inside and closed the door behind him. "I'm sorry, Imogen."

"For what?" Imogen's gaze darted from the ocean to Callum's face. "What's wrong?"

"I realize that I haven't properly thanked you for your help this morning. You saved the love of my life, and I owe you. While I don't yet know what I'll gift you with, I can give you this – you only have but to ask for help, and the Danula people will have your back. It is written."

"Oh, well, thank you. Really, you don't owe me anything. Lily seems really nice and I'm glad we were able to save her. And I'm just happy to get my boat home safely. I need it, you know?"

"That's right. This is your career. You make money from this, yes?" Callum looked around the boat as though seeing it for the first time. The man must have really been out of it on this trip, though she guessed she couldn't blame him. He certainly had other things on his mind.

"Yes. I do. I run passenger sightseeing charters."

"And you love this? It is a career that suits you?"

"I do," Imogen smiled up at him. "I wouldn't have signed my life away with the bank to get this boat if I didn't love this job."

"Ah!" Callum snapped his fingers. "There. That's the perfect gift. A life for a life. Well, metaphorically speaking, of course."

"I'm not following?" Imogen wrinkled her nose in confusion and looked back to the water. The boats had drawn closer, and they were intimidating in their fierce design. No, the Fae didn't roll lightly now, did they? With massive sails and glorious carved wood figureheads, the fleet was majestic.

"The bank, of course. Your boat is yours."

"Wait...what?" Imogen drew her eyes away from the ships. "What do you mean?"

"Your loan. That's money you owe, right?"

"Yes, it is."

"Consider it taken care of."

"Wait...no, you don't have to do that." Pride reared and

Imogen glared at the prince. "Saving Lily was payment enough. Truly."

"What's going on?" Lily asked, ducking into the wheelhouse. She'd showered, changed into a lovely purple sweater, and color had returned to her cheeks.

"I was just telling Imogen that I would pay off her boat loan as a reward for helping to save you."

"No, that's completely unnecessary. I pay my own way," Imogen protested, deeply uncomfortable with such a gift.

"Imogen." Lily walked forward and sighed, reaching out to pat her arm. "I love Callum dearly, but he is infinitely stubborn. If this is how he wants to thank you, he'll find a way to do so whether you like it or not. Can you receive this gift with the same manner in which it is given?"

"Um, no I don't think I can," Imogen laughed. "My world isn't like this. People don't just give you thousands of dollars for no reason."

"Thousands? Oh, that's nothing then." Callum waved her loan away like it was nothing.

"Hundreds of thousands..." Imogen amended.

Callum just shrugged one shoulder. Imogen gave Lily a pleading glance, and a smile spread on her lovely face.

"Listen, sure and I can be understanding where you're coming from. I was just a teacher on a small salary before I came to Grace's Cove. The riches that Callum has, well, his entire world really, is just...almost incomprehensible. But I promise you, he's giving this not only because he can, but also because he wants to."

"It's better than a ceremonial dagger, no?" Callum piped in. "You already have a knife you like, right?"

"I mean, yes, I do. But..." Imogen just shook her head and laughed. "This is just...it's too much, Callum."

"Nonsense. Nothing is too much. You saved the only

thing that matters to me, my sweetest Lily." Callum wrapped his arms around Lily, pulling her back against his chest, and Imogen couldn't believe the change in the prince now that he had her back. He was positively alight with joy, and it was contagious. "Please, let me give you some of my happiness."

"I just…" Imogen thought about not having the weight of the loan over her shoulders. Of owning her ship free and clear. She could take a vacation! Her first ever. A little trickle of excitement buzzed through her and she turned with a smile. "I really shouldn't…"

"That's a yes," Callum decided, and Lily clapped her hands and laughed.

"Oh, yay! I love a happy ending, I do. I'm so pleased you took the gift, Imogen. I hope it helps."

"Tremendously," Imogen admitted, feeling a lightness in her chest that she'd never really known before.

"We're close. Look, Lily. Mum's arriving."

"Your mother is here?" Lily's eyes widened as Imogen reduced their speed.

"Is that a bad thing?" Imogen asked.

"No, she's really nice. And intimidating. And nice…and…"

"Lily's just embarrassed because the first time they met, my mother appeared in our bedroom when we were both naked." Callum shrugged as though it wasn't a big deal and Imogen gulped.

"No way," Imogen said, instantly feeling sorry for Lily. "Oh, no."

"Exactly. I'm still recovering from that. But now that there's a wedding to be had, his mother has thrown herself into the preparations and I think I can…well, I'm trying to just forget about that initial introduction."

"You poor thing."

"Why is this such a big deal? Naked is beautiful. Sex is a normal and healthy activity." Callum whispered in Lily's ear and her cheeks flushed.

"Who is having sex?" Nolan asked, standing at the door, and Imogen kept her eyes on the boats ahead.

"Well, hopefully Lily and I, as soon as possible. But not when my mother is here. Apparently, that's not allowed."

"Of course, it's not allowed, Callum." Lily elbowed the prince in the gut and grabbed his arm to drag him from the wheelhouse. "Come on, let's go greet your mother."

"Why were you discussing sex?" Nolan lounged in the doorway, and Imogen refused to look at him. It was far more important that she not crash her boat into one of the glorious Fae ships that drew closer.

"I wasn't. They were. Go talk to them," Imogen ordered.

"Don't you like sex?" Nolan asked.

"No. Nope. No." Imogen shook her head fiercely. "I am not having this conversation. Not now. Not when I'm about to meet the Queen of Fae. And not later either. That subject matter is off limits." Imogen's insecurity with intimacy rose, reminding her she'd never casually bantered with a man about sex before. Not like this...not when there was some sort of link between them. It meant too much, and that scared her.

"Now I'm curious..." Nolan said, the warm timbre of his voice heating Imogen.

"I don't care what you are. That conversation is none of your business."

"For now..." Nolan said and ducked out of the wheelhouse. And not soon enough, Imogen thought, as she popped the engine into neutral and then reversed gently to steer the boat alongside the first ship in the fleet. Considering the angle and size of the two boats, Imogen dropped the *Mystic Pirate* behind, thinking it wiser to follow than try to tie up alongside the massive Fae ship. Callum and Nolan caught ropes tossed to them and tied the bow to the queen's ship so that the *Mystic Pirate* trailed in its wake. Good enough, Imogen thought, and shut the engines off.

Imogen glanced down at her clothes, the same she'd worn for battle this morning, and wondered if she was appropriately attired to meet a queen. It looked like she didn't have much choice, as Bianca swung the door open.

"We're meeting in the lounge. I'm opening some of your champagne. Is that okay? I know it is meant for guests."

"It's perfectly fine." Now that she didn't owe any more bank payments, Imogen added silently. Though, until she saw that title to her boat in her hands, she probably wouldn't believe it was true.

"Come on then. Wait until you see the queen – she is just too cool." Bianca grabbed Imogen's hand and dragged her down the stairs into the lounge where a woman with pink hair, presumably the queen, held court. Six men of varying sizes and dress flanked her, and Imogen blinked at them. There was just so much to take in, she thought, as their style of dress and ornamentation was just so unusual. The queen stepped forward and Imogen tore her eyes away from a man in the back who wore a gold circlet on his head in the shape of flames.

"You must be Imogen, the captain? It's an honor." The queen bowed her head to her – to *her* – and Imogen's mind blanked out before she dropped into an awkward curtsey. Well, at least what she thought a curtsey might look like. She'd never really practiced. The queen's violet eyes, yes violet, crinkled at the corners as she smiled. She wore a radiant tunic that shimmered and shifted around her, and slim pants that hugged her legs. A delicate crown, encased in tiny jewels, was twined through her hair.

"No, really, the honor is mine. Queen...Aurelia, is it?"

"Yes, correct. My apologies for not stating my name."

"Welcome to the *Mystic Pirate*. You are a most honored guest." There, Imogen thought, that sounded polite. "May I get you some champagne? Or a cup of tea?" Imogen paused. What would a Fae queen want?

"Champagne would be lovely. May we sit?" The queen gestured to the front of the lounge area where a cushioned half-circle bench hugged the wall.

"Please do." Imogen went to pour the champagne, but the queen waved a hand and one of the men behind her strode forward and picked up the glasses.

"Come, sit next to me."

It was weird, Imogen thought, to sit on her own boat and be served. But she did as she was told and soon the group of them all had glasses in their hands and were tucked next to each other on the bench. Nolan had plopped down next to Imogen, his presence a distraction, and she had subtly inched away so that her thoughts weren't so scrambled by his nearness.

"You should have sent word." Imogen blinked and realized she'd been thinking about Nolan and his kisses and not focusing on what the queen was saying. Currently, she seemed to be scolding Callum. "We would have been here."

"There was no time," Callum insisted, raising Lily's hand to his lips. "I had to go after her."

"Yet you could have been more effective, potentially, with back-up."

"Be that as it may, I made a choice," Callum said.

"Well, I'm eternally grateful it didn't backfire on you. I sensed a major magickal outburst this morning. How did you survive? It felt to me like a veritable army of Domnua. I was desperately worried we wouldn't arrive in time."

"It was an army," Bianca chimed in and then pointed at Imogen. "But she saved us."

Those violet eyes swiveled to Imogen, pinning her with a considering look.

"Is that right? How does this come to be, Captain?"

"Um..." What was a good way to describe something that she didn't yet understand? "It appears I have some sort of abilities. Particularly ones that are available during times of deep stress?"

"I have reason to believe she's the long-lost queen of the Water Fae," Nolan said quietly, and Imogen jolted, champagne spilling from her glass as she turned on him.

"You what?"

"Oh, that makes so much sense," Bianca squealed.

"I can't be...I'm not..." Imogen protested, furious at Nolan for even introducing such an idea. Particularly in front of a real queen. Was he making fun of her? Or just trying to make her feel awkward? Because this wasn't fair, that was the truth of it. "You've got this all wrong."

"Do I?" Nolan picked up Imogen's hand where she wore the ring and held his other up in the air.

"Ah," Queen Aurelia nodded knowingly.

"Ah?" Imogen burst out and jumped up. Nolan scooped the champagne glass neatly from her hand before she could spill any more. "How can you just say it like it is a foregone conclusion? I am not a queen. Of anything. What I am is Captain of this ship. A simple girl who comes from nothing. I am no queen."

"The Water Fae called you their queen though," Bianca reminded her, and Imogen whirled on her, nerves skittering across her stomach.

"That means nothing, Bianca. They clearly mixed things up is all."

"Did they? I mean, you basically held half an ocean in the air so Callum could rescue Lily and slaughtered a literal army of Dark Fae. Is it really outside the realm of possibility that you might actually be the queen of the Water Fae?" Bianca asked.

Imogen was shocked to find tears spike her eyes. This was all too much. She wasn't magick. She wasn't a queen. They were just putting her on, and she couldn't handle it. She just wanted her simple life back, before she'd met any of these crazy people, because at least that life she could make sense of. Imogen turned and ran from the lounge, not caring what the queen thought. Slamming the door of her cabin behind her, she plopped onto her bed and looked down at her hands, twisting the ring on her finger.

"Why does this scare you?"

Imogen almost jumped a foot off the bed as the queen materialized in front of her.

"You really need to warn people before doing that."

"My apologies. May I?" The queen gestured to her bed and Imogen nodded. The bed dipped lightly as the queen sat and contemplated Imogen's face. "You're a lovely woman. But beyond that, I see a strength that not many have. Born of hardship, I suppose?"

"That's one way to look at it, I guess." Imogen shrugged off years of struggle and angst.

"I am of the opinion that the best leaders are ones that have experienced the deep complexities that life can dole out to a person. Not ones who are coddled in cotton wool in rich families and know nothing of struggle. You, however, seem to understand hard work and responsibility. It also sounds like you are incredibly courageous, and though you didn't know my son and they abducted you against your will – you still stepped up to help a woman in need. These are all attributes of a fair and just leader."

"While I thank you for the compliments...I need you to understand I can't be the queen of the Water Fae. I mean, I can swim and all, but I can't live under water. I wouldn't know the first thing about...helping their people. Ruling their people. What their needs are. It's...it's crazy, Queen Aurelia. It's just crazy. Can you understand that? They'd be better suited to promote someone within their world who understands their society, and well, you know can like swim and hang out with them. I wouldn't do the job justice. So, I'll just...can you give this back to them?" Imogen slipped the ring off and held it out to the queen.

"It doesn't work quite like that, I'm afraid." Queen Aurelia smiled softly and pressed Imogen's hand back. "However, I don't think it would be a role where you have to change everything about your life. There are a lot of questions unanswered here."

"Yes, like why me?"

"Exactly that. Your mother...?"

"Could barely swim and wants nothing to do with me."

A quick look of sympathy passed over the queen's face. "Your father?"

"Don't know anything about him." Imogen shrugged.

"I suspect he's likely the missing key. While we are a matriarchal society, the males do hold power. If your father is Fae, it would make sense. However...even if you are the missing queen..."

"Wait. How do people know there is a missing queen? Like was she kidnapped at birth or something?"

"Ah, of course. You don't know the story, do you? Will you come back out and join us? If I promise you that you don't have to immediately take the throne of the Water Fae or change anything about your life until you are ready?"

"I can renounce the throne?"

"Of course, you still have free will."

"I renounce it then." Immediate relief filled Imogen.

"Well, let's just make sure we've got the right of it before you give up something that you don't really understand. But, for what it's worth, Imogen... you are a queen. Even if it's only ever of this ship. Some people have this power, and others don't. You do. I suggest you accept it and let that force drive your life – whatever decisions you make in the future."

"I appreciate that," Imogen said, and stood to follow the queen back to the lounge where the group waited for them. Heat flushed Imogen's cheeks as she looked around the room. "Sorry about that little outburst of mine. Sure, and it's just a lot to take in."

"Are you kidding me? I'd probably have a melt-down if someone suddenly declared me a queen. You're just fine, Imogen, don't you worry." Bianca patted the cushion next to her, and Imogen gratefully took a seat.

"Imogen wanted to know why we know there's a lost queen of the Water Fae," Queen Aurelia directed her attention at Nolan. "And I suggest you also explain to her about the rings."

"The Water Fae, much like the Fire Fae that Torin oversees," Nolan nodded to the man with the flame crown, "have their own leaders. All of the Elemental Fae do, actually. They have their own Royal Courts, special bloodlines, and ways of structuring their societies. However, because we are the higher-level Fae, we are given a ruling role in their society. So, for example, Torin could be considered the King of the Fire Fae, and the leaders of the Fire Fae are the court of advisors that tend to the needs of their people."

"You don't need to be of Elemental Fae blood to claim a role in the Royal Court," Torin chimed in. "However, the Elementals do highly revere lineage and bloodlines. Which means there can sometimes be more than one queen. More than one king."

"Doesn't that get confusing?" Imogen asked, studying Torin. His eyes were tawny, like a lion's, and his golden hair hid tints of red.

"Not if everyone works together. It is when someone makes a play for more power that things can get thrown out of balance. It doesn't happen all that often, and generally speaking, the Fae delight in celebrating their royals."

"So...wait." Imogen looked to Nolan who regarded her patiently. "Does that mean that Nolan's advisory role essentially makes him King of the Water Fae?"

"Aye, it does," Queen Aurelia smiled. "But it is a matriarchal society, as I mentioned. Therefore, more power is afforded to the women."

Which meant, if he was king and she was queen...were they fated mates? The truth slammed into her so hard that Imogen grabbed for a glass of champagne to soothe her now-burning throat.

"There was a child that went missing years ago. A baby born outside the kingdom of the Water Fae. The prophecy speaks of her," Nolan said, his words measured as he twisted the ring on his finger. "Created of four worlds – human and Fae – dark and light – and her return would save the kingdom from certain ruin. I suspect you are this missing child."

"I..." Imogen's mouth dropped open and she looked to the queen who nodded at her. "But how am I saving them from ruin? I can't help the Water Fae."

"We don't know that yet. Their amulet is still missing,"

Nolan said.

"And I'm to find it?" Imogen laughed – she actually laughed – because the thought of her saving an entire kingdom of Elemental Fae was just, well, it was ludicrous.

"We don't know that yet. But, potentially." Nolan studied her.

"And this?" Imogen held up the ring she twisted in her hand. "It matches yours. Does this mean...are we fated mates?"

"I...I believe so," Nolan said, his eyes burning in his face. His words took Imogen's breath away, and one thought made its way to the surface.

How could she be fated with a man whom she couldn't even trust with her secrets? What kind of cruel joke was this?

Sensing Imogen's distress, Bianca wrapped an arm around Imogen's shoulders.

"Maybe you aren't quite ready for that discussion. I think that might be a private moment the two of you need to have. Let's talk about this amulet, instead? It's gone missing and basically the person who has it is kind of the de-facto ruler or power holder of the Water Fae? Is that the gist of it?"

"Correct." Torin spoke this time. "All of the Elemental Fae have a charmed amulet or token of sorts that holds the power of the Elementals. If it falls into the wrong hands, well, it can be catastrophic for the world at large. For the Water Fae? Think flooding, tsunamis, hurricanes...that kind of thing. For my people? Wildfires and mass devastation. The Domnua are infiltrating our people and are after these items. We have to stop them."

"And we know the Water Fae's amulet has gone missing but have no clues who took it, where, or why?" Bianca ticked the questions off on her fingers.

"We have some ideas, but nothing substantial."

"Here's what I propose," Bianca held up a hand before Nolan could speak. "Let's return to Grace's Cove. I'm going to take some time reading through this fascinating book that Callum gave to me and look for any clues. You know, now that we're hopefully away from the threat of battle. All of us are going to take a night or two off to rest, fuel up, and all-around just reset before we try to find this amulet. The Water Fae will not let up until their leader has his powers back. So, there's more to do. Imogen will be no use to us if she's running on fumes and is filled with confusion and doubts. How does that sound?"

"It sounds like the perfect suggestion." Queen Aurelia bowed her head to Bianca. "Thank you, Bianca, for taking the lead here. I suspect Imogen's ring is an acknowledgement of her lineage, since the Fae do love giving gifts. I agree that Imogen will need a little time to understand her role in all of this, otherwise she'll be making uninformed decisions. And that's not fair to her or our people. Let's not waste any time then. We'll return at once."

The group immediately disbanded, the Fae disappearing from immediate sight and back to their ships, and Bianca stood, nudging Nolan away from Imogen.

"Don't crowd her now, Nolan. She just needs some space."

"She didn't say she needed space."

"Well, I'm saying it for her. Go on then."

Imogen could've kissed Bianca, she really could have. Because that was exactly what she needed – some damn space from all of this – just to catch her breath and figure out what her next steps were. Because right now? She had no clue.

26

IMOGEN SLIPPED AWAY from the dock during the flurry of activity upon arrival back at Grace's Cove. Bianca caught her just before she left.

"Wait..."

"Bianca, please. I just need to have a walk to clear my head. I've got my phone on me. Can you hold him off?" Imogen didn't have to say who she spoke of, and Bianca pulled her into a fierce hug before agreeing to help. Now, Imogen wandered the village in the early evening light, with no particular direction in mind, for once really just letting herself people watch. Rarely did she take time to wander, she realized, let alone watch as people went about their daily lives. Did they know that there was a magickal world operating just below the surface of their everyday lives? Did they understand how close they were to magick? Imogen wasn't sure she could ever really return to the life she'd known, now that her own world had been blown open with all this new information.

A young mother walked out of a restaurant, bending to wipe a smear of chocolate from her son's face, and he grinned up at her with a gap-toothed smile and said something that caused the woman to throw her head back and laugh. Scooping him up, she showered his face with kisses before turning the corner. Imogen's heart twisted. The easy tenderness and love was something she'd always wanted from her own mother. Not only had her mother resented her, but she wasn't affectionate. Rarely had Imogen been pulled in for a hug, and to this day, she still couldn't quite get comfortable with physical affection.

Imogen passed a group of women spilling out of a pub, snippets of their conversation reaching her. They spoke of clothing sales and makeup tips, date nights, and boyfriends. All things that Imogen just didn't identify with.

It was much the same when she'd first landed on the docks, Imogen thought as she continued up the street past a little bookstore with a pretty display of fairytale titles in the front window. She hadn't fit in there either. She still didn't, if she was honest with herself, but at least she'd earned the begrudging respect of a few old-timers.

Basically, the way Imogen saw it? She didn't fit in anywhere. She never really had. She knew absolutely nothing about parenting, so striking up a conversation with a new mother wasn't something that was easy for her. Not only did she not know anything about being a mother, but she also knew her home-life experience was likely far from normal, which made her even more of an oddball when it came to that particular subject matter.

Dating, latest fashions, and make-up? Imogen didn't have the time, the money, nor the inclination for anything like that either. What was the point in painting her nails when the varnish would get scraped off the same day as she washed the deck? Dating wasn't really possible because she was constantly on the water, and her free time was dominated by running her business.

No, Imogen had accepted that she was meant to be alone. In fact, she'd been absolutely fine with it. While she knew she couldn't be normal like the women who now clattered up the street like a flashy group of magpies, she'd also been content with having made her life into something she could take satisfaction from.

Now, Imogen feared she couldn't return to that existence and yet she didn't know what the future held either. It was this in-between that scared her, and she didn't like being blown off course. The uncertainty made her antsy, and it wasn't a feeling that sat comfortably with Imogen. Spying the door to Gallagher's Pub, she decided that a whiskey would pair well with such deep contemplations. Imogen swung the door open to find the pub bustling with activity but spied a few empty stools along the corner of the long wood bar. Perfect for her needs, Imogen thought and took the furthest stool away from people tucked away in a dimly lit corner.

"I remember you." A slim woman with a short crop of hair stopped in front of her stool. "Ship captain, right?"

Imogen had come for dinner a few nights with her crew before, well, before her world had been rocked.

"Aye, that's the right of it. I'm Imogen."

"Cait, nice to officially meet you. You're looking like you're a bit parched. What's your poison tonight?"

Imogen would have normally asked what the happy hour specials were, but since she now, apparently, had a boat that was going to be paid off – perhaps she could splurge a little.

"A Green Spot whiskey. Neat please. Oh, and a glass of water on the side."

"Coming up. Any food for you?"

"Not just now, thanks." Imogen wondered if her appetite would ever return. She'd never, *ever*, had so many consecutive days where the highs and lows of emotion had left her feeling like that one time she'd tried bodyboarding on a warm summer's day years ago. The waves had been far too large for bodyboarding, but Imogen had been stubborn and tried it anyway. When the wave had crashed over her head, as she'd been warned it would do, Imogen had been tossed around in a tumbling mess of sand and sea water before the ocean had all but spit her out – a dripping and bleeding mess – back on the beach. Yeah, that was kind of how the last few days had felt internally for her.

"Tough day?" Cait asked, a bar rag draped on one shoulder, as she slid the glass of whiskey over to Imogen.

"Tough life, really. But this will make it a touch better. Thanks." Imogen saluted the woman. Instead of turning to leave, Cait leaned against the bar and studied her.

"You ever see those bins of tumbled stones?" Cait asked and Imogen squinted her eyes at Cait in confusion.

"Like the real pretty colorful ones?" Imogen asked.

"Yeah, like the brilliant orange carnelian all smoothed out and soft to the touch, or a bright blue lapis. You know what I'm speaking of, right?"

"Aye, I do. They're lovely."

"Well, they don't start out that way. They're kind of ugly at first."

"Okay," Imogen sipped her whiskey, enjoying the heat of it as it warmed her core.

"And to make them all pretty and shiny and presentable to the world? Well, they're subjected to a shite ton of pressure. They toss them in these machines that tumble them so hard that they end up polishing them right on up. And it takes weeks and weeks to do so. This isn't an easy, overnight process, no it is not. But, after all that tough pressure is applied, you know what comes out of it?"

"A pretty rock?" Imogen asked.

"Aye, the rock's true colors. But you never see them for all their beauty if they aren't first subjected to intense pressure. The tough times? Well, that's what makes for beauty in this world, Imogen." Cait patted the bar once and went to speak with other customers. Imogen blinked down at the ring she still wore on her hand, wondering what others saw when they looked at her. Was she just an ugly rough-around-the-edges rock? Did she always want to stay that way?

Or was she ready to show herself to the world?

She already knew Nolan was in the pub before he'd made his way to the stool next to hers. Imogen had felt it as soon as he'd drawn close to the pub. It had to be this link he spoke of – this fated mate bond – the same link that had drawn Callum to finding Lily.

"Hi," Nolan said, not pulling out the stool.

"Hey," Imogen said, taking another sip of her whiskey and not looking up at him. Cait's words hovered in her mind.

"I know that you're wanting some alone time, and I respect that. But I wanted to warn you that everyone is coming to the pub to eat soon, so it's not likely you'll be getting that alone-time if you stay here."

Imogen thought about it. Was she up for a night at the pub with everyone? She still felt drained from the last few days, but as soon as Nolan had come to stand beside her, a little current of energy zipped through her.

"Can I get you anything?" Cait asked, coming to stand in front of Nolan.

"No," Imogen spoke for them both, having made up her mind. "We're just leaving. What do I owe you?"

"This one's on the house, but only if you come back to see me soon. I'd like to hear some of your stories from the water." Cait winked at her and walked away.

A queen wouldn't hide from her destiny, Imogen thought, as she stood and met Nolan's questioning eyes. A queen would face it head on. She might not be able to change her fate, but she could accept it and make her own decisions about her future. And what she really wanted to know about right now? The thing most pressing to her – more so than the magickal world of the Fae, more so than the missing necklace, and more so than the potential lineage of her family – was what it meant to have a fated mate.

And Nolan was the only one who could answer that for her.

She left the pub quickly, knowing he would follow her, and turned down a corner side-street so as not to run into the group that would be coming from the boat. Nolan matched her pace, but didn't speak, and again she could appreciate a man who didn't feel the need to break the silence with inane chatter.

It was fully night now, and the sounds of the village rose around them. Mothers calling their children home for the night, the clinking of silverware on plates, the laughter of groups of people in restaurants. A full moon rose into the inky night sky, shining a trail of light across the shimmering surface of the harbor. Imogen wasn't exactly sure what she was doing, but her skin hummed with anticipation as they neared the docks. She wasn't quite ready to return to her boat yet. Imogen needed answers first.

She walked along a little path that hugged the harbor

and pulled herself up to sit on the rock wall, her legs dangling over the edge. Patting the spot next to her, Imogen silently invited Nolan to sit with her.

Instead, he came to stand in front of her, stepping so close that he nudged her legs wide and she had to tilt her head to look up at him. His strong jawline was silhouetted in the light of the moon, and she could just make out his stormy eyes.

"Talk to me, Imogen. Please don't freeze me out. I want to know what's going on inside that beautiful mind of yours."

Nobody had ever really cared before, Imogen realized. Not enough to ask her something like that, at least. Her past lovers had been drunken one-night stands, and that had suited Imogen just fine. But this? This mattered. And she needed to understand the emotions that washed through her when he looked at her the way that he did.

"I'm not trying to freeze you or anyone out, really. I just needed a moment to walk. To think. To process. I...I can't believe it's not even a week since I was last here. And it feels like lifetimes ago." Imogen looked around at the brightly lit village behind her. "Do they even know? Do they even realize the magick that dances just outside their senses?"

"Some do. Most don't. More could if they took the time to look for it," Nolan said. He put his hands on her legs, stepping subtly forward, and ran his palms up and down her thighs in a soothing motion. "Is that what's bothering you? The state of the human world versus the Fae realm?"

"It's one of the things, yes. Particularly because I don't fully understand where I fit anymore." Imogen laughed and shook her head, her hair tumbling over her shoulders at the movement. "That being said, I don't think I've ever really fit in anywhere, Nolan. I've never had a family. I don't have friends. Not like you do. You're so sure of yourself and your place in the world. And me? All I know is my boat. It's my own little kingdom that I rule and the only thing that makes sense to me."

"And I'm a threat to that."

"Yes," Imogen tilted her chin up to meet his eyes. "You are. But so is...the whole queen thing. And everything else. I'm afraid if I take this next step forward, whatever it may be, that I'll never be able to come back to where I am now."

"Is that a bad thing?"

"Of course..." Imogen trailed off as his words seemed to unlock something deep inside her. *Was* it a bad thing? What was she giving up really? Sure, she loved her work, but that was really all she had aside from the respect and affection of her crew. "Actually...I don't know. It just all feels so big and scary and confusing and I don't know. I feel frozen, like I don't know if I should take a step forward or run away, and I don't like that feeling. That's not usually who I am or how I operate. I take life's punches on the chin and keep moving forward."

Nolan reached up and traced a thumb across her jawline, sending little shivers across her skin.

"You don't have to take those punches alone anymore, if you don't want to," Nolan said, his voice raspy with emotion.

"That's the other thing that scares me," Imogen laughed again, realizing she was dangerously close to tears, but already in too deep to hide anymore. "I don't know how to do this."

"This what?"

"This. You and me. I don't understand the fated mates thing. I...listen, Nolan. I've never even dated someone for a few weeks. I've exclusively had one-night stands. I don't know how to do any of this, you understand? I don't know how to be in a relationship. I don't know how to live with someone. I don't know how to consult someone before I make decisions. I don't..." Imogen's voice caught.

"You don't what?" Nolan's fingers held her face, turning it up to his.

"I don't know that I'm good enough for you, Nolan. I'm scared you'll realize that I'm not enough and you'll leave. Just like everyone else has." There it was, her stark truth laid bare, and Imogen closed her eyes because she couldn't bear to see the pity that was likely shining in his eyes.

"It's not you that should worry, Imogen. It's not you that's not good enough. It's me, don't you see? I do my best, but I'm still a flawed man, Imogen. I often put my duty above my own needs, to the point of hurting others. You aren't the first woman I've hurt with my loyalty to my role, but I hope you'll be the last."

"That's the other thing..." Imogen shuddered in a breath. "I don't know if I can trust you. And I hate that. I want to trust you and be able to rely on the person that I do finally decide to have as partner. You really hurt me. What you did...was shocking. And frustrating. And yet at the same time? I get it. I do. I really do. If I was in your position, I might have jumped to the same conclusions. So, I shouldn't feel as hurt as I do. And yet..."

"It eats at me, Imogen. What I did to you. When I thought you'd betrayed us? I...it destroyed me. Because I think I already knew, even then, that I was lost to you. That you were the one for me and thinking that maybe all along you were playing me for a fool? Well, it made me see red. No, Imogen, I may be magickal, but I'm still just a man. I'll spend the rest of my days making it up to you if you'll allow me to."

"The rest of your days?" Now tears did spill over onto

her cheeks as hope soared inside her. "You can't possibly think…"

"What do you think fated mates are, Imogen?" Nolan gently brushed the tears from her cheeks. "For me there will be no other. That's the way of it."

"But Seamus said that sometimes Fae can renounce their fated mates."

"They can…but not after they've been with each other. Once they have, there's nothing to break that bond, you see? It's only before the bond is sealed, that a person can walk away. At great personal sacrifice, but the choice is still there."

"Is that…is that why I can feel you near? Like we are linked somehow?" Imogen brought her fist to her chest. "Or how I know your emotions sometimes?"

Nolan lifted her fist and kissed it gently.

"Aye, that's how you know. It'll grow stronger if…if you accept me. What do you feel right now, Imogen? What do you feel from me?" Nolan brought her hand to his heart, and Imogen closed her eyes, allowing herself to listen with her own heart.

"I feel…like you…oh," Imogen gasped, almost pulling her hand back at the vision that filled her head. "You see me so differently than I see myself, don't you?"

"Tell me," Nolan whispered, still holding her hand to his heart.

"It's like…I'm just all sparkly and shiny and I…glow for you. It's what love would look like, I think."

"It is. Imogen…you're incredible. You're brave, you're loyal, you're whip-smart, and your beauty shatters my heart. You say you fear the future, but you're a warrior, *mavourneen*. You stepped right into a battle you didn't understand, and you showed the world just how powerful you are. The woman of my dreams, you are, and I don't know that I could go on without you by my side."

"Oh..." Imogen said, caught on his words. "I'm scared, Nolan. What if you..."

"I won't. I promise I won't. I didn't know then, but I do now. I'll never lead you to feel like you aren't good enough, I promise you that, Imogen. I promise on my mother's very soul, that I will spend my days making sure that you know just how loved you are."

"I think I need that," Imogen said, hiccupping through her tears. "I think I need someone to stand for me. I don't want to be alone anymore, Nolan."

"Then let me be your person, *mavourneen*."

Imogen blinked up at him through her tears and nodded, the pieces all fitting into place for her finally. Yes, this man was her future, and the rest would follow as it would.

Nolan pulled Imogen from her seat and wrapping his arms around her, he transported them with his magic. Someday she would get used to the strange sucking sensation of transporting, but she wasn't there yet. Steadying herself, she glanced around when her feet hit solid ground once more and realized they were in his cabin on the *Mystic Pirate*. Unlike hers, the guest cabins featured double beds, and Nolan was currently walking her back until the back of her legs bumped the edge of the mattress.

"You do something to me," Nolan said, bending so his lips brushed her ear. His breath against her neck was hot, and a shiver raced through her. "Since I first laid eyes on you. Since the very first touch, I've wanted you. I dreamed of my lips on your skin, of tasting your mouth, of feeling you beneath me...over me. Thoughts of you have consumed me to the point of almost madness, *mavourneen*."

"I..." Imogen gasped as he pulled her sweater over her head, and the shirt below it along with it. She'd only slipped on a simple tank bra that morning, and now felt somewhat frumpy as she stood before him.

"Yes?" Nolan asked, fiddling with the simple strap of her tank. His fingers at her shoulders sent little tendrils of heat rolling down her arm.

"Me too. I kind of hated it, too," Imogen looked up at him. "You were not very nice to deal with."

"Sure, and that was just me trying to keep you at arm's length. I didn't want to be distracted by you. To think about touching you." Nolan brushed his hand over her breast, her nipple puckering under his attentions. "Didn't want to be consumed with thoughts of claiming you."

Imogen's insides went liquid at his words. It was such a proprietary thing, wasn't it? Claiming someone. She jerked as Nolan dropped to his knees, his hands at her waist, unbuttoning her pants. She trembled beneath his touch, nerves making her anxious. Perhaps they should just get this over with?

"Oh, I can just take those off. And we can just get started."

Nolan hissed out a laugh, pressing his forehead to her stomach as he did, and Imogen looked down at him, finding she wanted to run her hands through his hair. But that seemed too intimate. Too...girlfriendy?

"Has nobody taken their time with you before?" Nolan's breath puffed at the sensitive skin of her stomach, and she shivered again. This was making her feel awkward, and excited, and unsure...there were so many emotions roiling around inside her.

"Um...no. I don't know...how to do it like this."

"Like what, exactly?" Nolan looked up at her from where he kneeled.

"Not half-drunk and not caring much about the other person?" Imogen said and then pressed her lips together. Probably not the best thing to say to someone who wanted to make love to her. Nevertheless, Nolan seemed to understand.

"Tell me what you want, Imogen."

"I want to run my hands through your hair," Imogen admitted, feeling foolish.

"You can do anything you like to me, my love. I'm yours to sample. Please, don't feel silly. And don't hold back – I don't plan to with you." At that, Nolan pulled her pants down, hooking her underwear along with them, baring her to him. Imogen's eyes widened.

"You take my breath away," Nolan said, scanning her body, before looking back up at her. "My love. My heart mate. Please, will you let me love you? I've dreamt about the taste of you on my mouth."

Oh my...Imogen was certain her entire body blushed, but she couldn't do much about her embarrassment before his tongue slipped between her folds and found where she ached for him most. Already liquid with need, Imogen's legs buckled as Nolan massaged her with his mouth, finding her most tender of spots and sucking ever so gently until Imogen felt ready to scream. She bowed backward, digging her hands into his hair, and closed her eyes against the wave of lust that washed over her. The sweetest of pressure began to build and her body trembled with need – need for release – need for Nolan – need for this connection with him. His tongue, oh but it was sheer madness. Surely the man was a magician, as he dipped and dived, swirling his tongue around her, tasting her as though she was a delicacy to be savored.

Imogen shuddered against him, the pleasure building to such a peak that she wanted to scream – to tell him to never stop – when he slid a finger deep inside her, curling it to hit her just so. It was at that moment that he pulled her over the edge, the relentless stroking of his tongue bringing her the release she sought, and she grabbed his shoulders as she broke apart around him. When she'd finished, Imogen blinked blurrily down at Nolan, who grinned lazily up at her, and began to kiss his way up her body, leaving a trail of heat across her skin.

"Exactly as I thought, my beautiful sweet goddess. Your taste...it renders me senseless. I'll never crave another the way I'll now crave you."

Oh, but the man had poetry, Imogen thought. She couldn't even string two words together at the moment, let alone think of something romantic to say. Her heart pounded in her chest, and she was just...overwhelmed by him. He was so much larger than her, and his hands and mouth were everywhere, kissing, nipping, tasting, sampling. It was like being pulled into a whirlwind of erotic delights, and Imogen couldn't even keep up before he'd brought her close to release once more just by lavishing attention on her breasts. Before she went over the edge again, she slapped a hand on his chest.

"Wait, please...I just..."

"Tell me what you need." Nolan stood now, nibbling at her neck, and lifted her gently to lay her back on the bed.

"I want to touch you," Imogen said. She'd done her own fantasizing, hadn't she? Here she was naked and the man was still fully clothed. Wasn't it her turn to enjoy some of the scenery?

"What the lady wants..." Nolan stopped and spread his arms wide.

"Well, first, you're wearing entirely too much clothing." To her delight, Nolan snapped his fingers and his clothes disappeared instantly from his body. "Wow, you'd be a hit at the strip club, wouldn't you?"

"I'm not sure what that is," Nolan admitted, and Imogen gaped at him in surprise.

"It's where people dance for money. They take their clothes off?"

"Interesting. Will you dance naked for me someday, Imogen?"

"What? No! I mean..." Imogen paused. Actually, the thought kind of intrigued her.

"Ah, you will then?" Nolan accurately read her inner commentary.

Imogen found herself laughing, something she hadn't expected with a lover. Nolan was playful, and sexy, and demanding, and...really well put together. Imogen trailed her eyes over his broad shoulders, his extremely well-defined abs, and...her mouth dropped open as the evidence of his attraction jutted out at her. He was...well, he wasn't lacking in that particular department, Imogen decided. Sitting up, she crawled across the bed to where he still stood. Tentatively, she reached out and traced a hand across his chest and down over his abs, feeling the dips and ridges of his hard muscles. He was perfection, this man before her, and he was hers if she allowed it.

Imogen looked up at him, her eyes caught on his, her mouth inches from his lips when she reached for him, sliding her hand over his hard length. He closed his eyes, a soft puff of air escaping his lips, and Imogen discovered she enjoyed having this power over him. Gently she trailed her hand back and forth, enjoying the feel of him, her hips starting to move in the same rhythm as her hand. Nolan bent, capturing her lips with his own, and Imogen moaned into his mouth. She tasted herself on his lips, and something more, a primal desire that seemed to swell up from her very soul, and she lost herself in the kiss, drowning, drowning, until he broke the kiss and pushed her back onto the bed.

"I need to feel you around me, Imogen. I need..." His voice had taken on that raspy quality that sent shivers straight through Imogen's core and she pulled him on top of her, needing to feel his weight on her body. Oh, but he was large...everywhere. Nolan ranged up on his muscular arms, holding himself off of her, nudging himself between her legs. He prolonged the moment, teasing her, as he slid his length between her folds, hitting her at just the right spot until she wanted to beg for him to take her that instant.

"Imogen." Nolan said, bending so his lips slid hotly over hers once more.

"Nolan." Imogen gasped against his mouth.

"You're mine. Now. Forever. Fated mates we are. Will you let me claim you?" Nolan asked, his breath coming in shallow pants, his control near to snapping. Imogen could tell, for she could feel his emotions for her reflected inside her, and it only heightened the moment, making the slide of his movements against her intoxicating.

"Please, Nolan." Imogen all but whimpered against his mouth. "I claim you."

"My queen," Nolan said, and slid deep inside of her, filling her in ways that nobody had before. Instantly, Imogen clenched around him, a sharp wave of pleasure cresting her neatly over the edge so that she shuddered around him as he held himself still, waiting her out.

"Nolan...I...love you." It seemed impossible. It had barely been a week since she'd thrown a knife at this man's head. But her heart knew – had known – the instant she'd laid eyes on him. Now, Nolan took her mouth in the softest of kisses before he began to move inside her, pulling all the way out before sliding deep once more, over and over until Imogen's pleasure spiraled up and threatened to spill over. But this time, she was determined to take him with her and met his thrusts, arching her back so he could slide more deeply inside, and together they shattered, forever cementing their claim to each other. Nolan stopped, dropping his head on Imogen's shoulder, and she wrapped her legs around him, needing to hold him close for just a moment longer.

"My queen," Nolan turned and pressed a kiss to her neck. "I look forward to showing you all the ways that I can love you."

"I...I'll look forward to that." Imogen couldn't quite bring herself to call him her king, for that felt a bit silly, but she'd be lying if she said she didn't feel a happy little zing shoot through her when he said she was his queen. For a moment, she settled back and felt his heart beat against hers. She'd never done this before, she realized, and enjoyed the moment of being entwined together with her lover.

"You're singing."

Imogen blinked up at Nolan as he grinned at her.

"I am?"

"Aye, you've sung it a few times now. I recognize it. It's our heart song."

"It is?" Imogen arched an eyebrow at him.

"It is. You've been singing it all along...I just refused to believe it. Remember? Love is an ocean both powerful and healing." Nolan sang softly to her, and Imogen's heart instantly reacted, flooding with warmth and joy.

"Oh, I've been hearing that song for ages now. I thought it was from a dream..."

"It is. Our dream, my love."

Imogen sank into his kiss, surprised when tears threatened. While she'd had some tough spots in her life, she'd never had a moment this vulnerable before. Or a week of emotions like this, for that matter. She sighed softly against Nolan's lips and drew back.

"Shall we have a whiskey on the roof? And wait for the others to come back?"

"Ah, yes, you know what? That would be perfect."

"Let's get cleaned up and I'll grab the drinks." And just like that, they fell into an easy rhythm that Imogen hadn't known with anyone else in her life.

This was good, she realized. It was right. She'd finally done it, she realized. Gone and fallen in love and found her person. It would take a little bit of getting used to, but...it was hard to worry in the middle of her after-glow. She could worry about life on another day. For now...she was going to enjoy a whiskey with her love on the deck of the boat she owned.

It was turning out to be pretty good day after all.

27

POWER SURGED through Nolan in a way that he hadn't felt since he was young. So, this is what they had meant about fated mates enhancing magickal abilities. It was as though his power hummed under his skin like a live wire, and he all but bounced around the boat. He'd had to leave Imogen before he took her once more when she'd joined him in the tiny shower in the cabin. The others would be home soon, and he wanted to take his time with her, and not be interrupted by the group. It hadn't stopped him from pressing her against the wall and slipping his hands inside of her to bring her to a sharp orgasm as she moaned into his mouth while the hot spray of the water pounded his shoulders.

She'd been everything he'd dreamed about and more. He loved the way her eyes went dizzy as he pleasured her, and the flush of pink that tinged her porcelain skin. With her flaming hair spread across the pillows, her lips swollen from his kisses, and her eyes hazy with lust – Imogen was every inch a Siren that sang her song only for him.

Whistling, Nolan padded in thick wool socks to the lounge area and poured them both glasses of whiskey before heading out to the deck. The night was still, with barely a hint of wind, and the moon shone brightly above them. He stopped at the ladder, considering how he'd climb it with both glasses in his hands, when a shock of pain choked him. Nolan dropped the glasses, reaching for his throat, only to sear them against the burning band of metal that now encircled his throat.

Iron.

Nolan doubled over, trying to wrench his neck free from whatever was holding him captive, but to no avail. He gasped for air, feeling his power begin to diminish, when a low chuckle greeted him.

"You know, I never expected you to find her."

Nolan tried to twist to see who was talking, but instead he was dragged along the side of the deck, the broken glass slicing through the wool of his socks and into his feet and tossed unceremoniously on the deck. Nolan twisted, trying to breathe against the fiery pain that raked through him as though he was being gutted with a hot poker from a fireplace.

A man stood before him, faintly glowing silver, his opal eyes narrowed at Nolan. A Water Fae. And yet, not a Water Fae. The shock of red hair was all Nolan needed to realize who had captured him.

Imogen's father.

And he wore the Water Fae's stolen amulet around his neck.

Nolan closed his eyes for a moment, trying to gather his strength as the iron sapped his power, furious that he'd finally found Imogen only to have this happen. Worry for her safety rose to the top and he tried to shoot her some sort of internal message – a warning.

"Nolan!" Imogen shouted, racing upstairs and skidding

to a stop on the back deck when she saw him crumpled. Her hair dripped down her back and she'd pulled on the bathrobe from his closet. The same one he'd used as a tie for her legs, and he winced at the pain of that memory. How foolish he'd been.

"Ah, there she is."

Imogen turned and locked eyes with her father and Nolan hated that he couldn't do anything, that he couldn't help her in this moment, but the iron rendered him virtually powerless. All he could do was watch as Imogen faced her biggest fear and her greatest threat in one.

"The amulet, Imogen. He's wearing..." Nolan choked out. He needed her to understand just how powerful her father was. Not only was he part Domnua, but he now commanded the Water Fae. They'd have to do his bidding, no matter their allegiance to Imogen.

"You've ignored me all these years. And yet I knew we'd come to this day. My darling daughter. Allow me to introduce myself." Imogen's father swept his arm out in a mocking bow. "Cathal is my name, and I am your father."

"You're..." Imogen's voice caught, and Nolan's stomach twisted at the anguish that crossed her beautiful face. She tore her eyes from her father and looked to Nolan. "I didn't know...I swear."

"Save. Yourself." Nolan gasped, little dots dancing across his vision.

"I think what he means is that it is time for you to step into your power, my darling love. You've eluded it all these years. But for no longer. Come with me."

"I refuse," Imogen said, crossing her arms over her chest and tossing her hair.

"Well now, darling, that won't work for me. Is it the boat you don't want to leave? It looks like you've done well for yourself." Cathal smiled at Imogen like they were having a wee chat over a pint at the pub. "I'm proud of you, you know."

"I *have* done well for myself. No thanks to you. What kind of father abandons their child?" Imogen demanded. Nolan wondered if she knew that the iron band around his neck was killing him. She still had so much to learn about the Fae world.

"A busy one, Imogen. I've spent years setting these plans in motion. Don't you see? Everything I've done up to this point I've done for us. Now we can rule the Water Fae *together*. I've come back for you. Because as family, we'll be more powerful."

More like he needed Imogen to make a rightful claim to the throne. Nolan knew how Fae rules went, and Imogen was part of the prophecy. Cathal was not. He'd tossed her aside as a child, and now he was using her to overthrow the Water Fae. Waves began to slap against the side of the hull, and Nolan knew the Water Fae were close. Had Cathal called them?

He sagged limply against the deck, furious that he couldn't help Imogen, that he couldn't do anything more in this moment. He shuddered in another breath, barely able to keep his eyes open.

"This isn't the way," Imogen said softly, turning to face her father directly. "You're hurting my partner, Cathal. This is my fated mate – the love of my life. Release him at once."

"No, unfortunately I can't be doing that for you, daughter of mine. I suspect he won't be pleased with our claim to the throne. It will take his power from him, and Nolan wouldn't like that, would he? He's prided himself on always being in power. He's no use to you now, Imogen. Don't you see? You don't need him anymore. And don't worry, once we take the throne there will be plenty of suitors for you to choose from."

"If I'm your daughter, as you say, then at the very least you can honor my request. Release him," Imogen said, her tone sharp. "You've abandoned me my entire life and I've never asked for or needed anything from you. Release him."

"Oh, already trying out your queenly ways? You'll do fine on the throne." Cathal's grin widened.

"You never once cared about me, did you?" Imogen asked, tilting her head to look at her father. Nolan's insides screamed, but the physical pain was nothing compared to what he felt from Imogen. To finally meet her father only to realize that he only wanted her for what she could do for him – it was heartbreaking to watch.

"Sure now, that's a harsh thing to say. I've kept an eye on you over the years."

"Is that right? Where were you when I was tossed out on the streets by my mother?" Imogen demanded.

"Ah, that slag of a mother of yours should've done better by you. Blame her – not me. Come on now, child. It's time to go. The throne can be ours. Just imagine all the riches we'll have – the power!" Cathal's eyes lit with excitement.

"If you let him go...I'll," Imogen swallowed, her heart-stricken eyes on Nolan's, "I'll go with you."

"No..." Nolan rasped, his throat closing up.

"You'll come with me either way, darling. I won't release him, as he'll only cause us problems once we leave here."

"That's it then? That's your choice?" Imogen asked quietly.

"Of course it is, silly girl. You're wasting time. It's time to leave, now." Nolan realized that Cathal was at the end of his rope and about to use his powers on Imogen. He raised his hand, trying to warn her.

"We all make choices, don't we father? And I choose him." Nolan barely saw the movement, before Cathal exploded in a spray of silvery goo, having taken the knife Imogen threw at him directly between the eyes. The Water Fae's amulet clattered to the deck, and Imogen dove for it, pulling it over her head before turning to crouch at Nolan's side. He blinked up at her, tears flooding his eyes.

"My warrior. My love. What a brilliant queen you'll make," Nolan rasped, barely able to lift his hand to stroke her face. "Proud of you."

"Nolan, please. Tell me what to do. How do I get this off you?" Tears streamed down Imogen's face as she reached for his neck.

"Can't. Magick." Nolan gasped, his vision going hazy.

"You know what I hate?" Imogen stood, fury thundering across her beautiful face. "Is when people tell me that I can't do something."

In that moment, she was every inch his queen, as she grasped the amulet around her neck.

"Water Fae!" Imogen shouted, and the ocean churned around the boat, waves slapping the sides. "Help me!"

Nolan blinked as the Water Fae poured over the side of the boat, and surrounded him, lifting him into the air. In seconds he was plunged beneath the surface of the water, the icy shock to his skin not nearly as painful as that from the iron band around his neck. Nolan blinked into the dark water as a soft white light approached, and he was held suspended, while a stunning mermaid, her hair twining around her head, reached out and deftly removed the iron band from around his neck. Instant relief coursed through Nolan, and he gasped for air as the Fae swam him to the surface once more, returning him to the loading platform at the back of the boat. There he found Imogen, kneeling, tears streaming down her face.

"Nolan!"

"Imogen!" A cry from the dock sounded, and Nolan glanced over to see Callum and the others racing toward him. They vaulted onto the boat, helping her to pull him to safety, and he collapsed into Imogen, wrapping his arms around her and resting his head in her lap. It was all he could do really, for his energy was gone.

But he was alive, and Imogen had vanquished her demons.

Well, one of them, at least.

"What happened?" Bianca said, dropping to her knees beside him. Queen Aurelia appeared, a glass bottle in hand, and Nolan was saved from answering when she unceremoniously dumped the liquid down his throat. The elixir worked almost instantly, like a shot of adrenaline, and Nolan sat up, though he knew his strength was low. At least he was alive.

"Imogen's father paid us a visit. He was the one who stole the amulet from the Water Fae."

Bianca gasped, her eyes stricken, as she looked to Imogen.

"Oh, you poor thing. That had to break your heart."

"I killed him," Imogen said in a bemused manner, as though faintly surprised by what had just happened. "I killed my father."

"And a good thing, too. He was part Domnua and trying to take over the throne. Imogen," Nolan reached out a hand and pulled her down to him. "He would have only used you for his own good. He did not care about you at all – only what you could do for him. You did the right thing."

"You made a tough decision," Queen Aurelia said,

rocking back on her heels. "The type of a decision a queen would make."

"I chose love," Imogen said simply, and then pulled the amulet over her head. "Here. Please return this to whom it belongs."

"I believe that might be you," Queen Aurelia said gently.

"No. It's not. Not yet at least. It's not fair to the Water Fae. Maybe, in time, I'll be able to help them more. But I'm not ready. I need to learn a lot more first before I can be of any value to them. Plus, what does that mean if I have some Domnua blood in me? Does that mean I am bad, too?"

"No, my child. It doesn't. You still choose your path, you understand?" Queen Aurelia pointed her finger to the loading platform. "If you aren't ready for the amulet, then it belongs to him – the elder from whom it was stolen."

Nolan turned to see an elder he knew well standing on the platform, patiently awaiting the outcome. Imogen stood and walked to him, looking as regal as she could in her bathrobe, and handed the amulet back to the elder Water Fae.

"I'm sorry my father stole this from your people. I hope you won't hold me accountable for his actions. I only wish for health and happiness for your people."

"My Queen." The elder bowed. "You are a blessing to our people. I hope, in time, that we can show you our world. You're welcome always."

A resounding cheer went up from the water, as the elder dove back into the ocean, taking the amulet with him.

"Does anyone want a whiskey? I could really use one," Bianca asked.

"You and me both," Nolan rasped out a laugh, before grabbing Imogen and claiming her mouth in a searing kiss. "Let's have a glass, shall we, my queen?"

EPILOGUE

"WHAT IS THIS?" Imogen laughed at Nolan as he tugged her into a little opening in a rock wall near the cove. It had been a few weeks since she'd learned she was part Fae, and Imogen had been all but taking a crash course on all things Fae from a delighted Bianca who loved nothing more than teaching about magickal myths and history. Between her teachings, and Nolan's demands on her time, Imogen had decided to reschedule some of her upcoming charters so she could take a small hiatus. She'd paid her crew handsomely for the time off, and found that for the first time in years she could breathe easily. So many issues that had plagued her for so long – like the man beneath the water – were now resolved. She almost didn't know what to do without the weight of those issues pressing on her shoulders.

Not that Nolan gave her much time to think too deeply about anything other than him. Oh, but the man was all-consuming and in the best ways possible. As Bianca had promised, the Fae were extraordinary and insatiable lovers, and Imogen was shocked to discover how much she craved Nolan's touch.

"Well, my love, this is a portal of ours." Nolan stood, ducking his head in the tunnel, near a stone circle. He wore the leather pants that hugged his muscular legs just so and Imogen sighed as her mind danced to other things. Reading her correctly, a sexy smirk crossed Nolan's face and he leaned over to run his thumb over her bottom lip, sending a little thrill of heat through her body. "Another time for those thoughts."

"Fine." Imogen fake pouted, but then brightened when he pulled her into his arms. "Wait...a portal? Does this mean?"

"Aye, we're going to the Fae realm."

"But..." Imogen barely had time to ask questions before that strange sucking sensation wrapped around her and she blinked when they landed in a field just lit by the last moments of sunset. She would have packed something, Imogen thought, as she peered around Nolan's arm to take her first look at the Fae realm.

A large castle sat directly behind where they stood in a field blossoming with yellow and pink flowers. Not flowers that Imogen knew by name, and she narrowed her eyes when she saw miniature beings with big butterfly wings flitting from flower to flower. One of them paused to wave at her mid-flight and Imogen found herself grinning at it and waving back. Little globes of light danced through the air, as though someone had strung the field with strands of fairy lights, except, well, these glowing lights seemed to actually be real fairies.

"This is incredible," Imogen breathed, following Nolan as he tugged her through the field and toward the castle. "Nolan, I can't go in there like this. I'm not dressed for it."

Nolan paused and turned to Imogen before looking her up and down. A cool breath of air washed over her and then

Imogen found herself blinking down at her body. Her canvas pants and jumper had been replaced with a flowing blush pink dress and she gaped at Nolan.

"Pink?"

"Sure and it goes nicely with that pretty red hair of yours, doesn't it?" Nolan said, beaming at her incredulous look.

"Pink," Imogen grumbled.

"It's the color that flushes your skin after I've made you beg for release," Nolan said, his lips hovering over hers, and damn it, but the man *did* make her flush Imogen realized as heat flooded her skin.

"Why are we here?" Imogen batted him away, yearning to soak up every minute she was in the Fae realm.

"You'll see..." Nolan dragged her through an archway, nodding to two guards standing in purple tunics with swords at their sides. Her gaze darted everywhere as she took in the colorful clothes of the people who all but danced through the streets, some flying, some running, some appearing out of thin air. The village contained inside the tall walls of the castle was a busy one, but cheerful shouts, laughter, and music dominated the scene and Imogen instantly relaxed even though she wanted to go and see everything. This was a happy place, that she could immediately ascertain, even while her brain tried to catalog all the various forms of magicks she was witnessing.

"This way." Nolan pulled her down a cobblestoned street and through a winding narrow alley before stopping at an arched doorway that was triple the height of Imogen. The doorknocker alone was the size of her head and shaped in the form of a rose with two swords crossing over it. Imogen caught her breath as the door swung open seemingly of its own accord and Nolan ushered her through, his hand at her lower back.

Still, at times, Imogen had to stop herself from flinching at his touch. She was learning to be more free with reaching out for him or allowing Nolan to hold her hand. The easy intimacy between couples wasn't something that she was used to, but every day she was getting better at it. It didn't hurt that she loved, as in loved, to run her hands over his body. The man was built like a fortress, and she was continually amazed at the strength of his body.

Nolan nudged Imogen through the doorway and she skidded to a stop when lights flickered on and sparkles rained from the ceiling.

"Surprise!" The shouts had Imogen clapping her hands to her face, even as Nolan steadied her from behind with his hands on her shoulders. Imogen peeked through her fingers to see a slew of people she didn't know, as well as many she did. Bianca and Seamus beamed at her from where they stood with Cait by a table overloaded with food. Queen Aurelia stood next to a man who was the spitting image of Prince Callum, which must make him the king. Imogen gulped when she realized she was in the presence of royals – at their royal palace. She was for sure going to screw up some protocol, and nerves twisted low in her stomach.

"Nolan? What is this for?" Imogen raised a questioning look over her shoulder.

"Your birthday, darling. I looked it up."

"My..." Shock stole the words from Imogen. She'd forgotten about her birthday, as she did most years. "You... this is a birthday party?"

"You told me that you'd never had one. I wanted to do something special for you."

Imogen turned back to the crowd of people and blinked

at the tears that flooded her eyes. Oh, but she was not a crier! However, this was just too much. The sparkles that rained from the ceiling turned out to be miniature Fae, flitting about and dancing, and food, drinks, and presents piled tables that lined the walls of the room. A band of colorfully dressed Fae struck up a tune in the corner, and immediately half the party began dancing.

Imogen's heart melted when she realized what song the band was playing.

"It's our song..." Imogen blinked up at Nolan, as the music twined its way around her heart. She felt his need for her deep in her core and moved into his arms.

"The Fae can't help themselves. We do love to dance." Nolan laughed, and his smile soothed her anxiety as he spun her across the floor and past a laughing Bianca. Imogen leaned into his arms, her heart so full to bursting. She'd never known she could feel this way – so full up on love and friendships. And, well, power. She was powerful, and magick, and oh, well, life was just...what a turn it had taken.

Hours later, full up on cake, dancing, and trying to remember the names of everyone she'd met – including his family – Imogen sighed with happiness as she finally took a seat at a long table. Bianca dropped down next to her, and Seamus and Nolan took the seats across the table.

"Truly, thank you for all of this. For never having a birthday party before, I am pretty sure that I've now had the party to beat all parties."

"I'm glad. I just wanted to make you happy." Nolan slid a box wrapped in purple paper with a brilliant pink bow across the table. "Also, I have a gift for you."

"You didn't have to do that," Imogen said, turning the box in her fingers. She'd never been good at accepting gifts.

"I wanted to. Go on...open it."

Imogen's pulse picked up as she carefully unwrapped the gift, smoothing out the nice paper, and admiring the small wood box carved with a vine of flowers.

"This is a lovely box. I can put my ring in it. Thank you, Nolan," Imogen said, smiling up at him and he threw back his head and laughed.

"Sure and I'm glad you're liking it, my love. But the gift is inside the box."

"Oh," Imogen flushed with embarrassment.

"To be fair, it's a really fancy box," Bianca said, patting her arm.

"Right? Thank you," Imogen said and then her mouth dropped open. Inside the box, nestled on a bed of purple silk, was a gold compass. *Mystic Pirate* was engraved in a gorgeous script, and Imogen gaped at the intricate scene she found when she flipped the compass over. There was a perfect replica of her boat, with her and Nolan on the bow, and the Water Fae flitting below the waters. It was museum-quality work, and Imogen was at a complete loss for words.

"It's so you can always find your way back to me," Nolan explained, reaching over to thread his fingers between Imogen's.

"I...Nolan. Nobody has ever given me such a nice gift before," Imogen said, her voice catching.

"I'm glad you like it. I made it myself. I've charmed it, as well. You can ask it to lead you to me, if needed."

"Oh, you're her True North." Bianca slapped a hand to her heart and pretended to swoon. "How romantic."

"It really is. I'm at a loss for words, Nolan. Please know how much this means to me," Imogen said, and standing she leaned across the table slightly to press her lips to Nolan's. She lingered there for a moment, feeling the compass heat in her palm, and knowing he'd made this piece for her with love.

"I hate to break this up..." Prince Callum's voice interrupted their kiss and Nolan pulled back before shooting a glare over his shoulder.

"Go away," Nolan ordered.

"I'd love to, as this is such a happy occasion, but we have business."

"What's happened?" Nolan asked, turning to the prince.

"Imogen, I'm very sorry to interrupt your birthday celebration. I understand this is a first for you?"

Imogen nodded, clutching the compass to her chest, waiting for what she was sure was going to be the thing that would burst her bubble. Torin, the man she'd met when the Fae ships had greeted the *Mystic Pirate*, stood next to Prince Callum. Both men held serious looks on their striking faces, leading Imogen to wonder who was in danger.

"It is, but that is fine. My heart is full and I've truly enjoyed my time. Please, it looks like you have something serious weighing on you. Won't you sit down and tell us?" Imogen prided herself on sounding polite and proper, even though inside she was knotted up with worry.

"Yes, tell us what's wrong," Bianca urged, patting the top of the table. Torin glanced at Prince Callum, and Imogen wondered if this was a break in Fae protocol. She waited quietly, still holding the compass in her palm, as the two royal Fae settled at their table.

"It's the Fire Fae," Torin said without preamble and Imogen's eyes caught on his face. He was a striking man, with chiseled features and tawny eyes. He reminded her vaguely of a lion, with wild red-gold hair and eyes that weren't quite human. The Fae were a striking lot, Imogen mused, as her gaze bounced between the cool good looks of Prince Callum, to the stormy dark handsomeness of Nolan, to the exotic beauty of Torin. Even Seamus, who at times struck her as lanky and awkward, carried his own quiet confidence that made him deeply appealing. Together, the men exuded a level of machismo that would have stopped more than one woman in her tracks. Herself included.

"I know..." Bianca leaned over and whispered. "It's like walking into a boxing gym or a sex club or something. Together they just pack a punch, don't they?"

Imogen gulped down a nervous giggle at the thought of these men in a sex club and schooled her expression even though Nolan's lips quirked as though he could read her thoughts.

"Prince? What seems to be the problem?"

"It's the Fire Fae." Torin cleared his throat. He wore all black, which made his gilded hair and tanned skin even more striking. "It's the same as the Water Fae. What we'd hoped was a one-off situation, due to her father," Torin nodded at Imogen, "is something more."

Imogen tried to push down the wave of guilt she felt about her father's actions. He'd hurt a lot of Fae, and even though it wasn't her fault, he was still connected to Imogen.

"It's the Domnua, isn't it? Like I had thought?" Bianca asked, drawing the men's gazes to her. "They're creating a divide between the Elementals, aren't they? If so, they can create an uprising and come for your throne."

"It seems to be that way, yes," Torin sighed, and pinched the bridge of his nose. "They've started fires. In Ireland. Their staff has gone missing."

"Their staff?" Imogen asked, before she could stop herself.

"It's like the amulet of the Water Fae," Nolan explained.

"The Fire Fae have a magickal staff that the leader carries. It wields incredible power."

"Oh, like a..." Imogen mimicked slamming a large stick into the ground. "Like Gandalf carries?"

The men just looked at her in confusion.

"They don't know our stories," Bianca said. "But yes, you are correct. Basically like a big magickal walking stick with some sort of charmed part on the end. Big magick. That kind of thing."

"And it's been stolen," Imogen said.

"Which means the Fire Fae are raging. They are a tempestuous and explosive lot, so this isn't something we can sit on. We need to help them before the Domnua creates absolute chaos," Torin said. Worry creased his handsome face, and Imogen wondered how they would know where to start or what to do.

"What do you need from us?" Bianca asked.

"The biggest fire is already raging and threatens a town. We have to stop it. From there? We need to help them and subdue the Domnua."

"Where's the fire?" Bianca asked.

"It's near a town called Grace's Cove. By one of our portals."

"No!" Bianca gasped, already rising, Seamus along with her.

"We have to go – now!" Imogen said, jumping from her seat. Queen Aurelia materialized by their table.

"There's trouble?" The queen wore a stunning white dress encrusted with crystals and her pink hair was entwined with sparkly combs.

"It's the Fire Fae. They've staged an uprising outside Grace's Cove. The town is threatened," Torin said.

"We'll go at once. Everyone to the portal."

At the door, Imogen stopped and took one last glance back at the room. Her very first birthday party. Though it was ending on an unfortunate note, she'd never forget that Nolan had given this to her – and that he'd made her feel loved. Well and truly loved. Nobody could take this memory or this feeling from her, and no matter what came next, she'd hug this moment to her heart forever.

"Are you well?" Nolan asked, wrapping an arm around her waist and she tilted her head up to his.

"Aye, Nolan. You've given me an incredible gift today. Whatever happens after this, I just need you to know how happy you've made me."

"Ah, *mavourneen.* It was, quite simply, my pleasure. I'm sorry it must end this way, but we're needed. That's my life, you know. I must serve the people."

"I understand. I want to help...if I can?" Imogen asked, searching his eyes with a questioning look.

"Of course you can...do you know what puts out fire?"

"Water," Imogen said, feeling her power surge.

"Aye, water. Let's go save our people."

Our people, Imogen thought, a sense of belonging and rightness flooding through her. She was a part of something bigger than herself now, and Imogen now understood that she held the power to make a difference.

Dying to know how Lily and Callum fell in love? Read their epic love story for free. Download Wild Irish Christmas for free at www.triciaomalley.com/freebies.

MELODY OF FLAME: BOOK TWO IN THE WILDSONG SERIES

CHAPTER ONE

Golden eyes, as though lit from within, stared at her through the flames of the bonfire. Sorcha Kelly prided herself on never stepping down from a challenge, so she met the man's gaze dead on, lifting her chin in acknowledgement. A smile quirked his lips, and heat seared her core as he raised a hand and beckoned to her with one finger. Pushing her instant attraction aside, Sorcha raised an eyebrow in disdain. The man had another thing coming if he thought she'd answer to a summons of that nature.

Servant to no one, Sorcha turned away from the fire, and followed the increasingly heavy beat of drums that made her insides thrum. Impossible to resist, Sorcha bounced to the rhythm as she made her way through the festival grounds, laughing as a random woman grabbed her hand and pulled her into an impromptu series of complicated Irish dance steps. Sorcha had all but danced her way out of the womb, and fell naturally into the beat, laughing and tossing her cherry red curls over her shoulder. Music, laughter, and creativity were her fuel, and this weekend's festival for artists filled her soul.

Billed as the Irish "Burning Man," the Ring of Fire Festival encouraged artists of all types to commune together for the weekend to create art that would set souls on fire. These types of events were like catnip to Sorcha, and she'd packed up Betty Blue, her trusty camper van, and had made her way to the festival tucked in the Irish hills with her gear in tow. She'd freelanced for years in the performing arts, mainly in dance and acrobatics, but was currently working on a new skill that had caught her eye – fire dancing.

The art had risen in popularity both with photographers and for audiences who wanted live performances. Sorcha had been booked for everything from wedding performances to photo shoots and was finally beginning to eke out a steady stream of income for herself. For the first time in years, she was allowing herself to embrace her art, and her lifestyle, without the heavy weight of guilt placed on her from her family.

With six sisters, Sorcha was but an afterthought in a long line of disappointments for her father. She'd watched the rest of her siblings try to live up to his expectations and quickly realizing that the only thing that would meet with his approval was if she were a male, Sorcha had opted out of the game of trying to win approval and set out on her own.

Oh, but she loved her life now! Sorcha laughed as the dancing woman plopped a kiss on her cheek, before wandering back to Betty Blue to fill her insulated cup with wine. Once there, she paused for a moment, leaning back against the cool steel of her car, and studied the scene.

The sun had long since descended, and the full moon shone brightly on the bonfires that dotted the hills. Fairy lights were strung up between campsites, and music and laughter rose to the gently sparkling stars above. Everybody here shared a common interest – to create – and the joy and love found among these people made Sorcha feel like she was burning from within. Aptly named, this festival, she mused as she took a sip of her wine.

"You ignored me."

Sorcha jumped, wine sputtering from her lips, as she turned to see the golden-eyed man standing beside her. He'd approached as lightly as a breeze, and Sorcha took a moment to study him more closely to see if she could get a read on him. She'd traveled alone for years now, and her instincts had kept her safe thus far.

"Sure and you can't be thinking that the way to a woman's heart is to beckon her with a single finger?"

"Oh? Do you prefer to be the one who makes the demands?" The man gave her a silky grin. The light dancing in his golden eyes told Sorcha this exchange amused him.

"I do prefer to be in charge, thank you very much. Do you have a name then? Or shall I just call you a cheeky lion?"

At that the man threw his head back and laughed, the huskiness causing Sorcha's toes to curl, and she found herself strangely entranced. While dressing in costume was encouraged for the festival, Sorcha was certain this man wore his own clothes. Red leather pants, a fitted long-sleeve black t-shirt, and a tawny head of gold hair with gilded red highlights contributed to her impression of him looking like a lion. It was the eyes though, that made her take a second and then a third look. Surely he wore color contacts, but the effect of golden eyes was both startling and arresting at the same time. Sorcha drew closer. Starkly handsome, with sharp cheekbones and a chiseled jaw, this man carried himself with a confidence that wouldn't be easy for most men to do while wearing screaming red leather pants.

"That would certainly be a first. My name is Torin. And what is yours, my enchantress?" The words purred from his lips and Sorcha felt their heat straight to her core.

"Sorcha." She took a sip of her wine, as her throat had gone dry, while Torin studied her with the same intensity with which she watched him.

"And isn't that the perfect name for a woman of your nature? I find you impossibly beautiful."

The words, simply delivered, struck Sorcha with their sincerity. For a moment, her tears welled, and forced herself to break his gaze and look away over the festival for a moment. *Quirky?* Yes. *Interesting.* Most definitely. But, beautiful? No, Sorcha had never fallen prey to those type of compliments before. While it might be just another line to get her into bed, the conviction with which his words were delivered resonated deeply within her.

"Are your eyes real?" Sorcha turned once more to Torin.

His lips quirked, the sulky half-smile that had captured her interest across the fire before, and he reached out a hand.

"Dance with me?"

"See if you can keep up," Sorcha said, raising her chin in a challenge once more. Downing her wine, she tucked the cup behind the wheel of Betty Blue and grabbed Torin's hand. A shock of heat rippled through her, and she gasped when his hand tightened on hers instead of releasing. Turning, she met his eyes in the moonlight and read the invitation held there.

Sorcha swallowed, not ready for the question he posed, and instead pulled him into a circle of people that danced around a large bonfire to a haunting Celtic melody. The pipers stepped forward, increasing the speed of the song, and Sorcha closed her eyes for a moment to catch the beat. Torin's hands circled her waist, and then he pulled her into his arms. For a moment, Sorcha floated along, allowing herself to be pulled into a fluid dance, the heat of his touch invigorating.

Time seemed to slow, as they fell into an ancient rhythm where music propelled them forward, twisting and turning, their bodies brushing, their gazes caught on each other. Torin matched Sorcha step for step, challenging her with his movements, his tawny eyes searing hers. As the night drew long, Sorcha found herself caught in whatever spell he was casting.

Intoxicated with him, Sorcha accepted his hand when he drew her back to Betty Blue, and she found herself pulling him onto her bed, twining her body around his as sinuously as they had danced together. Caught in a spell, the two feasted on each other's bodies, the pulsing of the drums mirroring the pulsing of their hearts, as lust and fire drove their most intimate of dances. Fire licked through Sorcha's veins, desire all but smothering her, as she met Torin's surprised gaze as he took her mouth once more. Only near dawn, once sated, did they fall apart, gasping for breath.

Sorcha blinked at the ceiling of her van, where she'd tacked up a hauntingly beautiful print of the sun slashing her fiery rays across a stormy sea, and turned to speak to...

Nobody.

Torin was gone. Gasping, Sorcha sat up and clasped her shirt to her naked chest, a trickle of sweat slipping down her back. Had she imagined the whole encounter? Her mind scrambled to make sense of the last few hours, for everything in her screamed that her meeting with Torin had been real.

Heat spread along her palm, to the point of pain, and an urge so deep-rooted compelled Sorcha to open her hand. When a single flicker of flame, no larger than that from a small candle, winked to life and hovered over her palm, Sorcha closed her eyes against the panic that threatened.

Had she danced with the wrong man this night?

Read Melody of Flame: Book Two in the Wildsong Series today!

ACKNOWLEDGMENTS

Thank you so much for joining me on this new journey through the Fae realms in Ireland. I always receive so many requests for more Irish books, so it was fun for me to dive back into the Fae realm first introduced in the Isle of Destiny series. There is something so delightful about writing about magickal worlds, and coupled with the charm of Ireland, I always find that I really enjoy my time spent in these realms.

A special thanks to the Scotsman for patiently listening to me bounce ideas off him, as well as helping me with some of the battle scenes. I suppose all those late nights of video game battles with his mates helped him to be an expert consultant.

Thank you to Dave & Rona for being some of the first to set their eyes on this book and helping me to shine it up.

And, as always, a huge thanks to my lovely readers who share in my delight of all things magickal and mystical. Sparkle on!

THE ISLE OF DESTINY SERIES
ALSO BY TRICIA O'MALLEY

Do you wonder just what the Four Treasures quest is all about?
Join Bianca & Seamus as they help the original seekers protect
Ireland from the Dark Fae in the best-selling four book series: The
Isle of Destiny series. Enjoy!

Stone Song

Sword Song

Spear Song

Sphere Song

"Love this series. I will read this multiple times. Keeps you on the
edge of your seat. It has action, excitement and romance all in one
series."- Amazon Review

Available in audio, e-book & paperback!

Available Now

THE MYSTIC COVE SERIES

Wild Irish Heart

Wild Irish Eyes

Wild Irish Soul

Wild Irish Rebel

Wild Irish Roots: Margaret & Sean

Wild Irish Witch

Wild Irish Grace

Wild Irish Dreamer

Wild Irish Christmas (Novella)

Wild Irish Sage

Wild Irish Renegade

Wild Irish Moon

"I have read thousands of books and a fair percentage have been romances. Until I read Wild Irish Heart, I never had a book actually make me believe in love."- Amazon Review

Available in audio, e-book & paperback!

THE SIREN ISLAND SERIES
ALSO BY TRICIA O'MALLEY

Good Girl

Up to No Good

A Good Chance

Good Moon Rising

Too Good to Be True

A Good Soul

In Good Time

"Love her books and was excited for a totally new and different one! Once again, she did NOT disappoint! Magical in multiple ways and on multiple levels. Her writing style, while similar to that of Nora Roberts, kicks it up a notch!! I want to visit that island, stay in the B&B and meet the gals who run it! The characters are THAT real!!!" - Amazon Review

Available in audio, e-book & paperback!

THE ALTHEA ROSE SERIES
ALSO BY TRICIA O'MALLEY

One Tequila

Tequila for Two

Tequila Will Kill Ya (Novella)

Three Tequilas

Tequila Shots & Valentine Knots (Novella)

Tequila Four

A Fifth of Tequila

A Sixer of Tequila

Seven Deadly Tequilas

Eight Ways to Tequila

Tequila for Christmas (Novella)

"Not my usual genre but couldn't resist the Florida Keys setting. I was hooked from the first page. A fun read with just the right amount of crazy! Will definitely follow this series."- Amazon Review

Available in audio, e-book & paperback!

ALSO BY TRICIA O'MALLEY

STAND ALONE NOVELS

Ms. Bitch

"Ms. Bitch is sunshine in a book! An uplifting story of fighting your way through heartbreak and making your own version of happily-ever-after."

~Ann Charles, USA Today Bestselling Author

One Way Ticket

A funny and captivating beach read where booking a one-way ticket to paradise means starting over, letting go, and taking a chance on love...one more time

10 out of 10 - The BookLife Prize semi finalist

Firebird Award Winner

Pencraft Book of the year 2021

STAY IN TOUCH

Join my newsletter list for fun island-living, travel, and book updates: newsletter sign-up
Or visit my website for more information:

Facebook:
https://www.facebook.com/triciaomalleyauthor

Instagram:
https://www.instagram.com/triciaomalleyauthor/

Website: www.triciaomalley.com